BEST
LESBIAN EROTICA
2015

BEST
LESBIAN
EROTICA
2015

Edited by

LAURA ANTONIOU

CLEiS
PRESS

Published in the United States by Cleis Press, an imprint of Start Midnight, LLC, 609 Greenwich Street, Sixth Floor, New York, New York 10014.

Printed in the United States.
Cover design: Scott Idleman/Blink
Cover photograph: iStockphoto
Text design: Frank Wiedemann
First Edition.
10 9 8 7 6 5 4 3 2 1

Trade paper ISBN: 978-1-62778-091-9
E-book ISBN: 978-1-62778-106-0

CONTENTS

INTRODUCTION

Over twenty years ago, I decided the world needed more collections of erotica. Erotica written with women in mind, with sexy, demanding, lusty, beguiling, furious, volatile, seductive, sensuous women as the featured characters. Women who were neither passive objects of desire nor fetishized simulacrums moving and acting according to a limited menu of activities and roles.

Twenty years ago, I put out a call for submissions, sending a carefully worded ad to three magazines, about a dozen newspapers and newsletters and a mailing list of my friends who I thought might know other writers, and waited for the typewritten manuscripts to fill my P.O. box....

Wait, wait, what now?

Things sure have changed.

For one, there are so many wonderful collections of erotica. The sheer wealth of delicious stories available for tantalizing enjoyment of every kind is nothing short of amazing. And of course, the Internet and e-books have revolutionized how we find these stories, whether we're readers (as I am), writers (that, too) or even editors.

Guilty. With pleasure.

And then there's the reach. I had trouble getting twenty submissions to some of my older anthologies, and often had to resort to begging fellow writers to please, please dash off something I could use—or writing things under one of my many pseudonyms. But now? One hundred and fifty stories came flooding in. Drenching me.

I know. I have your pity. And when you enter this steamy collection of stories, from the sultry to the sordid, I believe they will capture your attention.

Because some things have not changed. The thrill of a bar pickup, and the enticement of the new, will always be exciting. That's why you'll start this little erotic adventure with stories celebrating flirtation and spontaneous sexual combustion. With a nod to the cyber-age, it's only right that the first story, "A Knock at the Door," by Lee Ann Keple and Katie King, uses text messages to convey the courtship dance of getting-to-know-you and sexual negotiation. The instant ability to share thoughts and fantasies without even looking into someone's eyes is one of the wonderful and frightening things I couldn't have even imagined twenty years ago.

You will want to get to the eyes-meeting-eyes part though, even when we aren't sure what that hot woman's name is. Or… those hot women's. Picking up couples or finding lust backstage at a USO show; nasty sex in the ladies' room or the tempered and simmered heat of a meal designed to steam up more than the farm-fresh vegetables all await your traipsing. And if you're really ready to get down and dirty, "Wet Dirt," by Tina Horn, will serve a up potent concoction of humor and bodily fluids and "The Bullwhip and the Bull Rider," by Sacchi Green, will leave you with a taste of leather in your mouth.

And that's just the first section of this collection.

One of the things I love in a sexy tale is an unmooring from reality. Erotica has the ability to show us things that don't happen, can't happen, shouldn't happen, never happened. This is part of the attraction. So I am delighted to include in this collection two stories of magic and fantasy: one from pure Greek mythology and one from the quasi-mystical history of the Rain Queens of Balobedu. They serve as wisps of fancy between the three thematic regions of the collection.

The middle segment celebrates and explores existing relationships, because not all passion resides in first-times. Older lovers, established couples, recaptured memories and the urging of a friend to go for more and more—all these show up, starting with the wonderfully sensuous "Behrouz Gets Lucky," by Avery Cassell. Discovery beyond what we think we already know is just as intoxicating as any flirtation, and reawakening desire is like finding an old love we'd forgotten. So while "My Visit to Sue Anne," by Anna Watson, might seem like a first-time story—read it slowly.

And in the final part of this romp through the wicked worlds of wild women...go just a little crazy. Fancy getting sexed up while getting some new ink? Or maybe grasp a different kind of bull dyke and confront the challenge of saying "Fuck you!" to a debilitating condition while savoring every moment of actual fucking you can get. You'll be glad to have this collection discreetly on your reading device so your seatmate doesn't spy you enjoying the oh-so-public in-flight entertainment depicted in Andrea Dale's "Still Flying." But don't think you've landed safely; you'll still have a stunning swing through gender and what it means to be strong, and finally, that special sort of furious sex that can only happen in the presence of a lot of bad history.

It's been more than twenty years since I sat down to read the fantasies and myths and desires of hot femmes and butches, tops and bottoms and switches. I'm surrounded by married lesbians, polyamorous bi-dykes, and genderqueers with neutral pronouns, and the kinky sex that used to be way in the back is so mainstream the best-seller lists are packed with billionaires putting their girlfriends in bondage.

But some things never change. This shit is hot. And there's always more to come. I certainly hope you do.

Laissez les bons temps rouler.

Laura Antoniou
Queens, New York

A KNOCK AT THE DOOR

Lee Ann Keple and Katie King

I sit cross-legged on my ratty old couch, shaking my head at yesterday's encounter. *Get out and meet new women writers,* my friend said. *Come for sushi with us—it'll be fun,* she said. *Might as well,* I thought. I wasn't getting anything productive done with the one-two punch of a vicious case of writer's block and the worst dry spell of my life anyhow.

I went reluctantly, ate raw fish, engaged in chitchat and was about to bolt out the door when I saw the little cutie with the hazel eyes. Our eyes met as she popped a piece of spicy tuna sashimi into her mouth.

An hour later and the table is cleared of everyone but us, talking and laughing about everything and nothing in the way only total strangers can. She pauses, tilts her head and asks me if I'm up for a little experiment. A stupid smile takes my face hostage, and I find myself nodding agreement before I can think of all the excuses to say no. She asks for my email address and says watch for her message, subject line *Knock at the Door,* then saunters out. I'm watching her posterior geography in a bit of a daze when I realize—I didn't even catch her name. Idiot.

I fire up my laptop and check my inbox, just in case...

To: jabberwalker@notmail.com
From: stirstick@geemail.com
Date: 1 March 2014, 8:32 pm
Subject: There is a knock at your door...

You're sitting in your living room trying to write when suddenly there is a knock at your door. You cross the room, open the door and see:
    A) an appliance repair technician
    B) a pizza delivery gal
    C) a police officer
    Welcome to my new series: Choose Your Own Erotic Adventure. Make your choice—then write what comes next ;)

Shit-eating only begins to describe the smile on my face. I hit REPLY and start to type.

To: stirstick@geemail.com
From: jabberwalker@notmail.com
Date: 1 March 2014 9:38 pm
Subject: RE: There is a knock at your door...

Fantastic! OK—I'll play along. Decisions, decisions.
    C) police officer

My eyes travel upward from the spit-and-polish black oxfords, up the sharply creased pants, pausing slightly at the crotch line before appraising the fitted uniform shirt and the navy-blue peaked cap, and you say, "We've had another noise complaint coming from this location. Mind if I come in and take a look around?"

Me: (said loudly) "Of course, Officer. C'mon in—anything I can do to help Vancouver's finest." (Closes door and leans in.) "Tell me you have more than 20 minutes this time!"

You say:

A) "We can spend all the time I have talking about what I'm going to do to you," or

B) "You can shut that cute mouth and loosen my tie."

I read over what I've written and hesitate. My mind is racing with possibilities, but I barely know this woman. I decide to play it cool, and see where she takes it. I hit SEND.

To: jabberwalker@notmail.com
From: stirstick@geemail.com
Date: 2 March 2014, 8:33 pm
Subject: RE: There is a knock at your door...

B.

I let you loosen my tie. You slip it up over my head, unknot it and offer it back to me saying, "You may want to restrain me, Officer. I'm having the nastiest thoughts right now and could be a threat to public safety." I shove the tie in my pocket, grab your hands and walk you into the kitchen, eying you the whole way.

I shoulder you up against the refrigerator and grab my night-stick. I stroke the smooth tip along your jawline, across your neck and down your shoulder. It feels warm—almost alive—in contrast to the cold stainless steel of the fridge against your back. You can feel my hot breath against your cheek as the rod rolls down along your arm over your chenille robe, making a detour under the curve of your left breast. My belt buckle presses into your right hip as the oak stick describes the curve of your waist, left hip and outer thigh. Lifting the hem of the pink robe and rolling my nightstick toward your inner thigh, I say, "I'm hungry, babe—what's for breakfast?"

You:

A) cook me breakfast

B) push me away, throw off the robe, and drop to your knees

C) grab a ball whisk from the stoneware jar on the granite counter and get creative

Holy shit. She doesn't waste any time. I would never wear a pink robe, but damn. Game on!

To: stirstick@geemail.com
From: jabberwalker@notmail.com
Date: 2 March 2014, 10:30 pm
Subject: RE: There is a knock at your door...

C.

"Are you ordering on or off the menu today, Officer?" I ask innocently. I push off the fridge hips-first, and without losing contact with your belt line, grind and turn slowly until my body has rotated around and my ass is warming the metal on your buckle. Your right hand instinctively comes around my waist, traveling up my belly to rest flat just under my left breast, index finger tracing a line over and above the black lace of my bra.

I apply the whisk to a bowl of half-whipped heavy cream sitting on the nearby counter until peaks start to form. I flick the whisk back and forth, fast enough that there is the occasional whirring sound in the air to punctuate the tapping of the

whisk hitting the sides, faster and faster. You watch raptly while rocking ever so slightly from side to side against my back.
"I think it's ready now." I dip two fingers into the stiff peaks and scoop out a bit of the sweet cream. I reach my hand back over my left shoulder and offer you the first taste.
You...
Your choice!

I fall asleep thinking of inappropriate uses for dairy products, hoping that stirstick sends the next installment right away. I've been checking my email more and more during the day, as if this will induce the next paragraphs to arrive faster.

To: jabberwalker@notmail.com
From: stirstick@geemail.com
Date: 5 March 2014, 8:20 pm
Subject: RE: There is a knock at your door...

I lick the cream, then push my tongue into the web between your forefingers, sucking both fingers into my mouth. I turn you around so I can feel your breasts against mine as I push you against the counter and thrust against your belly with my pelvis. My left hand falls against a spice rack as my right reaches into your robe to encircle your waist and caress the small of your back. "A little spice with your cream?" I ask.
Your choice of spice?
A) cinnamon sugar
B) red pepper flakes
C) chocolate sprinkles

To: stirstick@geemail.com
From: jabberwalker@notmail.com

Date: 5 March 2014, 8:25 pm
Subject: RE: There is a knock at your door...

A.

You sprinkle some cinnamon sugar onto my upper chest and breastbone so that some falls into my lacy black push-up bra, your eyes twinkling the whole time. You drop your head and start butterfly-tonguing the spice, slowly moving over the warm skin on my lower neck and down the center, to the even warmer area between my breasts, darting from side to side, licking the top of each breast and allowing your tongue to roll over the top edge of the bra, then underneath. You are teasing me, and you know it. A small groan starts to build in my throat. As your attention is focused on my left breast and the taste of my skin mingled with the spice, I undo your starched shirt, one button at a time, from the bottom up. When I reach the top button, I pull the shirt open and off your shoulders. The shirt falls to the floor, revealing magnificent breasts straining against lingerie I am damn sure isn't department issue.

At this stage, you remember:
A) the bowl of whipped cream
B) your tie
C) your nightstick
Your move...

To: jabberwalker@notmail.com
From: stirstick@geemail.com
Date: 6 March 2014, 8:07 pm
Subject: RE: There is a knock at your door...

C.

The robe has slipped off your shoulders now, and as my

gaze falls on the creamy perfection of your skin, I can feel the fire building in my belly, my knees beginning to wobble. I have to do something to regain control. With my left hand I loosen your robe and reach around to stroke upward along the curve of your spine. With my right, I grip my nightstick, probing gently between your knees until your thighs start to fall open. In and out, up and down, the smooth dowel explores that soft warmth of your flesh. I press the other end of the nightstick against my crotch, feeling the sexual energy flow between us.

"It's time for a change of venue," I say. Let's continue the party:
A) on the stairs with the nightstick
B) by the fireplace with the whipped cream
C) upstairs with the tie

Ohh—I can totally see her on the staircase. I retrieve the nightstick, look at it, look at her, and balance one end vertically on the stair just in front of me, nesting the side of the smooth, hard rod against her very wet lips. Carefully, I squeeze my upper thighs and legs together, reach down and cup her asscheeks, urging her forward so that she is pressed against the top end of the rod, which has now become our own private and personal sized stripper pole.

She moves slowly against it at first, exploring the give and take between the stiffness of the rod and its slight soft pivot from the small undulations of my back and hips moving in response to her grinding. The rising sweet musk of her scent and mine—

Wait a minute. That would never work. The nightstick would have to be four feet long. Scrap that.

Could we just be straddling each other on the stairs with the nightstick between us? Oh crap. My back hurts just thinking about that. What was I thinking? Fucking on stairs is uncomfortable.

Start again.

To: *stirstick@geemail.com*
From: *jabberwalker@notmail.com*
Date: *7 March 2014, 12:39 am*
Subject: *RE: There is a knock at your door…*

C. Upstairs with the tie

I reach into your right pocket to find your tie. It's not there, but I take my time anyway poking around and rubbing your thigh through the cloth. I search all the pockets on the front and back of your pants and on your shirt before I eventually find it—taking your sighs and groans as signals in the best game of "You're Getting Warmer" ever. Taking one end of the tie in each hand, I toss it gently over your neck, pulling it back and forth lightly across your hairline and upper back. I realize we'll never get up the stairs at this rate. I fold the tie over itself and snap it against my hands. "Up the stairs, missy!" I say, and crack it once on your left shoulder and once on your haunch. "You know the way to my bedroom."

I'll leave the choice here to you—what happens next?

To: *jabberwalker@notmail.com*
From: *stirstick@geemail.com*
Date: *7 March 2014, 4:20 pm*
Subject: *RE: There is a knock at your door…*

I do know the way. I chase you up the stairs. Sitting on the bedside table are two empty cartons of chocolate-chili and tamarind-mango gelato from the last stolen lunch we shared together. My taste buds fire, remembering how we shared the icy treats alternating spoonfuls between the sweet and the spicy. I lick my lips. I push you back onto the bed so that you are sitting with your legs dangling off the end. I get down on my knees in front of you, and place one hand on each knee, running my hand up your thigh, then down the side of your leg to the ankle. On the way up, I turn my hand and lightly scratch your inner thighs. My hands find their way to your belly and then move downward to the light thatch of hair between your legs. I twirl my fingers through the curly hair, and then push your legs open wide enough for me to bury my tongue in your essence. Time stands still. I lap at the free-flowing juices. My tongue is dancing in a private playground the way a seal frolics in the waves. I lick your inner lips and then make slow radiating circles out until I've traced the topography. As your arousal increases and changes, that landscape shifts, and I must re-survey to see what's changed, darting around, delighted at every curve and texture. Oh no—your vagina is feeling left out so I rap on the door with my tongue, pushing in and out, and am rewarded with more of your oh-so-sweet nectar. Your pulsing hips and audible sharp intakes of breath spur me on.

You:

A) swing yourself around to have the opportunity to give as well as receive

B) urge me on in my efforts

C) reach for some of the ice cubes in the bowl on the bedside table

Ice cubes? Where the hell did they come from? How can there be unmelted ice? You know what? I sooo don't care.

To: stirstick@geemail.com

From: jabberwalker@notmail.com
Date: 7 March 2014, 5:20 pm
Subject: RE: There is a knock at your door...

I am powerless to do anything but enjoy the ride as your tongue has its way with me. The pleasure builds inside me until I feel myself move beyond that point of no return and my hips buck violently as an orgasm explodes out in waves rocking me from the inside out.

I reach for the ice.

"Ice cubes? You can't be serious—you know I hate the cold," you blurt.

With a sly grin, I put a cube into my mouth holding it like an icy tongue, and "lick" your mouth and breasts. I can feel and see your nipples harden and hear your breathing get a little jagged. I retrieve your nightstick, going into some patter about a bomb threat and needing to search the area, grinning archly. I point the end of the nightstick at the main heat source in the room and start probing the edges, occasionally and deliberately grazing the stick past your hood and "detonator button." I insert the tip of the stick into and out of you a few inches, teasing you and trying to keep you from going over the edge. Your heavy breathing says I'm failing so I reach for another ice cube with my right hand and start running it down your neck and over your breasts, bypassing your nipples. Such strange and enticing noises you make! I'd like to keep you on the edge for longer, but I'm barely hanging on myself, so I thrust the nightstick into your moistness, twisting and pumping it into you again and again. You explode in a torrent of gasps and contractions, and keep moving your hips.

What happens next?

A) use the nightstick as a double dildo

B) toss the nightstick and start scissoring
C) You look at me and know that my rational mind has left the building, and will do absolutely anything you want me to do.

To: jabberwalker@notmail.com
From: stirstick@geemail.com
Date: 7 March 2014, 6:03 pm
Subject: RE: There is a knock at your door...

I take A) followed by B) followed by C)!
  We fall apart on the bed, panting joyfully.
  I roll you over on your back and say, "My turn on top!" I kneel beside you, gazing on your naked perfection. I stroke your arms, one at a time, from wrist to shoulder, then I lean over you and brush my breasts gently against your upper chest, then up to your neck and cheeks, then down again. Your skin speaks volumes of poetry to me, and my nipples tingle with pleasure. I press myself against you, gliding up and down your torso, over your delectable tits, down amongst the soft folds of your belly. When our nipples touch, what a delightful shock! I climb on top to straddle you—I want to feel you against my pussy. I want to feel you everywhere. My hips start to grind against your belly, my breasts pressing against yours.
  I'm feeling the heat yet again! I move my legs between yours and start kissing you from your eyelids downwards, spending plenty of time at your mouth. Your teeth, lips and tongue are a world of pleasure. I stroke your side down to your hips—ah, that's where I want to be! Slowly I move downward, kissing licking and stroking the length of your body, until I reach your pussy, still warm and wet from fucking.
  I open your pussy lips with my tongue and taste your juici-

ness, Up and down the ridges of your labia, swirling and tickling with my tongue as I stretch myself full length, my legs off the side of the bed. I can hear and feel you respond, and that excites me even more. I push harder with my tongue, listening to your moans and gasps as I pound my hips against the mattress. My tongue is on your clit now, a delicious piece of heaven, and I lick and suck until I can feel you coming. A shudder runs through your body and mine, as I dip my tongue into your sweetness. As your orgasm recedes, I lift my head and you say—

Your choice.

To: stirstick@geemail.com
From: jabberwalker@notmail.com
Date: 7 March 2014, 10:20 pm
Subject: RE: There is a knock at your door...

Unh. Mmmmmm...uh...phhhh...grr...uhuh. Waves continue to pulse through me to you, or from you to me, as I lie back trying to control my breathing. We are slick with a most potent combination of sex and sweat, and I haven't the energy or inclination to move just yet. I have a drum between my legs that is causing them to tremble with aftershocks.

I crawl on top of you, hooking my right leg over your belly and right leg, and drape my arm under your breasts. I take in the full sight of you—the rise and fall of your chest and your magnificent breasts. The smoldering in your eyes: ageless, bottomless pools of bliss, wisdom, the pain of experience and the promise of what's to come. Dear Goddess—I've been pleasured into a state of stupefaction! Words are not going to be my strong suit for a while, though judging by your Mona Lisa/Cheshire Cat grin, your lips still have some energy left.

"Tell me a story. Share one of your fantasies with me. I wanna

*know what else revs you up." As you think about what to say, I
start letting my fingers gently do the walking up and down your
skin, contemplating the area under your breastbone, and the one
below your navel... You:*
  A) share a fantasy
  B) counter with a game of Truth or Dare
  *C) check your watch and say I think we have enough time
left for a dirty shower too*

*To: jabberwalker@notmail.com
From: stirstick@geemail.com
Date: 8 March 2014, 8:30 am
Subject: RE: There is a knock at your door...*

*I run my finger lazily along your spine, drawing circles through
the sweat-slick on your back.*

*"Ah, the old truth or dare game, eh? Well," I say, as I
stroke my hand down your thigh, "to tell the truth, I've always
wondered what it would be like to have Madonna go down on
me. I daresay she'd be quite proficient, although I think your
sweet mouth is much more talented."*

*I check the clock by the bed and give you a smack on the
butt. "If we don't wash some of this juice off, the citizens'll smell
the sex on me a mile away. Let's grab a shower and I'll, um, get
your back."*

*You roll off the bed and open the door to the bath. Yep, that
tub is big enough for two, with a double showerhead. I can see a
stack of fluffy towels and a basket of bath products and, oh yes,
toys! I follow you inside eagerly.*

*"Like it hot?" you ask, looking at me over your shoulder, as
you start the water flowing.*

"Mmm, yes, indeed," I reply running my hands down your

back, cupping them under your butt. We step into the tub and I grab for the hand shower, checking out the dial for the water-massage setting. I stand behind you and curl my left arm around your waist as I play pulsing jets of water over your back. I can feel you relaxing against me as I move my hand over your breasts and draw you closer. My hips push into your buttcheeks as I run the shower jets along your arms and chest. The water cascades over your lush curves. I want to drown myself in every part of you.

Hanging up the showerhead, I soap up a sea-sponge, covering you with soft slippery bubbles. I run my hands over your body from shoulders down to your luscious ass. My hand slides easily between your cheeks, and I can feel the warmth beyond. My fingers touch that heavenly wetness, and I am lost again in wonder and delight, caressing the folds of your pussy. I can feel you responding to my strokes, and my heartbeat quickens again. I draw back just for a moment—long enough to reach for the basket beside the tub. The water is still pounding over us as I point to the contents, letting you choose your favorite.

What's in the basket of goodies?

To: stirstick@geemail.com
From: jabberwalker@notmail.com
Date: 8 March 2014, 9:59 am
Subject: RE: There is a knock at your door…

A loofah, a dildo, a butt plug, a nylon harness, bottle of lube and a rubber ducky.

Do you want just one, or all of the above?

To: jabberwalker@notmail.com
From: stirstick@geemail.com

Date: 8 March 2014, 10:02 am
Subject: RE: There is a knock at your door...

Surprise me.

To: stirstick@geemail.com
From: jabberwalker@notmail.com
Date: 8 March 2014, 12:30 pm
Subject: RE: There is a knock at your door...

I smile when I see the yellow rubber ducky. His spelunking adventures last week had more than your feathers ruffled, I do recall. The noise he made was a little distracting...fun—but distracting.

I point to the butt plug and see your eyebrows raised in surprise. You know that's never been my thing. I've noticed you catch your breath every time you touch my ass.

You reach for the plug and the bottle of lube. You open the bottle and start to liberally apply the slick liquid from the narrow tip and then over the three other ridges that gradually taper out to the base.

You watch me for reaction as you lube up the toy. I turn around so that I am facing you and take the showerhead out of the base. I direct the jets over my face and hair so that the very warm water gushes down my front, running my other hand through my wet hair and tossing my head to keep it from falling into my eyes. I lower the showerhead so that the stream is now moving down between my breasts, then through the tangle of pubic hair before disappearing between my legs. My skin is still wet and slippery, which I find out as I run my hand over my breasts, lathering them up with the white, soapy bubbles. I soap around one, then the other, in a wide circle, pinching my nipples and watching you watch me.

A) As you come closer with a big smile playing across your face, I say I'd love to hear another fantasy/bedtime story while you find a new home for that lubed-up toy.

B) You come closer and say "I've been wanting to do this for a long time…"

To: jabberwalker@notmail.com
From: stirstick@geemail.com
Date: 8 March 2014, 2:22 pm
Subject: RE: There is a knock at your door…

B.

I pull out the harness and dildo and say, "Put this on."

I watch you while you get ready for action—and I do too! I stroke the slippery little butt plug in and around my labia, making sure I get every surface covered with lube. My own juices are flowing now and add to the mix. The sight of the black webbing against your smooth, pale skin excites me, and my other hand steals up to my right nipple, twisting it back and forth. I lean back against the shower stall, watching you adjust the dildo as the water cascades over your shoulders and breast and down your belly, wetting the harness. I can barely stand when I am this aroused. When you are strapped in—and strapped on—I grab the tube again, and reach out to coat the length of the dildo with shimmering lube. I look into your eyes, and say, "I'm ready."

I turn around, bend down and place my hands at the end of the tub. I can feel the warm water and cool air on my hot, hot pussy and I quiver with excitement, waiting for you to start. I wonder how long you will tease me before I feel those deep, strong thrusts.

You're in charge now, and I await your next move.

To: *stirstick@geemail.com*
From: *jabberwalker@notmail.com*
Date: *8 March 2014, 5:20 pm*
Subject: *RE: There is a knock at your door…*

I'd tell you I was ready too, but the words—any words—would catch in my throat. The combination of your beauty and your sexy confidence/comfort with yourself is potent enough. The sight of you bending over and presenting that hot primed pussy is intoxicating—so much so that I'm afraid I'll erupt without touching you. I close the distance between us and press myself against your backside, dildo up and between us. I lean forward into your back, placing my hands on your shoulders and raking them from your smooth white shoulder blades down your back and sides. You moan slightly as my fingers come to rest on either side of your hips, kneading into your soft, warm flesh. My hands drift down between your thighs, moving them apart a few more inches. Your legs are trembling just a bit. Mmmm…the steam from the shower combined with the sweet and salty scents has turned the bathroom into a veritable sex hot box!

Hands back on the sides of your smooth buttcheeks, I pull my hips back a bit so that the dildo dips down and you feel it bounce off your left thigh. Taking the shaft in my right hand, I move it to the top of your pussy and drag the head deliberately and slowly backward across your lips. The moan is still escaping from your throat as I thrust into you. Your breath catches. Again I find myself on that precipice—wanting to erupt while wanting to extend this moment forever—that primal desire to have every inch of you merged with me and to feel every nerve ending of your body tingle and broadcast to me again and again. I pull

17

back several inches and rotate my hips, pushing back and forth into you, plumbing the moist softness deep inside you. Deeper to the left, and then to the right, filling you and feeling your body's response. My pussy is on fire from the heat as it rubs against your ass through the harness, as well as from the feedback from the warm wetness of your sex tight around my cock. I pull back slowly and then slam forcefully into you full length again. Slowly drawing out the head, teasing your lips and then deep in again. You push back against me as I enter you again. And again. Your hips thrust and pussy contracts, trying to suck me in farther, and it is too much. Oh god, I can feel myself going, and you along with me, and my thrusts get more urgent and powerful. I support more of your weight as your legs start to give and we buck wildly. The telltale noises rise from you— Oohh. Ooooohhhh. Oooohhh. I cry out and groan loudly as the first wave of orgasm rushes over me. You tense and then relax against me as you come, moaning as pleasure washes over you. Wave after wave of aftershock orgasms course from me out through you and back. Our hips continue to pulse into each other, then come to a rest.

I pull out slowly, and gently turn you around so we are facing. Plans to push you up against the wall and take you again at a more leisurely pace in the shower are put on hold as you look just a little light-headed. Taking your hand, I lead you out of the shower to the marble countertop with double sink. I place your arms behind my neck so they're crossing and kiss you. Softly and slowly at first, then more insistently, I wrap my arms around your back and lift you onto the countertop so that you can lean into me as our tongues and lips and teeth commune and our bodies continue to sizzle.

What happens next?

To: jabberwalker@notmail.com
From: stirstick@geemail.com
Date: 8 March 2014, 7:15 pm
Subject: RE: There is a knock at your door…

With the cool smooth marble against my buttocks, your soft warmth pressing against me, I open my legs and wrap them around you, urging your hips against me as we kiss, deeply, hungrily. I can feel the dildo, now warm and slippery, against my thigh and I want to feel it within me again. You draw back slightly to position the head of the dildo against my crotch, rubbing back and forth, up and down. I look into your eyes, pleading for more, and with a sultry and mischievous smile you continue to tease my pussy until I am nearly ready to burst.

I can feel the heat spreading up from my groin as I lean backward, head against the steamy mirror, and push my hips forward to meet you.

I gasp as you enter me again, sliding in halfway up the shaft and then pulling out, as you ask, "Faster or slower?"

Through clenched teeth I cry, "Deeper!"

You're rocking your hips against me as our torsos press together, breast to breast, belly to belly. I lose myself in ecstasy and I no longer know nor care where my body leaves off and yours begins. As we meld more closely, my legs wrapped around you, urging you even deeper, I grip against the dildo with my inner muscles, feeling your blood pulse as if it were through my own veins, hearing your panting breaths as if they were my own.

I rake nails down your back and run my teeth along your neck as—

There is a knock at the door.

Who could it be at this hour? I hear a throaty and familiar chuckle coming from the hallway.

I think my dry spell is over.

ANDRO ANGEL

Deborah Jannerson

"I'm gonna get laid tonight!" I clinked my Lemontini Meringue against Carmen's. I guess I did it too hard, because we both lost a little precious alcohol over the sides of our glasses. The strangers around us probably just assumed I was drunk. But actually?

"You are hopelessly clumsy." Carmen shook her head, but she couldn't even pretend to be mad at me. "And, really? What's your plan?"

"I was hoping you'd help with that part."

My friend laughed. She glanced at her date, Myka, as if to warn me against painting her as a seductress extraordinaire, though she kind of is. "Just pick someone. Dance up, and go with it. If she's not into it, move on. No big deal."

"What's up?" Myka put down her beer and peered at Carmen. "Is she a hopeless romantic?"

"No." Carmen ruffled my hair. "She just likes to waste time letching after couples."

"Hey!" I pulled my head away. "I don't *letch*."

"My god!" Myka looked impressed with me for the first time ever. "Are you into threesomes?"

Oh geez, please don't offer, I thought with rising panic. *Not you and Carmen. That's too weird.* "Uh...no. I am decidedly outside of threesomes."

"What about her?" Carmen nodded at the door. "Your type, ain't she?"

I looked at the woman who had just walked in. Until that moment, I hadn't understood the meaning of *curvaceous*. The lady's big, shapely body was on display in a halter top, a tight pencil skirt, and...*nylons?* At a club party? She turned to chat with the bouncer, and I saw that her stockings were the type you never see anymore, the type with seams running down the back.

Wildly inappropriate for the occasion, but Carmen was right: the newcomer was my type. One of them, anyway.

I ducked under a HAPPY PRIDE banner and wandered toward the entrance. When I got within earshot—which was pretty close, considering the crowd—the first words I heard from the Nylon Angel's mouth were, "Yeah, my girlfriend went by the motel. She'll be here any minute."

Of course. I improvised by striking up a chat with a nearby acquaintance, as if that had been my intention all along. As we shouted our small talk, I scanned the room and saw plenty more women to whet my appetite. I reminded myself of Carmen's words: *Move on. No big deal.*

Righto.

After dancing with a couple of casual friends, I decided to wander. Yes, I still had sex on the brain. How could I not? It permeated the air, rising off the partiers' bodies. I was wet just from the energy in the room.

Now I'm not a religious lady, but I guess Moses took pity and parted the rainbow sea. Without knowing where I was going, I ended up face-to-face with an adorable androgynous chick and liked her instantly. She was petite, dressed down in a tank top, cargo pants and, weirdly enough, an Eagle Scout bandana. Well, why not? My body gravitated toward hers as our eyes met. She picked up my hand and spun me out then back to her, like a couple in an old film. I laughed and danced closer, our hips moving together.

When her short, shaggy haircut brushed against my neck, I felt the sweat that had mixed with her gel. She must have been dancing hard. It may sound gross, but somehow it turned me on even more. Maybe because I could imagine that hair trailing along my inner thigh... I breathed against her ear, grinding just a little. She intensified the movement, and I wrapped my arms around her, feeling the bones of her back move under my fingers.

By the end of the next song, we were kissing. At first, she was so gentle that it teased me, and I moaned a little as I pushed my mouth against hers. She chuckled but didn't stop, pressing her hand against my lower back as our kisses grew desperate. I sucked on her lower lip, aching below the waist. She brushed my hair away from my face, then, much to my body's chagrin, turned slightly away.

I had been dimly aware that my new crush was part of a group. They'd been hanging in a haphazard cluster in the middle of the floor, wing-womaning each other as they checked out the scene and danced up the guests around them. It wasn't until we came up for air, though, that I realized the friend nearest to us was the Nylon Angel. As if on cue, she leaned over to my Andro Eagle and said something I couldn't hear, then leaned farther. Their lips met, and both pairs of eyes went to me.

Oh.

Nylon and I each put an arm around each other as she moved into our space. Eagle watched, rapt, as I kissed her girlfriend's made-up cheek. *I can tease too.* Slowly, slowly, I moved in for my second first kiss of the night. Nylon had softer, fuller lips, but she didn't waste time being coy. Her tongue played with mine as our mouths got warmer and wetter, melting together like two parts of a whole.

But for once, I wasn't one of two parts—I was one of three.

I grabbed the cloth of Eagle's tank, over her belly, and pulled her in closer. Her mouth joined with ours. As you might imagine, it was a bit awkward, because I had never kissed two people at once before, but that didn't keep it from being hot. I gave them several brief pecks to start, then focused on each of them in turn until I lost track of who was who. It didn't seem to matter. I had these two sexy creatures licking my lips and caressing my shoulders, and I wished I had a wall to lean on. I was still nearly sober, but the couple made me so dizzy that standing felt like work.

"Shall we get out of here?" Nylon murmured, reading my mind. Eagle grinned in approval; all I could do was nod.

When Carmen and I had talked about my interest in threesomes, she had seemed puzzled by my desire to be the third party. "Don't you want to wait until you have a girlfriend who's into it? Then you could go prowling together. With a couple, you'd be the odd girl out." I saw her point, but the idea of playing with a couple had always been the sexiest to me. Maybe it was because I didn't want a girlfriend just then, or maybe it was the reassurance that if it didn't go well, I never had to see them again, but my fantasy felt like something deeper, something I couldn't name. As excited as I was, I couldn't help but shoot Carmen a smug look when we passed her and Myka huddled at the bar. Nylon and Eagle were on either side of me, holding my hands as we walked briskly to the door. *No odd girl out here.*

We talked for the whole drive to the hotel, and not small talk either. We talked about sex. We had all been tested recently (woo-hoo, responsible adults!) but would still be using condoms with toys—and as it turned out, we all liked our toys. Nylon shared that she didn't like being touched on her stomach, and I mentioned my passion for having my thighs played with. As soon as I said it, Eagle reached over and put a hand on my leg over my jeans, without ever taking her eyes off the road. That turnoff couldn't come soon enough.

I know that a lot of people avoid these conversations out of fear that they'll be "mood-killers," but if anything, getting this stuff out of the way made me more ready to go. Or let go, as the case may be.

I must have passed the motel a hundred times before, but I had never given it a good look. The Apple Inn sat at the intersection of two major city roads and was more the color of rust than red apples, but it didn't look particularly sketchy. I felt safe.

"Is the room everything we hoped?" Nylon Angel teased her girlfriend as we strolled toward door number sixty-seven.

"And then some!" Andro Eagle replied, pulling the key out of her back pocket. Catching my eye, she explained, "We reserved it especially. It's the 'Festive Room.'"

I blinked. "The what?" In reply, Eagle pushed the door open and hit the light. Rather, she hit the *lights*, because the switch didn't just turn on a yellowish lamp or two. It activated string upon string of multicolored Christmas lights, wound around every wall. "Ah," I breathed, looking around the sparkly, rainbow-lit shelter. "The Pride Room?"

"Tonight it is!" Eagle leapt onto the bed, which I could see had an autumnal, maple-leaf pattern. *Fall? Winter?* I wasn't sure what the Apple Inn was going for, festivity-wise, but it was good enough for me. As Angel dropped her purse and shut the door behind us, Eagle leaned over the bedside table. I thought she was going to turn a more normal lamp on, but no—instead, she struck a match and lit three scarlet candles, filling the patches of shadows with light. The wax gave off a strong floral scent, and something else, something fruity and hearty.

Of course: apple season had arrived.

The three of us gazed at each other stilly, taking in the strange ambiance. Eagle looked mischievous, grinning like the Cheshire Cat; Angel seemed shy but definitely happy. The air felt thick between us, and I wondered if they could hear my heart pounding. *I can't believe this is finally happening*, I thought. I swallowed and then turned toward Angel. "Come here," I whispered.

She put her hands on my hips and kissed me again. Everything about her was soft: her lips, her touch, the smooth skin of her shoulders under my palms, the tongue that lazily explored my mouth. I had planned on being confident, maybe a little aggressive, but Angel had already made me breathless. I felt weak with desire to have her body all over me. She kissed harder, trailing both hands down to my thighs.

I heard a soft moan from the bed. I could see Eagle breathing hard, her face flushed, as she watched us. I took Angel's hand and maneuvered us over to the bed before we resumed our making out, giving Eagle a nice, long, arousing look. Maybe it was my imagination, but I thought I could smell her getting super wet under her cargo pants.

Then again, it could have been any of us.

"Have a seat," Eagle hissed. I surprised her by sitting on her lap on the bed, still facing the standing Angel. I wiggled my ass against Eagle's groin, feeling her arms wrap around me from behind. When I wrapped my legs around the femme's pencil skirt, my face became level with her amply filled-out halter top. I laid my face against Angel's cleavage as I felt Eagle caress my tummy and begin kissing my neck from behind.

As Angel undid her halter, Eagle teased my right ear with her naughty, impish mouth. I ground my ass down harder as Angel stepped away, giving me a good look. She let her shirt fall down in front of me. She had gone braless, and her breasts hung round and gorgeous. She played with her nipples for just a moment then grinned as her hands moved to the back of her skirt. I had never thought that the sound of a zipper was erotic before, but the sound of that pencil skirt being undone drove me wild. It wasn't just that it was sexy, either; it was that now I was torn: I didn't know whether to let Eagle keep nipping and licking at my ear or get off the bed and go after Angel's luscious ass.

Luckily, Angel chose that second to quit her teasing and come back to us on the bed. I couldn't have gotten up even if I'd tried; Eagle moved her tongue farther into my ear, and I gasped. I couldn't believe how good it felt; if I'd heard it described, I might have thought the act silly. Angel pressed herself against us, knocking both of us onto the bed on our backs. The two of them held each other tight and kissed, and I felt my heart swell. Some people might have been jealous, but they were so beautiful together, and I could feel the love between them. Part of me thinks I could just have sat back and watched and been perfectly happy.

Still, the heat between my legs grew again when Eagle found my mouth. I helped her peel off my blouse, and when I saw Angel kneel next to me, looking inquiringly at my jeans, I nodded, hard. "Take it off. All of it."

I was, of course, referring to my own clothes, but I wouldn't have minded Angel finishing her own undressing job, either— or Eagle's, for that matter. Angel was now curled up on the comforter in only her ridiculous seamed nylon tights and a black thong underneath that covered almost nothing. Now I could definitely smell her. Angel opened my fly slowly and pulled my jeans down over my legs, leaving my panties on for now. Her boobs brushed against my thigh on the way down, and I nearly cried. I already wanted, badly, to come, but I knew that if I held on, this would only get better.

I ran my hand over Eagle's ass as she played with my breasts through my thin bra. It hardly seemed fair that Eagle was still nearly fully clothed while the rest of us were in our underwear, and I started to remedy that situation, pulling off her tank top as I played with her short hair with my other hand. We kissed fiercely some more as Angel moved her head back up to ours and buried her face in my neck. While still enjoying Eagle's lips, I caressed Angel's nearly naked body with both of my hands, from her smooth arms to her perfect breasts to her dimpled back. When my hands skimmed the top of her nylons, Angel nodded into my neck. I took a deep breath and wound one leg around Eagle as I slid my fingers past Angel's waistline.

I fondled the femme's ass and thighs, but I could sense where her most intense warmth was coming from, and I couldn't wait anymore. I moved my fingers into her crease, stroking her soaking-wet labia. It wasn't completely easy, having to move my hands under the confines of the tight, woven fabric that was the nylons, but that just made the friction more intense. As two of my fingertips moved inside her, Angel clenched and rocked and bit my neck hard.

Eagle, meanwhile, was moving her mouth down toward my navel. Then—*oh*—she was back to her skillful stroking of my thighs. I felt my panties getting moister and tried to maintain focus on both the sensations Eagle was giving me and the feel of Angel's sweet pussy. It wasn't too hard; the pleasures combined and my body moved as if this was what it had always been waiting to do. When I grazed the spongy texture of Angel's G-spot, I began begging Eagle to take my underwear off. I was sure I couldn't take it anymore.

Neither could Angel, apparently. "Fuck," she cried, riding my fingers for several seconds before pulling back slightly. I wanted to ask her what she thought she was doing, but I got the idea when she yanked open her suitcase's front pocket to pull out a dildo. Eagle stopped the thigh torture for just a minute and grinned at Angel. Eagle pulled a condom out of her back pocket then, apparently realizing she still had pockets, took her cargo pants off entirely. Her gray boxer-briefs fit her snuggly, and when I stole a look at the center of them, I no longer had any doubt that all three of us were dripping wet.

As soon as I had the condom over the toy, I raised my eyebrows at Angel and moved my fingers, still deep inside of her, the tiniest bit. I felt a small spasm for my effort. "You want me to fuck you with this?" I murmured, staring deep into her eyes.

"You better," she responded gutturally, and Eagle let out a short burst of laughter.

"I think you want something too, huh?" she singsonged. I looked down at her trailing her elegant fingers up and down my thighs, making my whole body buzz for more.

"Please," I said. I felt the air hit me between the legs as my panties went down. Angel finally broke our contact to get the last of her clothing off, and while I missed her pussy immediately, my mind nearly went blank at the first touch of Eagle's tongue. She teased my clit with gentle then firm licks, and, when I could find my voice, I had her put a finger inside me. We both groaned as it went in, and she lapped harder, getting me all over her face. As Eagle licked, she placed her now-naked legs on either side of my left one, and I moaned louder, feeling how wet she was.

"Didn't you offer to fuck me?" Angel inquired, sounding deceptively innocent. She now kneeled beside my torso, suited dildo in hand, one eyebrow raised.

I grabbed the toy and held it between my belly and my chest. "Hop on."

Angel straddled me, and it slid right in with me still holding the base. Her weight on my torso turned me on just as much as seeing her spread-eagled over me and feeling her soak my hand where I gripped the toy. She began riding hard, letting out small noises as her pleasure built. I barely had to move, but of course I was moving, because Eagle's skillful mouth was making me twitch. She licked my clit from top to bottom as her pointer finger filled my pussy, making my whole crotch tingle. She ground herself harder against my leg, and I felt each change in her breathing as she worked us both into a frenzy. Her girlfriend continued to ride me and moan, and I put a hand over Angel's breast and felt her shake against me with every rise and fall.

Soon, I began to feel light-headed. Angel's cries were getting more and more high-pitched, and I felt the tightness in my chest and knew what was coming. I can't know for sure, but I think I started to come first, my pussy gripping and releasing Eagle's finger violently as my legs shook. Angel began to climax too, pressing her thighs against either side of me as her body quivered, rigid around the dildo. Eagle, feeling my orgasm against her hand and mouth, rocked more aggressively against my leg, and then we were all there. Our gasps combined and parted for several long minutes, hovering around the incredible machine that was our spasming, wet, thoroughly pleasured bodies.

Even though nobody's head was on the pillows, we barely moved afterward. Exhaustion of the best kind radiated from my self, and I can only imagine that they both felt the same way. Eventually, we all began to doze, Angel lying next to me with her head on my stomach, Eagle curled up toward the foot of the bed with her head resting on my thigh.

I passed in and out of dreams, feeling so close to these women—these gorgeous, talented, damn sexy women. Even though I know they lived somewhere else, and that I might never see them again, I felt I knew them well. I knew the tricks of Eagle's devilish mouth. I knew the sounds Angel made when she came. I knew how they both liked to tease.

The only things I didn't know were their names.

LOVELY LADY LIBERTY

Nicole Wolfe

Justine knew as soon as Olivia Hill stepped onstage that the Axis would never win.

Justine and her fellow WASPs had crammed into the back of the crowd inside Hickam Air Force Base's mess hall. The USO crew had cleared the hall of tables and chairs earlier and put up their portable stage. All of the airmen on base had filled the hall to near bursting within five hours of the opening act—a live eight-piece swing band. Famous film comics Abbott and Costello had the crowd in stitches with jokes, ad-libs, and comments about the base commander.

Then came Olivia Hall, star of the newest MGM thriller—*The Silent Laugh*. She played the sultry, strawberry-blonde-haired, hourglass-shaped torch singer who pulled the detective into her web of deceit. She walked onstage in a sequined bikini designed like the American flag and held a burning silver sparkler. The Hickam airmen roared so loud that it would've drowned out air raid sirens.

"Happy Fourth of July!" she yelled to the crowd. The airmen exploded with catcalls, cheers and whistles. Justine could barely hear her singing a sexy rendition of "You're a Grand Old Flag."

Michelle, one of Justine's fellow WASPs, shook her head as she watched the crowd. "You'd think those guys had never seen a woman before."

Carla, Justine's other fellow WASP, just smiled. "That's fine by me," she said. "That means we'll have our pick of the litter after she's done warming them up."

Olivia Hill spanked herself with the sparkler, bringing wall-shaking cheers from the airmen. She finished her song, lit an airman's cigarette with her sparkler and then disappeared behind a curtain.

"Come on," Michelle said. "Let's work our way closer so we can rub against some of those fellas."

"I'm going to get some air," Justine said. "It's like an oven in here."

"We'll see you back at the bunks, then," Carla said. She and Michelle weaved into the crowd and were soon swarmed by horny pilots and mechanics.

Justine shut the mess-hall door behind her while she tugged at her uniform's collar. It was eerily quiet. She froze in place and thought for a moment that stealth Japanese commandos had raided the base. She let out her breath when she saw a couple MPs walk by.

"Hey, you!"

Justine turned to see another MP was moving toward her with urgency. She wondered if she'd unknowingly committed an offense or if someone had found out about what happened with that waitress outside Hamilton Air Force Base in Novato.

Justine stood at attention. "Yes, sir?"

"You have some hairpins, don't you?"

The question was so out of left field that Justine gawked at him.

"Hairpins!" he yelled. "In your hair! Right?"

She jolted out of her confusion and patted her pinned brown hair. "Y-Yes, of course, sir."

"Come with me," the MP ordered and then turned away without making sure she'd followed.

Justine caught up with him and he took her around to the back of the mess hall. Two more MPs stood at a door, but one opened it to let Justine and her escort inside. She could hear Abbott and Costello cracking more jokes. The swing band lounged in the kitchen's makeshift backstage area, smoking cigarettes and begrudgingly drinking bottles of root beer.

The MP held open a door to a storeroom. He pointed to the room and kept thrusting his hand to urge her along.

"Today, WASP!"

Justine scurried into the room and was greeted by the smell of lilacs. It had been so long since she'd smelled flowers that the scent almost gave her a head rush. She saw the racks of pots and pans and dry goods and then the mirror propped up on cans of beans. She saw the red, white and blue sequined bikini draped over bags of ground coffee.

Olivia Hall stood with her back to Justine. She was putting on a green toga and her beautiful bare back moved like a rippling bedsheet hanging to dry in a slow wind. Justine saw no lilacs and realized the smell was Miss Hall's perfume.

"Close the door, will you?" Miss Hall asked.

Justine shut the door. She was surprised at how quiet it was in the storeroom.

"Some dressing room, huh?" Miss Hall asked.

Justine swallowed. "It sure is, Miss Hall."

"Please, call me Olivia. You're the pilot here. I'm just an actress."

"I wouldn't say you're just an actress, Miss—Olivia. You've starred with Basil Rathbone. I thought you matched him."

Olivia smiled over her shoulder at Justine. Justine's hands flinched.

"Thanks," Olivia said. "Basil's a true gentleman. He made the job easy." She turned to face Justine. "What do you think of the outfit?"

Justine thought that the one precarious knot behind her neck in the green sheet Olivia appeared to be wearing would come undone with even a tiny tug. "It's going to drive those airmen out of their minds."

"They are sweet, aren't they?"

"I suppose so." Justine bit back the words, but it was too late. She looked down at a box of powdered eggs.

"It's supposed to be a Lady Liberty outfit," Olivia said. "I'll walk out there with another sparkler in one hand and a book of Air Force regulations in the other. I have a crown." She pointed to a green crown near the mirror. "But I forgot hairpins. Can you believe it?"

Justine looked up from the powdered eggs. "Oh! I wondered why that MP kept asking me about them." She took off her hat and pulled the pins from her hair, letting her brown curls bounce down to her jaw. She handed the pins to Olivia. The palm of her hand was soft and warm.

"It's a shame you can't wear your hair down," Olivia said. "It's adorable."

Justine blushed. "Thanks."

"Now will you help me with the costume?" Olivia asked.

Justine looked around the storeroom. "Which one?"

Olivia pointed at her chest. "This one."

Justine's lips curled out as she attempted to express her confusion but couldn't find the words to do it. "It looks great. I don't think it needs anything."

Olivia giggled. "Oh, darling, you've been on this base too long. It's a good thing you don't play baseball because you'd never make it home if you kept missing so many signs."

The room grew humid. Justine's hands twitched again. "Signs?"

"You threw enough at me the moment you walked in."

"I did?"

"It's in your walk, honey. And in your eyes when I caught you looking at my back."

Justine started to back toward the door. "Miss Hall, I can't—"

"Neither can I. It'd be quite a scandal if MGM found out, wouldn't it? It's a good thing the band's going to play a couple numbers and I have this dressing room to myself. No one will hear a thing." She took Justine's hands and moved them to the toga's knot. "Now help me with this outfit."

They started with a slow kiss as Olivia's toga fell to the floor. She was naked and Justine wanted nothing more than to get out of her WASP uniform, pop open a can of cooking oil and rub it all over both of them. Olivia kept it slow, however, and their tongues quickly met before Justine dared to hold Olivia by the head for a stronger kiss. She stroked Olivia's plump breasts and Olivia finally started to unbutton Justine's uniform.

She had Justine naked just as the band started up their set. She nudged Justine to sit back on a stack of sugar bags. Justine leaned against the cool wall as Olivia got on her knees. She didn't waste time. She licked down Justine's belly and soon Justine was holding her by the head and rubbing her pussy on Olivia's face. Justine closed her eyes and turned her head to make extra sure she wouldn't linger too long on the sight of Olivia Hall's movie-star mouth clamped onto her cunt. The image almost made her come and she didn't want things to end too soon.

Olivia stood up so they could kiss again. Justine let a little shudder escape, but held back the lurking spasms that struggled against the cage of her belly. She took Olivia by the shoulders and laid her back on the bags of sugar. She wanted, needed, to feel inside her. Olivia smiled as she spread her knees and stroked Justine's hair. Justine lapped at her clit and slipped one finger inside her. It was like reaching into a little jar of warm honey. She tasted just as good.

She wanted to feel more. She slipped another finger into her and used her other hand to rub Olivia's clit. Olivia rocked on her hand. Little cries popped out of her mouth that went unheard by the USO crew outside the room thanks to the swing band.

Olivia grabbed her by the chin and looked dead into her eyes. "Harder, pilot, harder."

Justine grinned. "How much harder?"

Olivia grabbed her wrist and pumped Justine's fingers deeper and faster. "Just like that. Like that."

Justine obliged as Olivia sat back to play with her own nipples. Olivia's little moans became little giggles and then joyful laughs as she soaked Justine's fingers. Justine pulled out her slippery fingers and put them in her mouth, humming as she sucked them.

"I love these USO tours," Olivia said.

She pulled Justine down on top of her and wrapped one leg around her back. She slapped Justine on the behind to encourage her, and Justine started grinding her cunt against Olivia's. Olivia nodded in approval and her short cries and moans, mixed with the smacks on Justine's ass, started to fill the little room.

Justine felt the fuse light at the bottom of her throat as Olivia kept spanking her and their pussies bumped each other so hard that the sugar bags started to shift underneath them. The fuse ran down over their sweat-beaded tits and between their bellies. It reached her clit, which she pictured as a big hard cock plowing into Olivia, and there it set off the charge. Justine's body snapped rigid, her eyelids fluttered, a sugar bag burst, and she let out a long grunt that she was sure could be heard even over the swing band.

They lay in a sweaty clench atop the sugar bags and stole little kisses from each other until there was a knock.

"Five minutes, Miss Hill," said a USO crewman from the other side of the door.

"Do you still want help with that outfit?" Justine asked.

Olivia laughed. "I sure do."

Justine helped her put on the Lady Liberty costume. They pinned up the toga so it showed off her shapely legs. Justine gave Olivia's hair a quick comb as Olivia scribbled a note with her lipstick on the back of a bag of coffee.

Justine put the crown on Olivia's head. Olivia grabbed the airmen's manual and another sparkler before heading for the door. She turned back and tossed Justine the bag of coffee.

Her phone number was on the back. Justine stared at it in disbelief. There were hundreds of airmen outside who would go on a hundred suicide missions for it.

Olivia opened the door and looked back before heading out for her next number. "Call me if you're ever in Hollywood, and stick around for now, pilot. I'll need help getting out of this in about fifteen minutes."

KRISTIE'S GAME

Alexandra Delancey

"I've always wanted to try it with a woman,' she said. I flicked a smiled at her and looked away again, too bored to put a response together.

It hadn't been a good night. It had started well, with a bunch of friends having drinks at my place. Melissa had come back from her trip to Europe full of stories, and there was Max, and Tina who I hadn't seen forever. But after that things had deteriorated, exponentially. In the rush of getting taxis, Adriana had somehow not ended up in my taxi, and I'd taken a taxi alone with Kelly. I could see Adriana's point. The feeling of Kelly's thigh pressing against mine during the journey, and the glimpses of cleavage she kept insinuating under my nose were probably the reasons why I hadn't immediately called Adriana when I arrived at the venue. And after that, I got swept through the door in a jumble of tickets and stamps and coats, and didn't stop until Adriana's small figure was three feet away, yelling into my face for all she was worth.

"How could you forget me?" she was screaming over and over, ignoring my attempts to explain myself. Then we'd ended up out in the parking lot. Me shivering hard, regretting putting my coat away before she'd had a chance to get hold of me, and her going at it, blaming me for everything that had ever gone wrong between us. If anything, Adriana was too beautiful for me. I remember looking down at her, my teeth clamped together, partly to stop them chattering and partly so I didn't scream back at her, with her flashing black eyes and flashing white teeth, and thinking there was something weird about someone looking so perfect when she was so angry.

When I wasn't saying anything, Adriana called her entourage, and they rolled up minutes later and swept her off, maybe for the last time. She was a firecracker. A tiny, Italian firecracker. Max had said it, before I'd even known who she was, and, of course, it had been part of the initial attraction. But it was our thirty thousandth argument, and I'd had about all I could take. I'd gone back inside and ordered a mohito to celebrate, and one for Kelly, and then a stray dab of coke had come my way and everything had gone fuzzy.

And then there was no more coke, and it seemed Kelly had left without me, and so had everyone else, and I had no idea how I'd gotten here. But here I was: in a grimy bar on the other side of the city, bored, bored, bored, and unimpressed by the straight girl who was straining for my attention. Short of anything else to do, I tuned back in.

"Or maybe you're not that kind of girl," I heard her say. I turned my head and looked at her properly. She was blonde, blue eyed and very slender, with naturally straight hair. Not my type. But she was exceptionally pretty. Prettier even than Adriana, maybe, and definitely prettier than I deserved right now. I turned back and surveyed my reflection in the mirror behind the bar. I looked wrecked by all standards; my eyes were big, dark smudges, and my hair was in tangles. But, I must admit, the effect was not unbecoming.

"Yeah, I'm exactly that kind of girl," I replied.

At last the bartender was looking my way. I waved a twenty and he came over.

"Two Sambuca shots!" I yelled, wincing at the alcohol-soaked rasp to my voice.

"Where's your boyfriend?" I said to the girl, more roughly than I would've liked.

"Oh, I've been single for a couple of months," she said. I looked her up and down, from the flawless hair, to the baby-pink dress, to the attack-me shoes. Girls like that didn't travel alone. They went in packs, more tight and complicit than Adriana's.

"And you're out by yourself?"

"I was with a friend," she said quickly. "She picked up."

"And dumped you?"

"I don't mind. It's kind of an agreement we have. And then I realized I wasn't far from here, and..."

"And you found yourself wandering in?"

"Yeah. I mean, I've passed it before and thought it was probably a gay bar."

The shots arrived, and we clinked shot glasses and swallowed aniseed intensity. With the heat glowing all the way down to my stomach, I leaned forward and kissed her, experimentally. At first, I felt her pull back. So, this wasn't some pickup line—she really hadn't been with a girl before. But then she kissed me back, really launched herself at me. Her lips were a sugary crush, and her tongue hungrily probed my mouth. It was a hot, sticky, arousing kiss, and soon the heat in my stomach spread down to my clit. I nudged my stool closer and pulled her toward me. My knee eased between hers and her thighs parted easily. Her skirt was forced up high enough to give me a glimpse of underwear: probably some butt-eating thong, but it looked like lace, at least. Out of the bartender's sight, I groped her breast over the fabric of her dress and felt the soft warmth of an unpadded bra. She moaned when I pinched her nipple, shooting another bolt of heat into my clit.

Already I was at my turning point—the ache in my cunt that rose up, obliterating every other sensible thought. All of a sudden, I really wanted to fuck this girl. And I had a place in mind—a staff toilet upstairs that another girl and I had stumbled into months before, on the hunt for a little privacy. But I also wasn't sure how wrecked I was. I pulled away from the girl and stood up. I stretched, ran my fingers through my hair, looked at myself in the mirror: no, I was good. I slipped between the girl's thighs again.

"So, let's try it," I said, close to her ear.

"Wait—I don't even know your name," she said.

"It's George. What's yours?"

"Kristie," she said. "George—so, that's short for—Georgina?"

"Maybe," I said. I reached for her hand. "It doesn't matter. Let's go upstairs."

"Uh, okay," she said, in a smaller voice than before. The hint of reluctance increased my desire for her. I cast a glance around as we walked away from the bar, but no one was paying us any attention. The bartender was talking to someone down at the other end of the room and anyone in the bar at this time of the night most likely had no idea what was going on anyway. I pointed out the stairs and made her walk ahead of me all the way, watching her hips moving from side to side in her ridiculous shoes, the curve of her ass, the candy-pink dress lifting high on her thighs. I felt like a predatory beast, about to eat the Sugar Plum Fairy.

The staff toilet was just past the top of the stairs. We stopped outside and I tried the door. It opened.

"Come on." I took her hand and pulled her inside. I flicked the light on. It was a bald strip light, concealing nothing. I bolted the door, and Kristie looked around dubiously at the small, shabby space—toilet, sink, mirror, bucket and mop, and a few coats hanging up. She met my eyes, hers showing apprehension. I moved close and kissed her hard on the mouth, twisted my hands in her hair. I was really turned on now, and I felt rough. I was still angry at Adriana, and I felt like I wanted to punish this pretty, expectant girl for it. I pulled the straps of her dress over her shoulders, and yanked the zip all the way down at the back. With nothing holding the dress up now, it fell to the ground. Kristie looked down at it, almost sadly, then stepped out of it and hung it up with the coats. Her underwear was pale pink as well, and matching. The mirror gave me a perfect view of her slender back and the round, firm asscheeks separated by what was indeed butt-eating underwear.

"Take your underwear off," I said. She looked at me, shocked by my abruptness, but I didn't say anything else. Self-consciously, she reached behind her and unfastened her bra. She slipped the straps down and pulled the lace demi-cups away from her breasts. My breath caught at their round fullness, the small, rose-colored nipples, but I concealed my reaction from her.

"And the rest," I said. After a long pause, she hooked her fingers into the sides of her thong and eased it over her hips, down her thighs, and finally slid it over her ankles. In the mirror, I caught a scorching glimpse of her pussy as she bent over to retrieve it.

Kristie stood up straight again, presenting herself to me. The elevation of her heels thrust her body forward. It was slender all over, with a nice, curvy waist and hips. She was perfectly smooth, every hair on her body immaculately waxed or shaved away. She was prepped like a sacrificial offering, I thought, smirking inwardly. Her bare pussy gaped very slightly, exposing a whisper of inner labia.

I caught her wrists in my hands and kissed her again. Her arms strained to be released, but I kept them pressed against her sides. My leg brushed against her pussy. She let out a groan of frustration, and her cunt left a gratifyingly wet trail on my pants.

"I'll only let you go if you keep your hands where they are, and don't touch me," I said.

"Okay." She nodded. I released her wrists and she obediently held her hands against her sides. Keeping my mouth on hers, I ran my hands over her waist, her shoulders, the nape of her neck, her soft, firm breasts, anywhere but her pussy. I dug my fingers into the tops of her thighs and pushed them farther apart. She wobbled in her shoes, and allowed me to spread her legs to shoulders' width. I wanted her to feel crazy with arousal, desperate enough to beg. Judging from her eyes, she wasn't far off. Her pupils were huge, her expression submissive and pleading. I felt her body trembling. I was almost crazy turned on myself. I'd ended up going commando today—washing machine issues—and the friction of my clit rubbing on the seam of my pants was almost enough to tip me over the edge. I ran my fingers along the tender crease of her thigh, barely brushing her labia, and, at last, I got the reaction I wanted.

"Please," she whispered. At the same moment, a silver drop of wetness ran out of her and hit the floor, and then another. We both looked down at the tiny pool and her face flushed crimson. I cupped my hand below her pussy and received another two drops. I closed my fist, as if I had a handful of diamonds.

"Maybe this is what I came for," I said, holding her gaze. "What if I left you now?"

"No. Please. I need you to fuck me!" she said, her voice breaking with desperation. All coquettishness was gone, replaced by pure, unadulterated need.

"Okay," I said slowly, as if I was deliberating. "But I'm only going to fuck you from behind. Do you want it like that?" She hesitated, then nodded, biting down on her lower lip.

"Yes, I do," she said.

"Then bend over the sink." Immediately, she did as I asked, putting her weight on the sink cabinet, thighs pressed against the edge and her face not far from the mirror. "Legs apart," I said. She widened them, and I gave her shoes little kicks until they were spread the width of the cabinet. Her ass was perfectly exposed. Her cunt looked swollen, and she was soaking wet.

I smiled to myself, deeply gratified to have turned her on so much without even touching her. I spread her labia with two fingers.

"Nice wet pussy," I commented. Then I spread her asscheeks. Her asshole was as immaculate as the rest of her. "And nice asshole." She whimpered, and in the mirror, I saw her cheeks reddening again. My hand brushed her pussy, just enough to pick up her wetness, but the contact made her body jerk.

"So what kind of slut comes to a gay bar and begs a lesbian to fuck her?" I asked, casually. Seconds passed and she didn't answer. "That was a genuine question," I said, and slapped her ass hard with my wet hand. She cried out, but still didn't answer. I slapped her again, and again, alternating cheeks, until her entire ass was red. She had pressed her own hand across her mouth, to stifle the cry that came out of her at each one.

When my hand was tingling with heat, I stopped, and stood back and looked at my work with pleasure. I brushed her pussy again, and her body jolted, even more violently than before. I had never seen someone so desperate, and I loved it.

"Where's your phone?" I asked.

"What?" she asked shakily.

"Your phone."

"Oh—in my bag—over there." I rummaged in her silly, girly handbag and found it.

"What's the code?" Her face showed reluctance, but she told me.

"Two-eight-six-one." I unlocked it. I found the camera app, aimed, and took a perfect shot of her red ass, and her swollen pussy and asshole. I put the photo in front of her face. "Looking pretty good, huh?" I said. She looked at the photo and her eyes widened. She made a small noise: "Um."

"Look, your asshole is even gaping, begging me to fuck it." I moistened my finger at the entrance to her cunt and circled it around her small hole. She gasped. "You want me to fuck you here?"

"Anywhere!" she said, her voice breaking.

"Well, I've decided I only feel like fucking you anally today," I said. "Are you sure you want it?" She nodded. "Then tell me."

"I want you to fuck me in the ass," she said quietly.

"Good. Keep looking at the photo." I circled my finger around her hole. It was truly gaping a little. Making sure my finger was wet enough, I pressed it against her anus. She groaned and my finger slid in easily, past the first joint, then the second. She felt tight and soft and hot. I moved my finger in and out, in and out, in slow strokes, and she started to breathe hard.

"Are you still watching the photo?" I asked. I could see she was, and that it seemed to be turning her on more. I slipped a second finger into her ass. Her anal muscles were tight around my fingers. I began to fuck her harder, all the way to the knuckle. She started to whimper and hyperventilate and I could feel her tensing around my fingers.

Suddenly, I pulled them out of her. She groaned, a sound of disappointment. Her asshole twitched closed, then opened again. I spread her cheeks, enjoying the sight of the helpless, pink gape. Carefully, I inserted three fingers into her, her small hole easily widening to accommodate me. She cried out again. She wasn't looking at the photo any longer. Her head was turned to the side, her eyes were closed tight and her breath came in gasps. I pumped my fingers in and out of her anus, and she pushed back on them, craving more. I wished I had my seven-inch monster cock with me. At last, I took pity on her. With my other hand, I found her clit. It was huge, bursting. I flicked it ten, twenty times, pressing my weight against the hand that was buried in her asshole, and she came violently, shouting out, her ass spasming hard around my fingers.

She stayed bent over the sink for a long time, and I carefully withdrew my fingers, feeling like they'd been swallowed. At last, she turned her head and met my eyes, her surprise at what we'd just done seeming to match my own.

"Give me the phone again," I said. Wordlessly, she handed it to me. I took another shot. From farther back this time, her face just visible, her pussy slick and glistening, and her asshole stretched open by my hand. I showed her the photo, and her lips curved into a smile. She eased herself up, as if her muscles were cramped from holding the position for so long. Her skin had a sheen of sweat. She turned the taps on and splashed her arms, her breasts, her stomach with water. She started to turn around, but I wasn't done with her yet.

I forced her back down, pressing the side of her face against the counter. I unfastened the fly of my pants and slipped them over my hips. Then, I pressed my burning clit against her asscheek. I loved to grind on girls' asses more than anything. The wetness from my cunt spread all over her ass, and I pushed her hard against the sink, riding her back and forth. My hand twisted into her hair, and I held her firmly, her sounds of discomfort increasing my arousal.

I was close, almost on the point of coming, when, suddenly, with an incredible force, she stood up and pushed me off her. She spun around to face me as I stumbled against the wall, completely taken unawares. I stared at her in amazement. This wasn't some fragile girly-girl; there had been real strength behind her actions. Dazedly, I noticed for the first time that her arms and legs were tautly muscled with the graceful athleticism of an athlete.

"I play football. For the state," she said, noticing my reactions. "You weren't expecting that, were you?"

"No," I replied, chastened, and embarrassed at the fact that I was slumped against the wall and my pants were halfway down. She stepped toward me and lifted me by the waist so I was standing up straight. Kristie had some crazy, Amazonian strength. She held me against the wall with a hand at the base of my neck, and I could only stare at her in shock. She looked into my eyes.

"I think I need to teach you some manners," she said. She slapped my cunt hard with her other hand. I yelped. She slapped me again, and again. I tried to get away from her, but she could have been made of rock—she didn't budge one bit. She stopped slapping me and looked me up and down. "Now, what should I do with you?" She paused, weighing up her options. "Hmmm... maybe I feel like bending you over the sink and probing your orifices?"

"No!" I almost shouted, struggling against her unyielding hand.

"Oh. Let me guess. You don't do penetration?"

"No, I don't," I said, with a stab of real fear. This girl was strong enough to hold me down over the sink, and there would be nothing I could do about it.

"But maybe that's what I feel like doing?" She pulled me away from the wall and dragged me toward the sink. I fought against her, but she resisted me. As she bent me over, my pants fell all the way down. She held me down and her hand brushed my cunt. I cringed, bracing myself for what was coming next. I felt her finger probing my entrance.

"Please don't!" I shouted out.

"What was that?" she said.

"I said, please!" I was breathing hard. "I'll do anything you want, just please don't do that!" She lifted some of her weight off me.

"Anything?"

"Yes!"

"Oh, okay," she said affecting surprise. "Well...in that case, I want you to fuck me again. But like a lady this time!" She pulled me back from the sink by my hair. Then, she lifted herself onto the counter and propped herself up with her back against the mirror and her ass just on the edge of the sink. I had recovered enough to be aware of how hot she looked, still naked, with her thighs spread, exposing her perfectly shaven cunt.

"Lick my pussy," she said. She didn't need to tell me twice. I leaned over her and slid my tongue into her cunt. She tasted good, with the sweetness of the orgasm she'd just had. I forgot about my ordeal and focused on pushing my tongue as deep inside her as I could. She sighed and jerked her hips. I licked her pretty, pink inner labia and then moved on to her clit. Her hips jerked again, harder this time, and I sucked on it a little, and her body responded, encouraging me to do it harder.

"Slip your finger inside me," Kristie commanded. "In my cunt." I did as she told me, the incredible softness bringing back my arousal. "And another one." I fucked her with my fingers, as far as I could move them in my position, and I let out a sigh of desire. "You can touch yourself if you want," she said. Keeping my mouth on her pussy and my fingers inside her, I fingered my clit with my other hand. It felt as swollen as hers had earlier. I was so turned on that the sensation was intense, and I felt my face flushing. I flicked my tongue against her clit quickly in time to my own finger on my clit, and before long, I was at the point of orgasm again. Then, I felt her go very still. She was motionless for a few seconds, and then she exploded again, her cunt spasming around my fingers. This made me come too, a rough, shuddering orgasm, my sounds muffled by my mouth on her pussy.

Kristie was the first to recover. She pushed me away from her and stood up. Then, she retrieved her underwear and started getting dressed. I fastened my pants up, as well as the buttons on my shirt that had come undone. Kristie took some things out of her handbag and started fixing her makeup in the mirror. I stared at her wordlessly. My ears were ringing, and I couldn't remember having felt so shell-shocked before in my life. She ignored me until she'd finished.

"Are you ready?" she said at last. She unbolted the door and we went out.

Dumbly, I followed her down the stairs, watching her stepping cautiously in her heels, once again looking like the girly-girl I'd mistaken her for. I rubbed my eyes, unable to square the sight of her in public with what had just happened. We walked back into the bar. It was still dark, but only just, and the place was almost deserted.

"Come on, let's get a drink to celebrate," she said. More than anything, I wanted to go home and digest what had happened, but I was now somehow under her power, and I let her pull me to the bar.

"The usual, Kristie?" the bartender asked, smirking at her. I shot surprised glances at each of them, but Kristie didn't acknowledge my reaction. She nodded to him.

"Please, Jamie." He came back a minute or so later and put two dark, alcoholic-looking cocktails in front of us. "I call these *transformations*," he said, with a cocked eyebrow. "Because once you've been with Kristie, you'll never be the same again."

"Cheers!" Kristie said, and bumped her drink against mine. She grinned at me broadly and, in a flash, I understood. She was ten times the player I thought I was. I grinned and toasted her back.

LEARNING TO COOK

Nan Andrews

Jackie glanced over her shoulder as she turned the corner and headed up the steep sidewalk, but there was no one there. No footsteps following her out of the fog. This neighborhood wasn't that safe, or so she'd heard. She'd never actually been here before, but that wasn't the real reason she was nervous. She reached number 714 and climbed the steps. The house was nondescript gray stucco with a metal grate at the entrance. There were no names on the three mailboxes, but she'd been told which buzzer to press.

Jackie hesitated, shifting the bottle of zinfandel from one arm to the other, the tulips tucked under her elbow. She felt so off balance, like the first time she'd ever worn high heels. Liz did that to her. She wasn't sure if coming here was going to help her find her balance or if she liked feeling askew.

She remembered the night they met. One of her business clients wanted to try a hot new restaurant called La Jetee, near City Hall. Jackie liked to eat out, primarily because she didn't cook. When she was home alone, she ate simply: fruit and cereal, salad, takeout. The restaurant was modern—dark wood, silver accents, spot lighting. The menu was very spare and wasn't at all what she expected; she'd assumed it would be a French place. There were large framed photos that the client said were from an obscure French film. That was as French as it got. The special that night was a fillet of beef.

"I'd like that cooked well done," she told the waiter.

"I'm sorry, but the chef has specified that this dish will be served rare."

"But I don't want it that way." She wasn't going to let the waiter or the chef tell her how to eat her food.

"Miss, may I ask you to reconsider? The chef has a very special way of doing this dish and I think you'll appreciate it." The waiter was trying hard not to offend, but she could tell he was hesitant to take her order to the kitchen. Was he actually afraid of the chef?

"I'd like to speak to the chef myself."

The server retreated into the kitchen; after a few minutes, the dividing door sprang open and the chef stalked out in a blur of black and white. She was wiping her hands on a pristine white apron as she made her way through the crowded restaurant to the table.

"What seems to be the problem?"

"I'd like the fillet and I'd like it cooked well done." Jackie smiled up at her certain that, as the customer, she would be obliged.

"I'm sorry, but this dish is served rare. If you'd care for something else, the pork chops perhaps, I can burn them for you, with pleasure."

Jackie stared at her, taken aback. She wasn't used to being spoken to that way by a service person. Who was this woman?

With creamy skin, flushed pink from the heat of the kitchen, and fiery red hair escaping from under her toque, she was whippet thin and had a stare that would frighten a pit bull. A shiver went down the back of Jackie's neck, straight to her pussy, at both the challenge in her manner and the intensity in her face. The hell with the steak; she wanted to rip off the white chef's jacket and fuck her right on the table.

"Why don't you make me whatever you think I'd like," Jackie suggested with a smile.

The chef stalked back into the kitchen. Ten minutes later, the server returned with an enormous piece of beef, bloody rare in the center. It was delicious.

Along with the check, she'd gotten the chef's name and number from the waiter. Elizabeth Brennan was twenty-nine, just a year older than Jackie, single and a rising star in the culinary world. It took Jackie nearly a week to catch up with her. She worked Wednesday through Sunday nights at the restaurant and spent her days god knows where. She didn't take Jackie's call until her next day off.

"Liz Brennan."

"Hi, Liz, this is Jackie Mathis. We met at La Jetee the other night."

There was no sign of recognition on the other end.

"I had a...um, a special request about the fillet of beef."

"Oh. Dead beef. Yeah, I remember."

"Look, I'm...I'm sorry about that. I really did enjoy the fillet that you cooked." She hurried on. "I was wondering if you've tried Atelier Crenn yet? Could I take you there for dinner?"

"Sure, I know Dominique. She was my sous-chef at Luce. Her food's excellent. She has a real feel for her product."

Jackie realized that she was hunched over her deck, her phone pressed to her ear, as if she were about to be yelled at again. She straightened up and pushed her shoulders back. "So, about dinner. Tomorrow night, eight p.m.?"

"Make it ten. I'll meet you there."

"Um, I think they close at ten."

"Then be a few minutes early."

She hung up before Jackie could say anything else. No good-bye, no polite conversation. What kind of evening was this going to be?

The next night, Jackie arrived at Atelier Crenn at quarter of ten and was seated at the bar. She had spent a long time after work deciding what to wear and settled on a short black skirt, a blue top that matched her eyes, and her favorite pair of boots. She ordered a martini and waited. At ten o'clock, there was still no sign of Liz. She was afraid she'd been stood up. She considered leaving, but the bartender asked if she'd like another drink, so she ordered a second martini. The last few tables were finishing up; Jackie watched the couples leaving in the mirror behind the bar.

Without warning, there was a voice in her ear. "Come with me."

She looked up from her drink to see Liz's retreating back. She was dressed in a pair of slim black pants and a dark maroon top that complemented her hair. Her hips were slim, but womanly. She had a sense of style, even in such simple clothing, which was very attractive. Jackie slipped off her stool and followed. Liz walked through the swinging door into the kitchen.

Jackie had never been in a restaurant kitchen before and she stopped just inside the doors and looked around. Everything was stainless steel or white tile. Enormous pots hung from a rack above a work area. The stoves were wide black expanses of metal, with looming hoods. Liz was leaning against a counter, a beer bottle in hand. She was talking to another woman chef, presumably Dominique. Jackie walked over to them, avoiding the waiters moving across the space with trays of dirty dishes.

Neither woman acknowledged her and Jackie stood by as they talked, completely out of place. It was the other woman, not Liz, who spoke to her first.

"Hi, I'm Dominique Crenn. Welcome to my restaurant." The hand she offered was very strong.

"Jackie Mathis. Nice to meet you. I've read some great things about your work."

"I'm glad. Why don't you go have a seat?" She nodded her head toward the corner of the kitchen. There was a stool alongside a high counter.

Jackie looked at Liz. Her gaze was neutral. This whole thing suddenly felt like a serious mistake on Jackie's part. Liz didn't want to have dinner with her. She must be planning to embarrass her for the incident at La Jetee. Jackie's face bloomed red, but she turned and took a seat on the stool. To her surprise, Liz picked up an apron and put it on. For the next half an hour, Jackie watched as Liz and Dominique worked together. It was a ballet—two bodies moving through space, aware of each other, barely touching as they passed, but in perfect harmony. The two women talked quietly and laughed together, occasionally glancing at Jackie, but never speaking to her.

Jackie would have walked out, except for the way that Liz moved. She was mesmerized by the way Liz handled the knife, the way her muscular arms flexed as she sautéed something on the stove, flipping the food with a neat twist of her wrist. The bumps of her spine showed through her blouse as she turned to reach for something on the counter. Jackie's body ached with the desire to take her into her arms, to feel the motion as she moved at the stove. Cooking had never seemed so erotic before.

Finally, the women joined her at the counter with a series of plates. Each was a beautiful presentation: a perfectly prepared scallop, three tiny lamb chops on a smear of green sauce, several spears of asparagus covered in something red and shiny.

Liz and Dominique took turns feeding her bites of food, describing the provenance of each ingredient, complimenting each other on the preparation. Neither of them ate a single thing. It was the strangest feeling, being fed by these two beautiful women, as if she were a child.

When they were finished, Dominique looked her up and down.

Jackie felt as if she were being considered for inclusion in some new recipe. "Thank you. Everything was delicious."

"Do you cook?"

"No, not really. But I really enjoyed watching you both work." She licked a bit of sauce off her lip and noticed Liz watching closely. "This was certainly not what I expected when I invited Liz to dinner."

Dominique laughed. "No, I'm sure it wasn't. But Liz isn't someone who does what's expected." She put her arm around Liz's waist and kissed her cheek. "Now get out of my kitchen, I have work to finish."

They left through the back door, and stepped into the alley. Liz walked with purpose and Jackie hurried after. Just before they came out onto the street, Liz turned and pinned Jackie against the brick with her body. The kiss was hard and hungry, Liz's tongue taking control of Jackie's mouth, her hand between Jackie's legs. Jackie was panting when Liz stepped back, a half smile on her lips.

"I like the way my cooking tastes on you." She reached out and squeezed one of Jackie's breasts, her thumb rubbing across the hard nipple. "You have potential."

"Do I?" Jackie's head was spinning from the whipsaw behavior; first Liz ignored her and then she fairly attacked her. What was going on?

"Perhaps." She stepped closer again and cupped Jackie's pussy, her fingers pressing in.

Jackie's pussy was slick and hot and she wanted nothing more than Liz's fingers filling her, her tongue parting her lips and suckling her clit. She leaned her head back and moaned. Liz pressed harder, her middle finger wiggling against Jackie's clit. She pinched one nipple and the pain speared her. Just as Jackie was about to come, Liz stepped back, dropping her hands. She had that look on her face, the one from the previous week, of intensity and challenge.

"Seven-fourteen Broderick. Nine o'clock. Monday. Bring some wine you like." Liz turned and walked away. Jackie stared after her, then pulled out her phone to save the address.

Liz welcomed her into a spacious third-floor flat, full of polished wood and lush textiles. The color palette was cool blues and greens, with touches of bright white. She led Jackie straight into the kitchen, which had obviously been renovated to the chef's specifications. The space took up most of the front of the building, with plenty of work space and high-end appliances. There was a long, narrow wooden table across the front, with tall chairs. Pendant lamps and ceiling spots gave the place a very theatrical feel.

Liz put the wine on the counter and found a vase for the tulips. She poured a martini and handed it to Jackie.

"How did you know I like martinis?"

"I saw what you were drinking at Crenn. Now don't get too comfortable. You have work to do."

"Really?" Jackie sipped the ice-cold martini and arched a

brow. "What sort of work?"

"You'll see." Liz went to a door on the side of the kitchen. Jackie wondered if it was a bathroom, but when the door opened, she could see it was a large pantry. Liz came back, tying an apron around her waist. "Take off your clothes."

Jackie nearly choked on her drink. "What?"

"You don't want to get them dirty while you're washing dishes."

"Is that what I'm going to be doing?"

"That's not all, but yes. You'll be washing dishes when we're done. You said you don't cook, so I'm certainly not going to trust you to do that." She cocked her head and looked at Jackie. "Take your clothes off."

Jackie walked toward the table and glanced back at Liz, who stood with her hands on her hips, waiting. This wasn't like disrobing for a lover; it felt more like an inspection. So why did it make her nipples stiffen? Jackie slipped off her skirt and pulled her blouse over her head. She stood uncomfortably in a set of pale-blue bra and panties, along with her heels.

Liz waved her hand. "Those, too." She reached under a bench and held up a pair of clogs. "You can wear these to protect your feet."

Jackie laughed nervously. What about the rest of her? Didn't that need protecting too? She walked naked back to the kitchen and stepped into the clogs. Liz stepped up and tied a handkerchief around her neck, the ends pointing to each breast. She caught Jackie's shoulder-length hair in a ponytail and tied it back. Jackie looked down. Naked between the blue neckerchief and the clogs, she thought she looked ridiculous.

"Now, stand over there." Liz pointed at a spot to the side of the stove. "Have you ever heard of the *brigade de cuisine*?"

Jackie shook her head.

"It's the French system of kitchen management. I'm the *chef du cuisine*, the head chef. You are my assistant, my *apprentice*, and also my *plongeur*. That's where the dishwashing comes in. Now, watch and listen, and hopefully you'll learn something." Liz laughed, as if she doubted Jackie would be capable of that.

Somehow, the sound of her laughter made Jackie wet. She realized she wasn't angry at being made to strip, being dressed in clogs and little else, not even at being the dishwasher. The way Liz spoke to her made her hungry in a way she'd never felt before.

Liz pulled some dishes out of the refrigerator and stirred something in a bowl. "Give me your hand," she said.

Jackie held out her right hand. Liz turned it palm up and painted some green sauce from the bowl onto Jackie's index finger and thumb. She raised the hand to her face as if to inspect her work and licked the sauce off.

"What is that?" Jackie asked, more interested in why Liz was doing it, than what was in the sauce.

Liz spooned some more sauce on Jackie's palm, picked a piece of papaya off a plate, ran it through the sauce and offered it to her. "Mint-chili sauce. Do you like it?"

"Very much." It tasted tropical: hot and spicy, with a cool mint finish.

Liz took the spoon and poured some sauce over Jackie's left breast. She took a bite of papaya, then bent and licked the sauce. The chili made Jackie's skin tingle and the heat of Liz's tongue made her pussy clench. She reached up to put her arms around Liz, but Liz pushed them down.

"Stand still and do what I say." She licked Jackie's nipple again. "I'm in charge of the kitchen."

Jackie stood still, trembling, as Liz continued to spread chili sauce on her breasts and then lick it off between bites of papaya. She fed Jackie a few bites and then put the dirty dishes aside, as if there were nothing unusual about the arrangement.

The next course was a sushi roll made of thinly shaved cucumber filled with crab and an avocado sauce. Liz showed her how to use a mandolin to make the strips of cucumber and then instructed her on what ingredients to bring her. Jackie watched her turn the simple items into a delicious mouthful, but Liz never touched her. Jackie ached to be touched again. The pile of dishes in the sink continued to grow.

The main course was a beautiful fillet of salmon. Liz seared it skin-side-down in the pan and basted it with hot butter. She tossed some freshly chopped herbs in at the last minute and their aroma rose in the kitchen. When instructed, Jackie carefully pulled a potato galette out of the oven, which Liz had made earlier. The rosette of thin slices of potato was crisp and smelled deliciously of garlic. A salad of lightly tossed greens completed the plate. However, there was only one plate. Jackie wondered what Liz was planning, as she opened the wine and poured a glass of the zinfandel.

"Bring those and follow me." Liz walked over to the table by the windows and lit the candles. Sitting in the chair at the end, she indicated where Jackie should put the food. Liz slid her hand up Jackie's leg, resting on the curve of her buttocks. "Tonight, I want you to feed me."

Jackie moved to sit in the chair next to Liz's place, but Liz stopped her with a stinging smack on the bottom. "No, stay here."

Jackie stepped back beside Liz's chair. Liz slipped her hand between Jackie's thighs and up to her pussy. Her fingers wormed between Jackie's lips and came out wet. Liz brought them to her lips and licked them. Jackie shuddered. Liz casually slid her hand back between Jackie's thighs and indicated for Jackie to begin.

There were no utensils. Jackie broke off a morsel of salmon and offered it to Liz. The first bite was taken delicately, but soon Liz was opening wide and sucking the food from Jackie's fingers. She licked off the fat from the potatoes and the herbs from the salmon. Her hand was doing a subtle dance against Jackie's pussy, rubbing and pressing. Jackie widened her stance, tilting her hips in hopes of more contact.

"Greedy girl, aren't you?" Liz asked, licking her lips. "Give me some wine."

Jackie picked up the glass to offer it, but Liz laughed. "No, I like this better." She took the glass and poured some over Jackie's breast. The ruby liquid ran over her breast and down her belly. Liz pulled Jackie close and reached up to suck the drops hanging from her nipple. Her teeth tugged as she flicked Jackie's clit with her thumb. Jackie caught her breath, desire snaking through her body. She wanted to put her hands in Liz's fiery hair, to press her face against her breast, but it seemed like the wrong thing to do. Liz was in charge of the meal and of her.

Liz ran her tongue from the bottom of Jackie's breast to her belly, gathering drops of wine as they lingered on her skin. The moment her mouth touched Jackie's mound, she began to come. The heat exploded in her belly, sending tremors from the top of her head to her feet. Her knees buckled as Liz pushed three fingers into her pussy. The wave of orgasm continued. Liz suckled her nipple again and thumbed her clit, causing Jackie to cry out. She had never come so hard, or for so long. When Liz released her, Jackie planted her hands on the table and dropped her head, panting.

Liz wiped her sticky fingers along Jackie's flank and smiled. "Delicious." She casually picked up the glass of wine and took a sip. "I'd like some salad, please. To clear my palate."

Jackie straightened up and laughed.

"What's so funny?" Liz asked.

"I may never learn to cook, but I'm certainly learning how to eat."

WET DIRT

Tina Horn

On days like this, Grace was so grateful to have short hair.

She glanced to her left and to her right, at the other girls in line for the bathroom. Their hair was either standing high on their heads in ponytails, or pulled to the side, framing their faces. *These bitches look good,* she thought, *but they must feel so stifled.* Her watch read quarter to noon, and it must already have been one hundred degrees.

Grace's hair was clipper buzzed in the back and asymmetrically long in the front, dirty blonde and curling ever so slightly over her brown eyes. Her bare neck was sweating with the heat of the first truly hot day of the San Francisco spring.

In Dolores Park, the public bathrooms are located in a small concrete building right in the center of the park's steep slope. A palm-tree-lined walkway led the length of one city block uphill. Flanking it on either side was another block's worth of green grassy slopes. Every single sexy person who lived in the Mission district, and many others from around the Bay Area, seemed to have "called in well" to work and headed straight to the park to lie on the grass, soak up the sun, day drink and cruise.

The line for the women's room was snaking up the hill. Grace had made the mistake of waiting until she really had to go before getting in line.

Grace wore leopard-print shorts, a neon-pink baseball cap and a black halter top. The morning's warmth was already making her feel limber and open. She traced her fingers over her golden-tanned skin, the smoothness of her abs and the soft beer paunch of her belly. Her pale-ale nipples felt puffy against the thin cotton of her shirt.

From the looks of it, there were about a dozen women in front of her in line. Experience had taught her that each one would take about five minutes for a simple piss while she stood there hopping from foot to foot in anticipation.

"Ugh," she muttered.

Discomfort or not, there was certainly plenty to watch while she waited. Bodies were bursting out of summer clothes like blooming flowers. Everywhere she looked there were perky asses in brightly colored spandex shorts, metallic triangles and string that counted as bikini tops, hairy calves in tube socks. Loose dresses revealed every curve and movement. Clavicles already shone with perspiration and vitamin D. Fraying T-shirts had been cut off that morning at the sleeves, sometimes all the way down the sides to the hip, revealing love handles and the sides of breasts. Backless dresses betrayed the absence of bras. Inner thigh flesh rubbed together. Pheromones steamed from belly buttons and biceps.

"I'll bet there's nobody in the men's bathroom at all," the girl who was getting behind her in line complained loudly.

"Yeah, I used to just go in the men's room," another girl chimed in, "but one time a dude complained, and I got a ticket with a hundred-and-twenty-five-dollar fine. Fuckin' gender policing highway robbery."

"What'd they do, a dick check? Different-gendered bathrooms are such bullshit anyway," Grace agreed.

"I've never understood why women take so damn long in the bathroom."

This last voice came from the person in front of Grace in the slowly moving line.

It was difficult to see her face; a dark umbrella obscured her. The umbrella was jet black with a lace-like bordering, and seemed to be made of a dense canvas.

"They're probably fucking, not pissing," Grace snorted.

The umbrella turned.

Beneath it was a girl. A girl that Grace instantly found enormously attractive. Her hair was dark, like her umbrella, with a flat shine to it. She wore enormous dark shades adorned with silver rhinestones, the kind that movie stars wear to both conceal their identities and call attention to themselves. Grace couldn't exactly tell, but it looked like the girl was staring directly at her.

She wore a dress that was knee length and strapless, with sheer black nylon material that covered her cleavage and arms to her elbows. The skirt billowed around her, obscuring her thighs. Though the dress was far from formfitting, it was clear this girl was well-endowed and luscious. On her feet she wore ankle-high leather boots with pointy toes, and nylon stockings also covered her legs. Her skin was pale as a sheet of paper, completely unblemished, which perhaps explained her need to shield it from the sun.

They held each other's eyes for a moment.

"Nice umbrella," Grace said. They were now far enough ahead in line that she could lean against the wall.

The girl sniffed.

"It's not an umbrella. It's a parasol with UV protection."

"Wow," said Grace with the sarcasm of someone whose method of flirtation is teasing. "So it's like a giant pair of fancy sunglasses for your entire head."

The girl was unfazed. Her obscured face made her expression nearly impossible to read, which gave Grace much-welcomed cold shivers.

"The sun gives you lots of healthy vitamins, you know," Grace continued. She was also wearing shades, of course, and a billed cap, but her body was much more expressive than this girl's, and her intentions were more difficult to hide.

Grace was not good at being coy.

"The sun," the girl replied in that same impassive tone, standing still as if she was an ice sculpture of a swan, "makes you wrinkle."

"Your skin does look fantastic!"

The line continued to shuffle forward.

"You have a funny way of flirting. You make fun of me and then you compliment me. You're like something between a ten-year-old boy and a debonair dyke."

"I'm Grace," Grace said immediately, holding out her hand. "I would ask you for your number but it seems you already have mine."

This melted the ice swan ever so slightly.

"Claudia," the girl said. As they shook, Grace imagined this pale hand being used to pick up teacups and re-shelve reference books.

"Aren't you hot in all that black?" Grace asked, resuming her boyish method of picking on girls she wanted desperately to kiss.

"I like black. Goes with everything."

"No offense, but I can't stand to see people covering their

bodies on hot days like today. I take one look at you and I feel oppressed. Especially places like underarms and the back of the neck and ankles. Don't you get irritable?"

"No. I keep cool."

"All right, ice princess over here. Don't let me tell you what to do. I just hope you'll let me buy you a Popsicle is all. Don't worry about the bright colors, I think coconut would go great with your skin."

"You are very entertaining. I bet you'd enjoy watching me eat a Popsicle."

"Are you kidding? The only thing I love more than a girl with a push-pop in her mouth is a straight dude eating an ice cream cone. It is so clear that someone doesn't know how to suck dick from the way they eat something cold and sweet that's melting all over their hands."

"You are vulgar."

"You like it."

Claudia's red mouth turned up ever so slightly.

Grace couldn't help but grin a wolfish grin. "You know, there are other places to pee in this park," she said.

"You don't say."

"I do say. I could show you."

"But we're finally at the front of the line," Claudia noticed.

Grace leaned over and looked inside the dingy bathroom.

"Please," she said. "Has anyone who wasn't at least a little drunk taken a piss in that disgusting bunker?"

"Maybe that's why everybody takes so long."

"Or maybe, like I said before, they're too busy getting off."

Sure enough, at that moment a loud moan and a wet sound that was definitely not urine hitting porcelain emitted from one of the stalls. Everyone in line started angrily complaining.

"Wanna get out of here?" the ice princess asked.

"Well, what is summer for if not instant gratification?" Grace agreed.

They began marching side by side up the hill.

Grace and Claudia came over the crest of the hill on the west side of the park, and looked down at the Muni tracks below.

"I've never been over here," Claudia said.

"Really? It's so great." Grace pointed to their left, under the tunnel made by a cement bridge that ran over the tracks. "That's where boys go to cruise."

"Is that so?" Claudia was smirking now, twisting the handle of her parasol so it spun.

This drove Grace crazy, and she reached out to grab both of Claudia's hands in hers.

"Sometimes," she said, "When people are doing really cute things I feel like I have to stop them."

"Is that so?" Claudia repeated deliberately, but did not pull her hands away from being enclosed in Grace's.

"I think it's a control thing." Grace stepped closer.

"Fascinating."

"Yeah. Mind if I join you in your little tortoise shell?"

"You have to be invited."

"Ah, this is like a reverse vampire thing, huh? Day walkers have to be invited out of the sun?"

"Something like that."

"Well," Grace suddenly remembered her rather urgent need. "Who needs you and your transportable shade?"

She turned, and pulled her Hanes boxer-briefs and bike shorts clean off her body, stepping out of them one foot at a time. She then squatted into a wide-legged position, bracing herself with the heels of both hands.

It didn't take long for a strong stream of piss to shoot from her urethra. Grace gave a satisfied sigh as it did. The position combined with gravity combined with Grace's strong pelvic muscles sent the piss in an arch on its way down the hill.

Grace had drunk a lot of beer already, and a lot of icy lemon water. For a while, she watched her own piss with fascination and pride. It smelled potent and sour, though not unpleasantly so. Then she turned her head to look up at Claudia.

"Show-off," Claudia said.

Her piss finally over, Grace shook the remaining drops off by thrusting her hips into the air a few times.

"Maybe so," she replied, pulling her boxer-briefs and shorts back on. "I read somewhere that Sharon Mitchell, who was this badass seventies porn star, was once arrested when the cops were busting a Times Square live sex show. So she's in drag, and the cops are arguing over whether she's a boy or a girl. They say they want to watch her pee, and if she can pee standing up she must be a dude. And she's learned how to pee standing up from doing golden showers, you know. So she walks up to the urinal and pisses and so they agree she must be a man."

"Is that how you learned to do it?" Claudia asked.

Grace's face blushed redder than it was already from the sun.

"Nah," she said, "I like people pissing *on* me."

"Is that a fact?" asked Claudia, with the even tone of someone who was asking someone else to read between the lines.

"Want me to hold your panties?" Grace asked, holding out a hand.

"That won't be necessary," Claudia replied.

Grace paused, then grinned, and threw herself on the grass, on her back.

"Com'ere."

Claudia faced uphill. She bent and picked up her skirt

one-handed, without disturbing the parasol's position protecting her head. She stepped to the side over Grace's face and squatted as daintily as one could expect someone to squat.

There was a moment, as Grace stared up into the dark folds of Claudia's skirt, during which she could see that the other girl's nylons were lace stay-ups.

And that she was not wearing any panties.

Then Grace's world went dark.

It was humid under Claudia's skirt and pitch black. The noise of the rest of the park was muffled. Bereft of all this input, Grace was in a world of scent. Claudia smelled like she spent a great deal of time making sure she didn't smell like anything. She probably exfoliated and moisturized and wore things that were very laundered. But the heat has a mind of its own, and the ripeness of her cunt hit Grace like a freight train.

Grace had just begun to marvel at this when she smelled something even riper. And then the first drops of piss hit her face.

Claudia had been drinking coffee, perhaps several cups, with sugar but no milk. Grace knew coffee-piss well. It was dehydrated and suffocating and she loved it.

Grace had a date named Sally who loved to piss on her in the morning. It had gotten so she could recognize what the piss had once been. Sally would deliberately arrange quizzes, and reward her when she was correct.

Sally's piss was thrilling, but Grace knew her, fucked her, slept next to her. The intimacy of being someone's routine had always been a clear part of the fun. But Grace didn't know this Claudia person at all, except that she was kind of a bitch and Grace definitely loved that. All of a sudden, piss tasted humiliating and powerful. It was new to Grace and very, very good.

Claudia had good aim, though *Not quite as good as mine,*

Grace thought. She was, admittedly, also doing it without seeing what she was aiming for. Which may have been part of the point. A lot of urine found her mouth, and Grace worked to swallow it, becoming a gulping machine. Some of it hit her chin and throat, dribbling down her neck into the grass, turning it muddy. The piss heated up Grace's little head cage considerably. The smell of piss-mud and grass took over what little air there was, like eucalyptus oil and ice water poured over steaming hot sauna coals.

The piss ceased, and Grace lay there panting. Her head was in a haze and her cunt was instantly wet. As fun as this was, she was looking forward to a breath of fresh air.

But Claudia didn't move. What felt like minutes went by in seconds before Grace realized what she was being invited to do.

Obediently, she opened her mouth and searched blindly for Claudia's bare, piss-soaked cunt. It may have been dark but it was pretty much the only other thing under Claudia's skirt besides Grace. All she really had to do was follow the substantial thighs.

As soon as Grace's mouth found it, Claudia's pussy opened, pleased. Grace felt her shift slightly, placing her knee on the ground in the piss mud. Now that's dedication, thought Grace, who was pretty damned dedicated herself.

Not every cunt is wet to the touch. Some require a spit in the palm of the hand, or a push-bottle splooge of lube directly dripping onto it. Some cunts require finesse, slow warmth, tenderness. Grace loved to make sure they got it.

Heat-wave cunt has a life of its own.

Heat-wave cunt is insane, and manic. It's hungry not for sustenance but contact. Heat-wave cunt is hungry, eager, sucking you right up inside like a matter of life and death.

It was muffled, but Grace could hear Claudia whimpering

that obscure language of nonverbal instructions from head-getters to head-givers.

Claudia's pussy was totally bald and smooth as an egg, and her outer labia were slender. Her inner labia hung down ever so slightly, and Grace tugged on them.

Grace stuck out her tongue and flattened it, licking one long lick from Claudia's hole to the base of her clit. Undulations of pleasure rewarded her. Repeating this a few more times, she reminded herself to be slow—although all she wanted to do was lap ferociously like a puppy at a water bowl. She brought Claudia's lips back into her mouth and pouted them out.

It didn't take long for Claudia's pussy to heave, and pour cum all over Grace's already piss-covered face. Sticking out her lower lip, she dragged it along the same sweet route. She rubbed her lips together against Claudia's hole. Piss and cum and mud were starting to mat into her hair. Grace lapped up the cum like the piss. It wasn't dissimilar—Grace was getting a taste for Claudia's juices. They tasted somehow cool despite being so hot, like peppermint tea.

The cum only encouraged Grace further. She was past the teasing phase. She knew what Claudia wanted. She wrapped her lips around Claudia's clit hood and tugged lightly, using the warm folds to jerk Claudia off. The clit began to grow fatter and longer in her mouth as she tugged, emerging from inside the hood. Grace continued to work the hood and stuck her tongue onto the clit itself, just touching it as if testing something she wasn't quite sure about (though that was certainly not the case). She was rewarded with another orgasm, a tensing up that pushed the clit deeper into Grace's happy mouth. As it got longer from cumming, Grace pushed the hood back and began to work on the clit itself. She pursed her lips together and pulled them along the short length of it, sucking and hollowing her cheeks. Her head bobbed, and she could feel her hair squishing in the mud.

She wished she could see Claudia's face but there was something incredible about being trapped under this skirt. Pussy was her entire world and she had one job to do. She just wished she could see Claudia's labia—wished she could see it change color as it got more engorged and aroused. She wished she could see how it looked drenched and shuddering.

Grace began licking again. Instead of flat, full-pussy licks, she pointed her tongue and pushed between all the folds of Claudia's pussy. She loved the crevice between inner and outer, finding it often got neglected and responded well to attention. Her tongue was a paintbrush trying to get into a complicated door-frame molding, like those of so many Victorian Upper Haight apartments Grace had helped to paint robin's-egg blue or cabernet red. She wiggled in these little canyons, first the left then the right, teasing Claudia, who was clearly ready for another cum. Just when she was sure Claudia wouldn't be able to take it anymore she returned to the center of her project, sucking on the clit, which shuddered into her mouth in about five seconds flat. She kept sucking through this orgasm, licking up and down and side to side and diagonally, stirring it like something she was trying to get to dissolve in a soup. She even dared to nibble gently, and was rewarded with another thrusting orgasm.

Claudia's pussy was now so open over Grace's mouth that it would have taken some effort *not* to begin fucking her hole. She did this with animal lust, turning her tongue into an erect undulating phallus for Claudia to ride. It was already difficult to breathe, but Grace just relaxed and concentrated, taking small gulps in through her nose in time to Claudia's thighs bouncing against her ears. Her own pussy was sore and ravenous, but she couldn't really reach it, and Claudia was certainly not obliging.

Grace remembered reading some magazine factoid that the

most sensitive taste buds are at the tip of the tongue. The magazine explained that this is why we love to eat ice-cream cones even more than a bowl of ice cream. It's the licking that sends our sensory receptors into pleasure frenzies. Ice cream, Grace thought, is great, especially on a hot day. But if that thing about taste buds is true, it would be much more effective to explain why we love to give head. Or why she loved it anyway. Grace could never understand why people treated it as a chore, or even something nice to do for your partner. For Grace, pussy eating was 100 percent self-gratification. The front of her tongue, one might reason, had some very greedy buds.

By now, Claudia was full-on riding Grace's face, and who knows what anyone might have thought if they had walked by and seen her crouched and humping in ecstasy. Grace was mostly concerned at this point with keeping her tongue boner up and useful in Claudia's vagina. Every so often she would grab Claudia's entire labia, and suck it into her mouth before thrusting up again with her tongue. This released the cum that had built up inside, drowning Grace's face even more.

Finally, as Claudia was grinding her entire crotch onto Grace's face, she came one last, shuddering, convulsing, lovely cum, pouring out another offering. Grace knew she was finished, at least for the moment, as the pussy hovered, shaking over her face. After a moment, Claudia stood with surprising swiftness. Incredibly, the early-afternoon summer air felt cool on Grace's cheeks after the pussy steam room she'd been enjoying. She lay there gasping in a puddle.

Claudia burst out laughing.

"You look horrible," she said.

"Well, I feel great, so fuck you," Grace grinned.

Claudia snorted. "You should be so lucky." She twirled her parasol, smoothed her skirt.

Grace pushed herself up on her elbows. "Well, what do you call that?"

"I call that a good alternative to that stinking little girls' room."

Grace was a little pussy-drunk, and stunned to realize just how thoroughly she had been used.

Then she remembered that she loved being used, and fell back again to revel in the mud.

The sky above her was clear blue and the air was beginning to feel hot again as she acclimated back.

The day, she realized, was still incredibly young. And she'd already had the hottest pickup scene she could ever hope to pull off.

Suddenly she heard a sound from down the slope:

"Ohh Daddy, *fuck!*"

"I told you it's the best cruising spot," she muttered, and struggled to her feet.

"I never said I didn't believe you," Claudia replied. She turned and headed east down the hill, twirling her lacy black parasol as she went.

Grace watched her for a moment. She was sure she could make Claudia feel eyes on the back of her neck, just as sure as she knew her crotch was soggy with piss, sweat, saliva and cum.

When the other girl didn't turn, Grace picked up her soaked hat, gave it a shake and headed north back to her friends, grinning like the cat who got the ice cream.

THE BULLWHIP AND THE BULL RIDER

Sacchi Green

"Hey, wildcat! Come with me!"

That throaty female voice would've snared me any other time, but not now. I kicked and thrashed and kept on struggling against the two guys who'd pulled me off my brother Ted. Cindy knelt beside him, all cooing and lovey-dovey—Cindy, with her full, smooth curves, who'd been all for a little mutual exploration at last year's rodeo but brushed me off this year and ran to Ted.

I'd beaten him at bull riding! Beaten 'em all! I'd won the trophy belt buckle. But no matter how much I could work like a man, even thrash the men at their own games, their more fleshly rewards were off-limits to me.

Life sucked. My blood was up, the pressure building until I had to explode or die, so I damn sure chose the exploding option. Nobody was gonna hold me back!

Except that the sultry voice came again, much closer now.

"Let me handle her, boys. This calls for a woman's touch."

The calloused cowboy hands trying to hold me back dropped away. Slender, satin-clad arms wrapped around me, long, dark hair smelling of sweet lemons brushed my cheeks, and my face was pressed against a scarlet blouse that barely covered the peaks of a magnificent pair of breasts.

I had the sense to stop struggling.

"Come along with me now, *tigrina*," Miss Violet Montez, lead singer of the intermission entertainment act, murmured into my ear. "I know what you need. And what you don't even know you need."

And, as it turned out, she surely did.

Her trailer was cramped, but I saw right away that it had a narrow, built-in bed. She saw me eyeing it.

"Not yet." Her voice turned stern. "Wrangling a bull is one thing. Treating a lady right is something else. Especially your first time."

Well, there wasn't much I could say to that. In fact, I couldn't think of anything to say, and, while I surely knew some things I'd like to do, I didn't know how to go about them with a gorgeous, worldly woman like Miss Violet Montez. I'd seen her before at rodeos and suchlike gatherings, and fantasized a bit like I did about movie stars and photos in the kind of magazines cowboys tucked under their mattresses in the bunkhouse, but never imagined I'd get this close. "Yes, Ma'am," I said, trying to sound polite with just a hint of cocky, but it didn't come out right.

"You sit down in that folding chair and don't stir while I change into something more comfortable." I perked right up at that, but then she added, "And while you wait, give some thought as to whether you want things sweet, spicy or downright nasty."

I knew my preference, even though I wasn't exactly sure what she meant, but I'd got my brain working enough to know the right answer. "Whatever a lovely lady like you wants is what I want, too."

"We'll just see about that." She scooped up some clothes from the foot of the bed and edged into the tiny bathroom, leaving the door open. I knew better than to get up from my chair, but I did crane my neck to see what I could see. It wasn't much.

The low-necked satin blouse sailed out through the bathroom door, followed by her voice. "Never came across a girl bull rider before in a regular rodeo. Things must be changing for the better."

"Not yet," I admitted. "Not officially. Except at small local shindigs where anything goes." And where my dad was the biggest rancher around and chief sponsor of the rodeo association, but I didn't say that.

Her short black satin skirt with rows of gold spangles followed the blouse, and so did her high-heeled, sparkly cowgirl boots and a pair of nylon panty hose. I wriggled in the chair to see if I could hook that last with my foot, with no luck, but I did get a glimpse of a bare shoulder through the door.

"Well, you can sure handle a bucking bull, but you need to work on self-control," she said over that shoulder. "And it remains to be seen how much else you can handle."

"Yes, Ma'am." It seemed like the safest thing to say. Now I could see that she was shrugging into a blue-checked shirt, which didn't fit much with my hopeful notions of "something more comfortable."

I looked idly around the trailer. It was dented and shabby, but with colorful pictures on the walls, mostly old rodeo posters, and some fancy duds hanging on hooks, along with…

I only just caught myself from bolting straight up. On one hook, coiled neat as a rattlesnake, hung one of the longest bull-whips I'd ever seen. I looked wildly around again at the posters, and there it was, in a corner of what looked like the oldest one: MISS VIOLET MONTEZ, QUEEN OF THE BULLWHIP.

I'd seen her way back then! She'd been performing her tricks at the State Fair when I was just knee-high to a fence post, and she couldn't have been much older than I was now. That'd been the day I'd known for certain that girls could do anything boys could do, and better, if they put their minds to it.

Did she still use the whip? On what? Or maybe who? Some of the racier pictures from those bunkroom magazines came to mind. So did stories from a few paperback books I'd mail-ordered from ads in the back of those magazines. Not enough room in here to swing a whip like that, though. I didn't know whether to be relieved, or disappointed. So many thoughts whirled through my mind that I didn't hear Miss Violet stepping out of the bathroom.

"Like whips, do you?" Her voice, right behind me, made my head swing around so fast my neck cracked.

Right in front of my eyes and nose, close enough that I could tell she didn't shave her private parts but did wash them with lemon soap—though not in the last few hours—was a pair of denim cutoffs so short and tight even Daisy Duke couldn't have got away with them. Looking upward, I saw an expanse of bare midriff topped by the blue-checked shirt, unbuttoned and tied tight under full breasts half-uncovered and straining against such confinement as there was.

I wrenched my gaze upward to her face, trying to tell whether I was being challenged to release those breasts, or even unzip the shorts and give those private parts an airing.

She read my mind. "Don't get big ideas, cowboy. You only get what you earn."

"Yes, Ma'am!" I'd do most anything for a woman who knew not to call me "cowgirl."

"All right then. You can stand up."

Fast as I stood, she backed up quick enough that I didn't get to brush my own tingling chest against her bountiful one. Then she was sitting on the edge of the bed, one of those high arrangements with drawers underneath to save space. She crossed her long legs, bare all the way up to kingdom come and down to a pair of dusty boots that had seen real work, not like her fancy sparkly ones.

"Now take off your belt."

My belt? With my brand-new, shiny, trophy buckle? I unbuckled and slid the worn leather out of the belt-loops so fast my split-second of hesitation couldn't have showed. I hoped. She just held out her hands, palms up, and I laid my prize possession across them like an offering.

I was all set to reach for the zipper of my jeans, but she ordered briskly, "Now turn around."

I turned.

Faster than I'd got it out, she had the belt back in the loops with the buckle perched between the small of my back and my ass. "Slip your hands down in there right over your butt."

It was awkward, but I did my best, ending up with the backs of my hands right against my skin and the belt buckled around both hips and wrists. I could've wriggled loose, of course, but by then I was bound and determined to please her enough to earn, well, whatever reward there might be. Besides, the feel of my own hands against my buttcheeks, especially if I wiggled my fingers, was tantalizing in an odd sort of way. Maybe soon it would be her hands there. One way or another.

"Turn around again."

I turned. She leaned back a bit. Her shirt looked likely to slip right off one or another of her breasts, if not both, and I could see the outlines of her nipples poking out like they wanted to speed up the process. It occurred to me that she was enjoying all this a whole lot, which made me enjoy it even more.

"Not bad," she said. "I'll give you a little reward you haven't really earned yet." She stuck out one of her boots and nudged me in the crotch with its toe. "You can clean up my boots."

The boots were even grubbier than I'd noticed at first, with worse things than dust on 'em. Well, so were mine just now, and the crotch of my jeans wasn't much better after riding the bulls. It was getting mighty damp, in fact, which could be a help in the cleaning department. I mounted that boot.

My elbows stuck out enough to give me some balance. Carefully, so as not to put much downward force on her foot, I squeezed my thighs around the stiff leather and moved myself back and forth, first by tilting my hips, then taking tiny steps forward and back. My jeans got a whole lot wetter. My rhythm got faster. The pressure between my legs was building so high I could hardly stand it.

Her face didn't give me any clue as to whether I was pleasing her, but her nipples seemed to be poking out even more, which didn't soothe my state of frantic arousal one bit.

"Self-control, hotshot, self-control," she scolded. "Keep your attention on your work."

That last part sounded so much like my mother you'd think it would dull my urges, and it did for a bit. "Toby, pay attention to your work!" Ma had scolded, time after time. She'd come West as a schoolteacher, a good one, and even after she married my dad she kept on as principal when the area got populated enough to need that big a school. Ted and I had got pretty well educated in spite of ourselves, even though we tried not to let on. It was a strange feeling to be minding Miss Violet Montez the way I'd never minded anybody since my mother passed away. Strange, but exciting, and that was downright weird.

"Don't slow down! Where's that bull-riding stamina?" She slid her foot free and ground the boot's toe into my denim seam right where it crossed my clit. I jerked and bit my lip to hang on, and dug my knuckles into the flesh of my butt, which made me jerk even harder.

"Time for the other boot, before you run out of steam."

If I got any more steamed up I'd explode all over her trailer. I almost said so. Luckily her other foot creeping up my inseam distracted me. I didn't know whether talking back would bring on a punishment, or make her give up on me, but I sure didn't want to risk the second. I stared down and concentrated on rubbing that second boot with my thighs and crotch. It didn't seem to be getting any cleaner, in spite of how wet I was.

"Ma'am," I said, meekly as I could manage, "I'm afraid my pants are so grubby by now they're just adding dirt to your boot."

"I believe you're right," she said. "I can smell those britches from here, reeking like a cross between a bull pen and a harem full of horny women."

I dared a quick look. Her tight shorts were looking damp at the seam, too. "I could wash up," I offered.

"You just stay dirty until I tell you otherwise! Now pick up those panty hose and use them to clean my boot."

Pick them up while my hands were still stuck down the rear of my pants? Impossible! Which was likely the point. Punishment was on the way. That was fine with me, but I still did my best to follow orders, hooking the toe of my boot under the panty hose, kicking them high up in the air, and ducking my head to try to catch them on my neck. Nearly made it, too.

But crooked elbows weren't enough to keep my balance, especially when something, maybe even Miss Violet's other foot, tripped me up. I went down on my knees, hard, my upper body sprawling over her thighs and my face planted right down in her crotch. I tried to act like the wind was knocked out of me, but to tell the truth I was gulping in her warm, rich woman-scent.

Miss Violet wasn't fooled. She lurched her hips up, and for a brief second I even got to taste the wetness seeping through her shorts, but then she threw me off onto the floor. It was only when my hands broke the fall that I noticed they'd come out of my pants.

She stood above me, arms crossed over her breasts, a fierce frown on her face that didn't quite go with the gleam in her eyes. "Get up. And get the whip." I got up.

There might have been others in the trailer I hadn't noticed, but I went right for the coil upon coil of the bullwhip. My pants, loose now that my hands were freed from the belt, rode dangerously low on my hips, but I managed to lift down the heavy coils, carry them to her and loop them over her outstretched hands.

She looked down at the whip for so long I was worried she'd forgotten me. Finally she looked up. "High time this lady got to dance again. It's been too long." That fierce look took hold of her again. "Take off your shirt, go stand right up against the door and keep your hands raised to the top of it. Surely you can do that much right!"

I did just what she said, not even pausing to straighten out and tighten my belt. Chances were she'd order me to pull the pants down anyway. But for what seemed like a long while nothing happened, except a few sounds of motion behind me like she was looping and relooping the whip. I tried to remember things she'd done with it at the State Fair: hitting targets, flipping fence posts end over end, sending wagon wheels whirling through the air, even making pictures with its curves and loops high over her head, outlines that looked like ocean waves or a mountain range or even handwriting in some unknown language.

She hadn't used it on living flesh, human or animal, but I had no doubt that she could kill or maim with it if she had a mind to, or just etch lines into skin precisely where she wanted them to go. Maybe even my skin. A shiver, more of anticipation than dread, ran all the way down from my scalp to the soles of my feet.

But nothing happened. "Ma'am," I said finally, when I couldn't bear the wait any longer and my upraised arms were aching, "Miss Violet, please, Ma'am, can I look around at you?"

"When I'm good and ready," she said sharply, and before I could draw another breath something lashed out fast as lightning, wrapped around my butt, and jerked my pants down to the floor, belt, underdrawers and all.

"Now," she said, "you can turn around."

I turned and stared. Naked now all the way down, pants tangled around my boots so I couldn't walk if I tried, I should have felt shame, embarrassment, confusion or fear, but something more powerful swept over me. Something like, like…awe, but even stronger.

Miss Violet stood tall, shirt, shorts and boots discarded, naked as I was except for the bands of bullwhip wrapped from one forearm up to where they bound the whip's grip to her shoulder. Shortened like that, there was no more problem with lack of space to swing it. The tightly plaited strips on the outer layer of the thong looked like the patterned skin of some exotic snake climbing down to her hand that gripped it three feet or so above where the long, narrower fall piece was attached. When she twitched her hand, the thin cord at the end, the "cracker" that makes most of the noise when the whip slashes through the air, looked like the tongue of a snake flickering just before it decides to strike.

There'd been a snake charmer lady at the State Fair, too, in skimpy, gaudy duds meant to look Oriental, with a snake around one arm and another draped across her neck. Miss Violet was as far beyond that sideshow faker as a statue of a Greek goddess is beyond a kewpie doll.

What went before had been some kind of game. Now, however much Miss Violet's curving hips and full, luscious breasts tipped with jutting brown nipples made me want to fuck and be fucked, I wanted even more to fall on my knees in front of her. To show respect for her greater power and let her use me any way she wanted.

I almost did fall on my knees, but she motioned me to turn back to the door, and I just managed it without stumbling. The whip teased me at first, trickling down my spine, curling around to nip at the sides of my breasts, drifting across my buttcheeks. My legs were as far apart for balance as the pants at my ankles would allow, and when the whip's tip rose up between my thighs to tweak my tenderest parts I jerked so hard I almost toppled backward. In my imagination first it was a real snake, then it was Miss Violet's finger, and I couldn't even tell which made me the wettest.

When the pain came, it was more like ice at first than fire. Thin slices across my shoulder blades, buttcheeks, thighs, too random in the beginning to brace against, accelerating after a while into a storm of strikes that inflamed already-sore places until I felt like I must be red-hot as steel being forged into a blade. A blade to serve Her.

I may have cried. If I did, it wasn't for the pain. The pain was just the means to bring it out. The unfairness of life...of death...Cindy, my mother...the huge, unknown world stretching in front of me...

When the whipping stopped, I didn't know for a while if it was just another pause. Then Miss Violet's whip-free, snake-free arms came around me from behind, her breasts pressed into my sore back, and she wriggled her cunt against my butt. "You sure stripe up nicely, *tigrina*. Don't worry, hardly any blood. Guess you'd better ride on top tonight, though, for the sake of my sheets."

So I did. Miss Violet was still a goddess, with or without a whip, far better in the glorious flesh than any Greek stone statue. I paid close heed to what made her writhe and cry out with pleasure, and went over the edge a time or two myself when she pumped her knee into my crotch while I was sucking her breasts so hard she yelled but kept hold on my short hair to urge me on. After a while she showed me just how far my own body could rise above anything I'd ever imagined, spurring pleasure with pain to newer, sharper peaks, until we were both so worn out we could scarcely twitch, and her sheets were soaked with sweat and our mingled juices and the occasional streak of blood after all. Even the leather-bound handle of the bullwhip had come in for some soaking and lay pungently damp beside her pillow.

After a while I asked drowsily, "How come you gave up on your bullwhip act, Miss Violet? You were the best! Doesn't seem as though singing at small-time rodeos would pay better."

She propped her head up on one hand. "There's things men will stand from a young good-looking girl that they won't abide anymore when she's a grown woman. You'd find that out soon enough even with bull riding, so you might as well understand it now. There's a big world out there with chances for you, so don't get stuck here if you can help it."

I didn't want to think about anything but being there with her right that minute, but deep down I knew she was right.

When I rode back to the ranch at daybreak, too drained to sort out the remnants of pleasure and pain and smoldering resentment, Daddy was waiting in the barn. He couldn't quite meet my eyes. "Looks like maybe you'd better go back East to school, Toby, the way your Mama always wanted."

"Looks like," I agreed. And that was that. I knew he felt guilty for the way he'd raised me, but I'd never have survived any other way. If he thought going to school back East would teach me properly womanly ways, though, he was dead wrong. Going to a women's college didn't make a lady of me, but I sure learned a lot about women.

And thanks to Miss Violet Montez, whip artiste extraordinaire, I had a good deal to teach, as well.

ARACHNE

Catherine Lundoff

Warp and weft, shuttle and thread, the cloth springs from my fingers like a blossom. Its bright threads will call to passersby in the marketplace, coaxing them to my father's stall. Its beauty will cry out for them to touch it, to possess it. Warp and weft, gold and silver. My hands fly.

So passes my youth. No young man or village matchmaker comes to see my father for my hand because I am stooped from bending. My dark eyes are wide from staring at the loom morning and night and my fingers curve more easily into the threads than into the cupped fingers of a young man's hand. Still, my cloths are worth more drachmae than those of any other weaver in this city, enough so that my widowed father can hire help at the stall and can buy a husband for my sister. I find that I want none of my own, even if one wanted me.

Sometimes at night when I rest from working, Father tells us stories about great heroes and battles. I think that I am like Penelope, Odysseus's wife, endlessly weaving and picking apart her work to fend off suitors. Except that there is no hero I wait for. Except that no cloth of mine is ever picked apart and done over because there is no need. But I am skilled and patient at my loom like her, caught up in the fibers of my web. Still, I wonder how she could have loved so much that Odysseus was worth more than her weaving. I wonder if I could love anyone or anything like that.

Other times, Father tells us tales of the gods and these I despise. They are nothing but shadows of human failings, full of rage and lust and deceit. I listen because he is my father and both he and my sister enjoy such stories, but in my heart I feel only contempt. I do not believe in gods or their followers. My faith hangs on the power of my shuttle alone.

And for many years, it is justified. I sit at my loom like a spider in her web and my cloths fly through the cities on gossamer wings. Great citizens and their wives come to watch me while I weave and to marvel at the results. Tapestries and chitons, hangings and coverings for wall and floor and door, all these and more climb newborn from my loom. They leave the city, my children do, to go to foreign lands and across strange seas. I long for them, each one beloved, brought to life with infinite care by my fingers.

But leave they must, for my sister's wedding approaches and my father longs to be splendid among the merchants in the agora. I cannot disappoint them for they are the only ones that I love. My winged fingers trail feathers of wool and flax behind them. The beauty and fame of my weavings grow until the day when I weave with threads of gold and silver. The cloth on my loom is terrible as a thunderstorm, beautiful as the sea at rest. A merchant's wife lays her unlovely hand on its edge and says, "Your work is a great tribute to Athena."

I meet her empty eyes with a cold gaze of my own and answer her. "I owe nothing to any god. This work is born of my body alone, and I say it is better than anything you can imagine made by your so-called goddess."

She flinches and runs off like a startled doe and Father shouts that I will be his undoing. First he demands, then he begs that I take back my words, so fearful is he that I will bring the curse of the gods upon this house. He and our slaves go to all the temples that day bearing gold and dead birds in a frantic effort to appease those who do not exist nor would care for such sacrifices if they did.

Word of my foolishness, for so it is seen, spreads quickly and soon our shop is filled with philosophers and priests who buy no cloth. They speak and their words are filled with anger and belief and fear. There is no joy, nothing of the feel of silk, the light touch of linen and I say one word to them, "Enough!" and then two, "Get out!" After a time, they leave and only one old woman stays to give me a last dire warning.

I look upon my loom and at the beauty glowing there. I turn it so she can see it, too, and I answer her, "What goddess of yours could do such work? Can her phantom fingers fly over the warp threads and birth such children as this? I think not. The gods are nothing but our vices given form and I do not, will not believe in them."

She gives me a strange smile and when I look at her again, she is growing, straightening the bent back of age, wrinkles fading into the smooth skin of youth. Her rags turn to silks so fine, so blue and gold and purple that I reach out to touch them, longing to feel their glory beneath my fingers. But her eyes blaze with black fire and I stop my hand where it is, halfway between us. Her black hair cascades down to the floor and when I look upon her face, I know that I have never seen such beauty, such fury. But I will not be afraid: that is the only gift the gods of my people have to give us and I will not accept it.

"Ungrateful girl." Her eyes burn into mine but I will not look away. I force myself to bathe in them until their heat warms my skin and my heart. I shiver a little, still refusing to believe that this is real, despite the evidence of my senses. She smells a little of olives, of wildflowers on the hillside, and her pale brown hands are broad, with long fingers, longer even than my own. I imagine them on my skin because real or not, I want to feel her touch. I realize that I would give myself to her for the slightest hint of her smile, and I yield to love for the first time. But I am proud and I will not kneel to beg forgiveness for my boast or my disbelief.

My father falls to his knees instead and begs for me, his voice breaking, pleading for her mercy. Athena looks upon him and gestures toward the door. "Go," she says in a voice like thunder. "I would speak to your bragging fool of a daughter alone." He crawls out on hands and knees and my sister and our slaves go with him with many a backward glance at me. Cowards. I draw myself as straight as my back will permit and wait for whatever comes next.

She looks at me with immortal eyes and I know she sees all that is in my heart. She holds me in the palm of her hand, and I am hers. With a single gesture, she captures the shuttle and holds it in her light brown hands. "I could strike you down at your loom but I will be merciful. I will challenge you to a contest instead and prove that I am the best weaver. But if you lose, you are mine to do with as I please."

"And if I win?" My voice rasps, as with unaccustomed use, and I dream of her desire consuming me until nothing is left but ashes. I find that now I want to believe that she is more than mortal anger and jealousy given form, and because I want it so very badly, I do believe. My longing almost leaps from my lips, held back only by the fear that such as she cannot love.

She smiles, and I see my fate in her eyes. Either way the outcome is the same and the knowledge fills me with fierce joy and great terror, bound as one. A loom appears before her, already strung and ready to be worked. At the same moment, my work vanishes from the loom before me and I too, have nothing but a blank warp. I cry out in rage at the destruction of my work and her smile remains. "Did you think to anger a Goddess and pay no price for it, mortal?"

My pride rages within me. "I will win. I am the best weaver in Athens and you cannot defeat me."

"I give you your gifts, child. Of course I can defeat you."

I reach blindly for the wool and flax, for the threads that will display my rage more splendidly than any words I know. I turn away while the Goddess Athena, who I denied, sits before me and laughs quietly as her shuttle embraces the loom like a lover. I force myself not to watch the way she holds the thread, how she calls the design from it as I do myself. Shuttle and shed, my fingers fly.

When I finish, I am stiff and tired, but the beauty of the tapestry before me draws tears from my eyes. This is my most glorious work, the most blessed child of my fingers. It is the glory of the rising and setting sun, the pasture in spring, the olive grove at harvest time. But more than that, it is the truth as my heart knows it. She is finished moments after me, but I wait before I look at her loom.

Athena rises first and turns my loom with a gesture so that the tapestries stand side by side. Hers is lovely, a moonlit pool in the forest, a mountain in winter behind it, each detail lined in shimmering beauty until I could weep to see it. Yet, mine outshines it and when I look upon her face, I see she knows it, too.

I have woven my father's tales in threads of many colors: the sins and deceits of Zeus, the betrayals and cruelties of Apollo and Aphrodite and Hera. Here Europa, there Leda, Echo, and others, lovers and would-be lovers cast aside or ravished or transformed, punished without cause. Their pain shines from their faces, their bodies as they flee or are changed and suffer.

She looks at my loom and her face grows dark as a storm cloud. Her black brows draw together and I wonder what I shall be changed into, how I shall be punished for my superior skill. I nearly laugh in my triumph, for whatever she may do, I have won.

Her gaze fixes upon me and my shuttle flies from my fingers and wraps the threads around my wrist until I am forced to my feet, my right hand bound tightly to one corner of my loom. The shuttle sails on, guided only by her gaze until I am fastened, each limb to a corner and my face toward the weaving. My back groans at being so suddenly straight and my heart races as I wonder what she will do next. At the thought, her hand splits my chiton to my waist and she snarls through clenched teeth, "Do you believe in me now, girl?"

Rather than answer, I sag against the loom and it stands firm as if by magic. My body begs wordlessly for her touch but I will not let the words pass my lips, will not let her see my weakness. Wool and linen braid themselves together in Athena's hands until they are like leather in their strength. I watch from the corner of my eye as they swirl, whistling in the air around her before landing on the exposed skin of my back. They trace lines of fire over my skin, tearing a muffled groan from my firmly closed lips. I tell myself I will say nothing, that no cry of pain or desire will she draw from me but the threads pull the words, the sounds from me, despite my efforts.

I can feel her smile, reveling in her mastery over me. For a moment, I hate her for her power to see into my heart and draw my desires out. I hate myself for desiring her as well as for my failure to speak, to banish her from my world. But I long also for the touch of her hands, her lips, I who have never known love or desire for anything except the work of my hands. I want her to weave me anew, her hands coaxing me into a new shape, one that she could love.

Fire sings along my skin, and I melt into the tapestry before me. Again and again, she strikes until welts dance over my back and my juices pour down my thighs like rain. I think that she may never stop. I close my eyes and imagine myself a sacrifice to love. Surely capricious Aphrodite must exist if Athena can make me love her. The thought shakes me to the bone and moans and pleas pour from my lips now, a torrent of sound and desire.

Behind me, Athena laughs and the room goes gray around me. I can no longer stand on my own, and I collapse into my bonds. I hear her voice around me like a cloud: "I see I have a warrior of my own now, one like my sister's Amazons," and I wonder who she means. Jealousy sears my heart like a bolt and I want to cry out that I am better than any Amazon but the words, too long held back, will not come.

This, then, is the moment when she throws the whip from her and her lips touch my skin. Like water, they cool the burning touch of her hands as they explore my flesh. The loom releases me into her arms and I fall almost to the floor. She holds me up with one mighty arm while her eyes once more examine the tapestry before us. This time, her expression is rueful and anger is pushed gradually from her face by admiration. "It is a master-piece, for all I despise the topic, Arachne. You are well named, spinner. Perhaps you can weave yourself a tapestry about this day."

I surrender the last of my pride and reach up to pull her face down to me so that I may cover it with kisses. Suddenly, we are lying on my bed and her lips own mine, devouring them with the last of her fury. I cry out at first as my swollen back meets the fabric, but she drives the pain from me and soon I think of nothing but her. Her fingers find my sex and twist themselves into my wetness, into my being, until I am filled with them. I meet her eyes as my body writhes into a new, straighter shape beneath her caress.

She takes me then, her mouth consuming me like a ripe melon and I cry out like a Maenad possessed by Dionysus. I imagine my spirit and flesh roaming wild in the olive groves, dancing ecstatically to the unseen music that flows from my beloved. My body is like the fire-mountains in the sea and I writhe and twist beneath her. Her tongue cleaves my lips to find the center of my being, and I am hers.

Slowly, slowly I return to myself and begin my own timid effort to taste her flesh. She permits me to explore her body, the rounded swell of her breasts, the curve of her hips and thighs and belly with my lips and tongue. Her skin glows as if lit from within and her thighs, too, are wet like a mortal woman's. Delight shines from me when I see that she, too, knows desire and I set out to coax more from her. I want to know her flesh, to know her heart as she can know mine with her fiery glance. She tastes of honey and of the sea and the scent of olives fills me as my fingers find a road inside her.

Athena cries out beneath me, her voice like a temple trumpet, and my heart sings at the sound. She rocks under me and her legs tremble as mine did at her touch. For a moment, her eyes open and fall on me and I shudder at the lightning I see there, fearing, yet almost longing to be turned to ash by her fierce gaze. Instead, she strokes my cheek and her voice whispers softly, "My little spider, you will be mine for the rest of your mortal years and beyond." My heart sings.

When she sees the answer in my eyes, she sweeps me, loom

and all, from my home. Housed in the secret chambers of her temple, I learn how to please her until I am sure of her heart, or as sure as mortals can be. I never forget that she is a Goddess first, though she blesses my body with her hands and tongue and my loom with her eyes. But it is enough. I will live out my days in her temple, known only to those I love because I want nothing more.

Outside in the agora, the foolish merchants and the priests who want to believe in such things speak of my destruction at the hands of the Goddess. Only my father and sister know the truth and they are happy to keep my secret because I ask it of them. I want no more fame, no more watchers at my loom but one. Athena herself acknowledges my skill and what more can any weaver want than that?

My sister visits the temple to tell me that she hears I killed myself in shame at losing the contest to the Goddess. They say, too, that she revived me and turned me into a spider as an act of contrition. She tells them nothing in return and I smile a quiet smile as I weave both for my beloved and for the pure joy of it. Her spider, my Goddess calls me and so I will remain. Warp and weft, my fingers fly.

BEHROUZ GETS LUCKY

Avery Cassell

I was sixty, and long past the age of hope, young lust, love and bewilderment. I was sixty, using my senior discount to buy oatmeal, black tea and ginseng at Rainbow Co-op, and silk neckties at Goodwill. I was a time-traveling, part-Persian expatriate. I had been an outsider all my life and felt insulated that way. Insulation is protection, but it is also isolation. Even though I lived in San Francisco, that bastion of sexual and gender freedom, I lived outside of the galaxies of the butch, FTM, genderqueer and leather communities. I'd hitchhiked across the country, been a streetwalker, smoked opium with princes, raised children, been fisted on Twin Peaks, sung in punk bands, grown up in Iran, had threesomes with bikers and members of British parliament, followed family tradition and become a librarian. I'd buried one daughter and two lovers, spent decades in the Midwest, kneaded bread, gotten sober, been homeless, pretended to be a boy wanting to be a girl, driven across town in a blizzard at five a.m. to slap a gigolo who was wearing pleated black silk panties, taught preschool, attended PTA meetings and tickled grandchildren. It's-a-long-story was my middle name.

At sixty, and in my considerable dotage, I spent my evenings wearing a quilted, charcoal velvet smoking jacket, foulard silk cravat and worn, cuffed flannels while delicately sipping English Breakfast tea with my cat, Bear, strewn across my lap, a pile of tattered paperback Dorothy Sayers mysteries at hand, and vacillating between wanting to manifest a lover and relishing each delicious second alone. Between chapters and inspired by Lord Peter Whimsey and his paramour Harriet Vane, I imagined a lover, a you. If I could manifest you at six a.m. when I was lolling between the sheets distractedly having my morning pre-work come, or on Sunday afternoon when I was settling in for a leisurely fuck session with myself, my two biggest silicone dildos, nipple clamps, my S-curved metal dildo, a metal sound, a stainless-steel butt plug, Eartha Kitt wafting from the stereo, a fountain of lube, dim lights, and a cushion of towels and rubberized sheeting to soak up the spillage…I would imagine a you.

Sometimes I craved you when I came home, tired from a day of advising patrons, giving restroom directions, problem-solving minor computer issues and searching for copies of the latest best-selling romance. Sometimes I craved that moment of perfect domesticity when I'd open my door to the oregano- and tomato-scented smells of minestrone soup wafting from the kitchen, and you in the rust velvet armchair in the living room. I'd fall to my knees on the rough wool of our Tabriz carpet, start to crawl across the red-and-gold fibers. Your pipe would be smoldering in the ashtray, filling the air with the sultry sweet aroma of tobacco and cherry. You'd lean back and spread your denim-clad legs, rubbing your cunt as I approached on my knees, the workday rolling off of me the closer I got. Reaching your cunt, I'd rest for a minute, my lips caressing the bulge in your crotch, as grateful for your hand on the back of my neck and your packed jeans as I was for salt. I'd growl softly, nipping at the thick blue fabric, damp from my spit and slightly threadbare from past ministrations. You would unbutton your fly slowly, each button releasing with a soft pop; I'd cover your cock with my mouth until it reached my throat, then ease up and lick the shaft, lost in your smell and your palm firmly pushing my head into your cunt. Your cock would shove the outside world aside, erasing demanding supervisors, aching joints and crowded MUNI buses until all that was left was it in my throat.

I had a shallow, translucent blue glass bowl on the dining room table that I filled with garnet-colored pomegranates, dusty plums, phallic bananas and tart green apples, and sometimes I longed to see your house keys on the table next to the bowl of fruit. Did I want this complication to interfere with my quiet life? Did I really want someone to know my quirks and fears? To discover that I sometimes ate cheddar cheese, figs and cookies for dinner, to twist her hand into my silver-haired cunt, to be privy to my mood swings and self-doubt, to be content to live with my need for solitude? I'm Middle Eastern to my part-American core, and as such have a deep belief in fate. At a jaded and indecisive sixty, I decided to leave love and lust to fate.

How did we meet? How does fate decide to roll her dice? Was it at the park, commiserating over fawn-colored pigeons fighting for brioche crumbs at our feet, while the ginkgo trees shed golden, fan-shaped leaves on the park bench? Was it in an airport while listening to the murky flight update announcements, wondering if we should grab an overpriced stale croissant and latte before our flight, and finally reaching for our lattes at the same time, our fingers touching over scattered copies of *USA Today*. Maybe it was at work, sighing and rolling our eyes over gum-snapping coworkers, discovering mutual tastes in movies and politics in the lunchroom, meeting outside of the office on the sly and texting filthy thoughts to each other across the table during meetings.

In reality, we met prosaically. Lacking a noisy yet accurate village matchmaker, we filled out our profiles on OK Cupid, rolled our mutual eyes at the idiocy of naming the five things one could never do without and updated our profiles earnestly and regularly. I worried about whether I sounded too shallow, and you fretted about sounding too serious. We both were annoyed at OK Cupid's lack of queer identity choices. I changed my sex from male to female and back again monthly, while you identified as bisexual so as not to leave out possible FTM matches. You put up an out-of-focus picture of you repotting plants, said you spoke French and ironed and starched your sheets, didn't mention your sexual proclivities at all. I mentioned flagging red, gray, black and navy right in the first paragraph, said that I cooked Persian food and collected bird skulls, put up a photo of myself half-dressed and playing an accordion and said that only butch dykes need apply. You were eleven years younger than I was, a rough-hewn-looking butch, and gave me five stars, which made my heart flutter and my cunt get wet in anticipation. I rated you five stars back, and nervously sent you a short, overly edited but carefully flirtatious email suggesting that we meet for tea and conversation. Then I heard nothing for five months. In the interlude I went on a series of fruitless first dates, but I had not forgotten you. In spring you finally wrote back, suggesting that we meet for coffee. Your name was not Amber or Dixie or Tyler, but Lucky. And I wrote to you, signing my name Behrouz, which means lucky in Farsi.

We met at Cafe Flore, the classic rendezvous for queer blind dating in the Castro. Public transportation was two steps away, so it was easy to flee from the date if it was awful. Cafe Flore was loud and gay as fuck, with mediocre food and sweet servers.

We were both on time. I wore pleated gray flannel pants, a white shirt with a Campbell clan wool necktie, my tattered gray Brooks Brothers jacket, purple silk socks with striped garters, horn-rims, my hair slicked to one side and my favorite butterscotch-colored brogues. You wore a stately pompadour, a red, ribbed, wool sweater with frayed cuffs over a white Oxford shirt, black 501 button-fly jeans, three gold rings on your right hand and harness boots. You were stocky and muscular, a little shorter than my five-eight, had deep-brown hair threaded with gray, small breasts, olive skin, a chipped front tooth, hazel eyes, a large aristocratic nose with tiny nostrils, and a beguiling swagger. You drank black coffee, and I sipped sticky sweet soy chai latte.

I was immediately turned on by you, trying not to look too eager as I glanced at your rough-hewn gardener's hands, evaluating them for size and dexterity. I was nervous and unsure if you liked me back. I was never good at reading signs and knew that my reserve was often read as disinterest. I wanted to feel your hand in my cunt. We started slowly; we talked about our cats, the general state of classism and disrepair in San Francisco, our jobs, food, and our upbringings. Your tuxedo cat, Elmer, had died two months ago, after living a long and productive life of catching mice, napping in your oval, vintage, pink porcelain bathroom sink and skulking on bookshelves. My ginger cat, Francy, had one bronze eye, a puffed out tail that was longer than her body, and liked to pee with me when I came home from work.

I told you about my love of books, organization and social service, which led to the good fortune of a job at the San Francisco Public Library. After studying biology, you'd fallen into gardening, and spent your days planning gardens and fondling manure and plants. We agreed that the recent invasion of stealthy, gleaming-white Google buses with black-tinted windows that transported entitled tech workers from their cubicle penthouses in San Francisco to their jobs in Mountain View were shark like, and wondered why they hadn't been violently defaced yet. We mourned the loss of Plant It Earth, Osento bathhouse, Faerie Queene Chocolates, the dimly lit Mediterranean place on Valencia with Fat Chance belly dancers swiveling sensuously around the tables, The Red Vic Movie House, and Marlene's drag bar on Hayes Street...and then we sighed like curmudgeonly old farts wondering where the past had disappeared.

You were raised Jewish in Columbus, Ohio, a hotbed of Republican ideology and Christian intolerance, graduated a year early from Bexley School for Girls and then fled to UC Berkeley for sexual and intellectual freedom. Your dad was an insurance adjustor and your mom worked part-time in the ladies' undergarments section of Lazarus department store. Your father worked late hours and fancied himself a suave businessman, leaving the house each morning awash in citrusy Spanish cologne and cigarette smoke, and sporting a flashy gold Rolex wristwatch that he won while playing cards. Your mom was bitter around the corners and sentential in the middle: a brunette in turquoise double-knit pants suits and the sweetly floral scent of Chanel No 22. You told me about coming home to find your mom drinking endless goblets of chardonnay while listening half-cocked for the metallic sound of your father's key in the front door, and the sneaky shuffle that announced his belated presence home. You were an only child, but lived in the same Tudor-style home in the same quiet middle-class neighborhood your entire childhood, the oak-lined streets, your aunts, uncles and cousins, and your friends and their families protecting and loving you even when your folks were distracted. Our family had moved every two years, from state to state, country to country, and continent to continent. I found your childhood geographic stability both exotic and enviable. At age seven, you decided you wanted to be a boy. Each night you'd stare dreamily out of your bedroom window while stroking the faint down on your upper lip to wish a mustache into existence. Wryly, you told me that it didn't work, but now you're content with your hard-earned butchness. As a child, you escaped into books, and spent hours in the Bexley Public Library, scouring the shelves for anything related to sexuality and gender, which wasn't much in the 1960s. Your curiosity and scholastic diligence paid off with a full university scholarship and an early release from Ohio. I'd also grown up immersed in books, hiding in odd corners of the home with a stack of paperbacks and a pocket full of raisins. I related to the escapism that they provided to desperate kids like us, junior outsiders and renegades.

After three hours of exchanging stories and too much coffee and chai, we started to talk about sex and desire. Our drinks cooled as our temperatures heated. We both lived in San Francisco, home to sexual freedom and excess, with everything from International Ms. Leather, to the Eagle, Mr. S, the 15 Association, the Exiles, regular play parties for every identity and orientation, BDSM coffee houses and more. One-time hookups, public play and casual sex were easily obtainable, but I was embarrassed to admit to you that in my midfifties I'd grown out of the ability to do casual play and sex. It didn't work for me anymore, and although I missed the immediacy and physical relief of instant sex, I needed lovers, continuity and intimacy. You commiserated, and said that you'd felt the same ever since turning forty-three. Even though we agreed that we both wanted love and deeper intimacy, everything felt dangerous and forbidding—like we were getting ready to foolishly leap off an emotional cliff, our hearts potentially shattering on the shoals below.

I flushed as our eyes met. We both stopped breathing for a second, unsure if we wanted to continue. Finally, you inhaled, leaned forward, pierced me with the possibility of a future, and murmured, "Tell me. What do you want? What do you need?"

I blushed, my eyes widening and quickly looking down, and my cunt tingling. I admitted to wearing my hankies on the right, and a proclivity for getting fisted, giving head, ass-fucking, bondage and getting beaten. You reached across the table and held my hand with my palm facing up and your calloused hand beneath mine, leaving me feeling exposed, trapped and cradled all at once. I swooned a little at your touch. You smiled a lopsided, sweetly sly smirk, and I imagined one pointed incisor sharply peeking through your lips, your teeth hard against my neck and biting my flesh. You told me you were a top and a sadist, and had been that way since you were a baby dyke in plaid flannel shirts, Frye boots and Carhartts. I blushed again, and felt my nipples harden painfully in the tight confines of my binder, as I whispered through dry lips that although there was no accounting for chemistry, thus far we seemed to have chemistry just fine. I told you that I had simple tastes really, all I wanted was to suck you off, then be beaten and fisted until we were swimming in a pool of come.

You said, "And what do you call your top? Daddy or Sir?"

And I answered, "I call my top, baby."

You looked at me with your hazel eyes turning green like polished sea glass. You leaned closer, took my hand and bit the side of my palm while looking into my eyes. As you bit harder, my hips lifted, and I groaned. I wanted your teeth on my neck, my breast, my ass. There is a vulnerability to a hand's underbelly. It is my favorite place to be bitten, so tender and so blatant—I melted. I wanted you to read my desire with your mouth, you hurting me because you need to, and me letting the sharp sensations course through forming a loop of desire between us.

"Baby," you said, managing to draw the word out like we'd already taken our clothes off and were lying hip to hip. You didn't huff up in toppish indignation, weren't quizzical or offended, but you understood that "baby" was my code for hotness, tenderness and love.

After four hours at Cafe Flore you murmured, "Let's go."

You stumbled lightly over the shallow steps leading down to the sidewalk, exclaiming that your new bifocals were a bear to get accustomed to, then leaned in to kiss me good-bye on the sidewalk in front of a gaggle of Sisters of Perpetual Indulgence and next to the organic stone-fruit stand at the farmers market. "It's Raining Men" was playing tinnily through Cafe Flore's speakers. You kissed exactly correctly...and if that sounds dry, it isn't meant to be so. Your lips were firm and pliant, and fit mine like a T-shirt on a teenager. You'd mastered the art of the tender lower lip bite, and as I delicately licked the corners of your lips, we quickly became breathless. We pulled away a quarter of an inch to prolong the anticipation and fell onto each other after five seconds. I pulled you closer as a Sister with a violet Marie Antoinette wig wolf-whistled in our direction. You slipped one muscular thigh between my legs as my cunt melted and throbbed. I moaned into your mouth as your wide palm smoothed my back under my jacket, and I whispered that I wanted your hand inside of me. Now. You growled—a low sound from deep in the back of your throat. I know that the Sister with the lime-green boa passed us a fistful of condoms. I was starry-eyed and damp as we stumbled to my apartment near Duboce Park on Steiner.

It was dusk, that magical time where the day ends and night begins, when responsibilities dissipate, and mystery and longing fill our hearts. The evening air smelled of jasmine, anticipation and piss—the violent and sweet scents circling us as we walked. The moon was rising as bright as a streetlight, and the sidewalks were full of early evening dog-walkers, with their pups tarrying by trees and potted plants while the owners peered into their palms at their phones. We barely talked. We'd talked through an entire afternoon. Words mean something, but I needed to know how you tasted, how you touched, how we smelled together as we heated up. All I could think of in that fifteen-minute walk was your hand in my cunt, your gardener's fingers entering one by one, packing me full of you. Anything else was gravy on the cake. You knew.

By the time I unlocked the door to my flat, it was dark and the full moon watched us. The streetlights had followed us home, lighting one by one as night fell and we were closer to my apartment. I unlocked the top bolt, and then struggled with the pesky bottom one, trying to make the stuck key turn. As I jiggled the lock in the dark hallway, you pressed your body against mine from behind, rubbing your cock against my ass, and reached around to untuck my shirt and run your hands up toward my nipples. I moaned, humping the doorknob with my clit and almost dropping the key. Finally the brass key turned, and the door flew open under our weight. You pushed me suddenly through the dim foyer, down the hallway and into the sandalwood-scented living room, then to the floor. I wasn't expecting the quickness, and fell to the Persian carpet, my jacket still on and my shirt half-untucked. You stood over me, unbuckled your black leather belt, threw off your sweater, unbuttoned your jeans, pulled out your dick and started stroking it with your hips insolently cocked forward.

"On your knees. I want you to suck my cock. Now."

I crawled over, leaned forward and opened my mouth. I loved filling my mouth with stuff, whether it was cock, chains or fingers. My cunt was soaked, my dick was throbbing and I wanted nothing more than to suck your cock. I wrapped my lips around the black silicone and took it to the hilt while looking up greedily at you. You thrust your hips forward, then drew away, teasing me with just the head until you roughly pushed it all the way in again, banging my throat rudely. I could smell your cunt heating up and sucked your cock, pushing it hard against your cunt, then letting up, and pushing it in again. I was lost in the rhythm, smells and sounds of cocksucking, feeling my cunt muscles spasm the more turned on I became by your moans and growls, and the feeling of my mouth being stuffed.

You grabbed my head, shoving me harder into your groin while letting loose with a stream of fuck noises and words: "I'm gonna fuck your mouth until I come. Suck me, my little invert."

I was slobbering down the sides of my mouth and making slurping and snorting noises as you pulled my hair and fucked my mouth. I desperately wanted to jack off but even more desperately wanted to suck you dry. I wanted you to come down my throat and out my asshole, your heat burrowing into my body. I wanted you to come like lightning through my cunt. I fucked your cock harder with my hot mouth, until with a tremendous series of guttural grunts you came, my swollen lips wrapped around you.

Your hand loosened on my hair for a minute, then you pushed me backward on the rug. I fell awkwardly on my back, supported by my elbows and looking up at you dazedly. You kneeled over me, your pompadour disheveled, your cheeks flushed, your eyes half-closed and blazing, and then took my face between your calloused hands and we kissed, a long luxurious smooch, full of promise. I shrugged off my jacket as you did the same. As I was unknotting my necktie, I heard the swooshing sound of your leather belt being jerked rapidly through your belt loops and looked up to see that you'd doubled it up and were grinning at me evilly.

You shoved me sideways. "Bend over the ottoman."

I kneeled over the high Moroccan-leather ottoman, as you

yanked my flannel trousers and my briefs down to my knees. Your hand reached between my thighs, cupping my cunt, then withdrawing slowly, your fingers separating my labia and running from my cock to my cunt to my asshole. I could feel salty-sweet precome drip down my thighs. I moaned and pushed back, trying to draw you inside. I didn't care where, I just needed your fingers inside of me pumping and rolling and fucking…filling my hungry holes. Instead, you stood up, hovering over me, letting the heat between us build. Suddenly you drew back and went at me with your belt against my ass. The first hit was a kiss. My cunt was slammed into the ottoman, and my ass reached up for you. You hit me harder the second and third times. I still wanted to jerk off, but didn't want to come yet, so I shoved my clit into the side of the leather, forgetting about the belt and spreading my legs to expose my cunt to your touch, then closing them rapidly as I remembered and the leather flew through the air. The next hits were harder and faster, and I could feel your grin and your hard-on behind each swoop of the belt as it thumped my ass. I was making whimpering noises, and each time your belt hit me, it drove my chest forward, pushing the air out of my lungs with a whoosh. My ass was on fire and my cunt felt hollow. Suddenly, I heard the snap of latex. You dropped to your knees and started grabbing my burning ass, twisting my newly bruised, tender flesh. I moaned at the fresh pain. Then there was a cold slurp of lube and one finger circling my hole. I was frantic for it and bucked, trying to suck you in, but you slapped my ass with your free hand. One finger, a second finger and finally a third, with your thumb rubbing against the side of my engorged, stiffened clit.

"Please fuck me. Please! I need your hand inside my cunt," I begged.

You groaned, but pulled out, prolonging my agony as you teased my cunt by barely dipping your fingers inside of me. I sobbed as you finally started pushing four fingers into my cunt while biting my shoulder with your pointy teeth. By now I was inarticulate with wanting to get fucked; the world had shrunken to your hand in my cunt and your breath on my neck. Then you were twisting your hand inside, I opened to you, pushing back, and we were fucking—your gardener's hand in my cunt, the wettest nest, everything swollen and rippling. Your mouth. My cunt. Your cunt. My cock. Your cock. I was fucking you back and you were growling. I was making noises that said, "Fuck me fast and hard." I could feel my orgasm start in my belly—a heavy roll undulating from my chest down to my cunt as I shot out a gush of come, my cock swelling and my cunt clenching around your fist. You were shouting as I sputtered hoarsely, my salty come squirting out a second time, soaking us both.

I slid off the ottoman to the carpet, panting, my pants tangled around my calves and come dripping down to my knees. You fell down to the floor and we held each other close until our breathing slowed down. We were still mostly dressed, our clothing soaked with sex and sweat. I tried to get up, and my knees creaked as I stumbled over my twisted and damp trousers. I tipped over onto the floor laughing. You were in better shape, but your wrist joint ached, your shirt was wet up to the armhole with my come and your cock was listing perilously to the left. I sat you down on the olive mohair sofa, put Eartha Kitt crooning "C'est Si Bon" on the stereo, poured you a snifter of cognac and hung up our jackets. Woozily, I staggered into my bedroom, fetched you a fresh shirt from my cedar-lined wardrobe, changed into a dry pair of pants, and made my way to the kitchen to fix us a postcoital snack of a simple omelet, à la Alice B. Toklas.

In the kitchen, I turned on Marlene Dietrich dramatically singing "Black Market" and swung my well-oiled hips. I let the warmth of the after-fuck flow through me lazily as I vigorously beat the eggs, water, cheese and a hearty sprinkle of coarsely ground black pepper with a fork, then slid them into the hot skillet. Soon the omelet was bubbly and I plopped bread into the toaster, singing along with Marlene's racy double entendres.

I could hear Eartha Kitt's husky voice as I strolled back into the living room, carrying a silver tray with plates of hot omelets and crisp buttered toast. As I walked through the French doors into the living room, you were humming to Eartha while rubbing your wrist. I cleared the low engraved-copper-tray coffee table of leather-bound books, dime-store mysteries, a prickly tomato pincushion and a clutch of fountain pens and put down the tray, then sat down next to you, massaging your wrist and hand, pressing my thumbs into your over-fucked joints. We ate, denim knee to flannel knee, and shoulder to shoulder, devouring the steaming eggs quietly.

Eggs and toast finished, I suddenly became nervous and insecure. Was this just a queer, kinky, senior-citizen version of the one-night stand? Did I want this invasion of heat and conversation in my midst, winding its way through my apartment and life? It was easy to know what I wanted when my legs were spread—my cunt and your hand conversed fine. What the fuck was I doing? I must have jolted in panic, because you removed my empty plate from my lap, leaned over and snuggled me against your shoulder.

You said softly, "Hey, you."

I said, "Hey, you too," back. And this is how it all started.

SECOND DATE

Miel Rose

It is our second date and I still don't know what to call you as your fingers wrap themselves around my throat. You haven't told me, and it didn't occur to me to ask. My back is pressed firmly against the wall of this hallway and as your hand squeezes, your lifeline heavy on my windpipe, words well up in my mouth like saliva. *Yes, please, more, thank you,* and behind them this desire to name you, name exactly what you are to me in this moment.

Sir feels most safe, standard, but there is a little girl deep inside me who has already claimed you for her Daddy and that word feels large and weighted in my mouth, a stone held protectively underneath my tongue. This girl is desperate to know what she has done to make her Daddy so angry he would wrap his fingers around her throat, constrict air and blood, choking out his sweet-princess-baby-girl-sugar-darling in the hallway between kitchen and living room. Because this is what she wants to be to you: treasured and precious and small and cared for, Daddy's angel, sheltered in his strong arms. Made to do unspeakable things, knowing she is safe because her Daddy would never truly hurt her...not really.

The problem is, I haven't told you about her yet. The problem is, while you are my perfect wet-dream butch Daddy, I have no idea if this is a role that has found a place within your desire.

I have told you about other aspects of my need to submit. The part of me that is loving every ounce of brutality dealt by your hand, that longs for force and velocity to bring your palm to my cheek, that wants your teeth sinking deep into the meat where the base of my neck joins my shoulder. Tomorrow morning I want to wake up to a visible map blooming on the surface of my skin, undeniable evidence of where we have been.

I've told you that I like to be roughed up during sex, told you what kind of pain I like and to what degree. I have not told you about how this kind of treatment has the tendency to open a deep and vulnerable rawness inside me, to crack me open like a pomegranate, my red jewels spilling everywhere.

Because, baby, it has been a while since I let a butch touch me like this and it is only our second date, and I like you way too much for the small amount of time I have known you. I am not ready to be cracked open for you, all seeds and red juice, all that potential sweet and tart and available. I want to stay inside my own skin, contained, private. I do not want to be that girl who gives you access to her pussy and her heart on the same night.

But your hand grabbing my throat is so many things. It is sweet and delicious and causing this fierce panic to blossom in my stomach. My heart is swelling and cracking open, and I know that all of this is visible in my eyes. I can tell that you have recognized what you are seeing when your grip relaxes to a caress and you ask me, "You all right honey?"

This and the tenderness in your eyes could undo me, could reduce me to a sobbing mass on the floor. But I am committed to this course of action, determined to have sex with you tonight without breaking open, without making accessible the tender regions beneath my ribs and without the word *Daddy* accidently slipping past my lips.

So, "Yeah, fine," I say, pushing past you and heading for the bedroom, pulling my dress over my head, hoping to distract you with skin and curves and flesh spilling from foundation garments.

While I haven't known you long enough to fully realize exactly who I am dealing with, I get the feeling as you cross the room toward me, your eyes intently locked on mine and nowhere else, that I should have known better than this. That I have highly underestimated you if I think I can get away with smoke and mirrors, this slight of hand, as if my internal process were a shiny coin I can hide up my sleeve. I am not wearing sleeves and your hand is hot and dry where it grips my bare arm. Your other hand comes to rest on my cheek as you continue to look me in the eye, gaze sharp, mouth quirked slightly at the corner.

"What's going on in there, darlin'?"

I see calm and confident strength in your eyes, a soothing counterbalance to this anxiety riding the swell of feeling inside me. That look in your eyes makes me want to believe in a world where I was never labeled "too much," where that fertile and messy and powerful landscape of emotion is not only tolerated, but maybe accepted and a little sought after. I want to believe in a reality where you can handle me, in all of my parts. My insides ripe and accessible, burst open and artfully arranged for you on a platter.

I make a decision and say, "Can we just talk a bit?"

You nod and I take your hand and lead you to the couch. I tell you a story of a little girl whose needs were not met, of a teenager bleeding internally. How she was told that she cried too easily, cared too deeply, laughed too loud and wanted too much. I tell you how that little girl inside me wants so badly to feel cherished and cared for and as the words *want* and *Daddy* come out of my mouth, you pull me deep into your lap and cuddle me close.

This one gesture is like salve on old, festering wounds. Layers of neglect, calcified like limestone, start to loosen and prepare to slough off. I lean my head against your chest and breathe in your cologne as you stroke my hair: musky sandalwood, a suggestion of pepper. I let myself relax and feel what this safety is like, even though I know it is a fleeting thing. I am a grown woman, struggling to integrate my past with my present, and wanting desperately to embrace my future. This small moment of time, relaxing into your lap, being held in your strong arms, is a precious gift.

My nose is pressed against your neck right above your collar and I shift so my lips fall to your skin. A low rumble comes from your chest, a purr or a growl, and your hand tightens on my hair, tugging at the roots. My tongue snakes out to taste your skin and you groan, "Sweet baby, you wouldn't tease your Daddy, would you?"

My body turns into yours, my tits pressing against your chest as my mouth makes its way to your ear. "No, Daddy. I just want to make you feel good."

I rock my ass into your lap, feeling what you packed for me. Your hand grips my jaw, and you kiss me for the second time ever.

Your tongue slips inside my mouth and this small entrance into my body triggers a massive need to have as much of you inside of me as possible. It feels like summers when I was a kid and would cram as much Bubblicious bubble gum inside my mouth as would fit. I would work my jaw furiously, chewing the wad, and loving the feeling of my mouth so full. At the same time there was this inexplicable and overwhelming desire to swallow the whole mass down my throat and this is what your tongue in my mouth is like. I want to swallow your tongue to make room for your fingers, your cock, your cunt, hard and wet underneath, whatever part of you I am allowed to bring into myself. I want to bring you into myself, want to be stretched by you, filled to capacity, brimming over.

In this moment of feeling overwhelmed I whimper around your tongue and you stop, say, "You all right, Princess? Does it hurt?"

"Yes, Daddy." I feel small and fragile and hovering on the verge of panic. I am walking an edge here and while it looks like your desires are the mirror image of mine, I am still terrified I could lose it all.

"Show me where it hurts, baby."

I hide my face in your neck and mumble, "It hurts everywhere, Daddy."

"Show me."

I sit up and point to the spot between my breasts where the pain is radiating from, right over my beating heart. Your lips are so soft when you lower them to my skin, your hands firm on either side of my rib cage. My heart is beating so fast under your lips, and I can't seem to get enough air into my lungs.

I gasp out, "Daddy, that's making it worse!"

Your eyes are saturated with desire and your voice is a rasping husk. "Where else does it hurt, sugar? Tell me where I need to make it better."

There is a conflict of need inside me. My little girl is turning my cheeks bright red, ashamed of how much she wants her Daddy's hands in forbidden places. The masochist inside me wants you to slap me across the face as hard as you can, hold me down over your lap and spank my ass until I bruise, then fuck my pussy with vicious precision. Anything to drive me deep inside my body and quiet this overwhelming internal cacophony.

I start to hyperventilate and you sandwich my face between your hands. You give me a shake that is both small and fierce and say, "None of that, now. Use your words, baby girl."

You take a deep and obvious breath to show me the way and I follow your example. When I have some breath back, I lean in and whisper, my cheek flaming hot against yours, "It hurts between my legs."

You clear the tension from your throat. "That sounds serious, darlin'. I better take a look."

You lay me down, my back sinking into couch cushions. You peel my panties away from my body and when you spread my legs my hips feel spring-loaded, like a bear trap. Your brow creases in mock concern as you stare down at my pussy, holding my legs firmly open so they won't snap shut.

"Hmmm. It is really swollen down there, sweet girl. Does it hurt more here"—your thumb strokes my clit—"or here?" Now the circumference of my opening.

I am squirming out of my skin. I am shy and breathless and desperate and I want you everywhere at once. "It hurts both places."

"That is serious. But don't worry; Daddy's going to take good care of you."

The tears well up in my eyes all on their own and they are spilling down my cheeks before I can stop them. You lie down on top of me, your hips spreading my legs wide, and trace a tear's path down my face with your thumb. I try to hide my face from you but there is nowhere to go. You grab my chin and make me look at you. "None of that," you say, "I want to see it. It's sexy when my little girl is so open and vulnerable for me."

You rock into me, a small, slow movement. It is just enough to feel the hardness of your cock through your jeans and suddenly I am on fire.

"Oh Daddy, please." The tears continue to stream from my eyes as your hands swallow my wrists and bring them up over my head.

"Please, what, baby?"

You continue your slow-motion rocking and I am trying to thrust myself against you, but your weight is solid, pressing me into this couch, hampering my movement.

"Please Daddy, please, please..."

The dam has burst and my mouth is on autopilot and it feels so fucking good.

"Tell me what you want. I want to hear you say it."

I feel little and grown at the same time.

"I want you inside me, please Daddy? I want your cock inside me."

The noise that comes out of your mouth is both amused and satisfied. You lower your lips to mine and your tongue is in my mouth again, thick and hot and then gone.

"I'm not sure you deserve it yet," you say and suddenly your weight is being removed from my body. Before I get the chance to feel completely unmoored, your hands are there, pulling me up to sitting and back onto your lap.

Suddenly I am all petulance. "I thought you said you would be good to me," I say, hot and embarrassed, more tears welling up in my eyes.

I am full-on pouting and you chuckle and bounce me on your lap. "I am being good to you, sugar. I'm giving you exactly what you need."

There is a bubble expanding in my chest and I give in to it, letting it pop and come out as a sob. You make mock-soothing noises, still laughing at me, but it feels somehow safe and incredibly sexy that you are being mean to me like this.

You let me cry it out, your hands roaming over my body, and as my tears slow to sniffles, you ask, "You want to prove yourself, baby? You want to show me how much you deserve your Daddy's cock inside you?"

All my petulance is cried out and I cannot think of one thing I would not do to please you and show you that I am deserving of your attention.

I lean in and nuzzle your neck. "Yes, please, anything."

You sigh. "Sweet baby, you almost make me want to go easy on you." Your hand fists the hair at the back of my neck and you force me down and over your lap. I am all adrenaline, heart expanding, blood pulsing between my legs, angling my ass up underneath your palm.

"If you want to be my sweet little princess, you better take this spanking for me." Your hand that is not on my ass is firm on the back of my neck, pushing my face into the couch, and you squeeze down for emphasis. "Show me how brave you can be."

"Yes, Daddy." My ass is moving against your palm in anticipation, and then empty air as you raise your hand and let it fall with a loud smack on my bare skin. You repeat this again and again, the pain hot and sweet, sharp and then diffuse in the moments I am allowed to process it. I am counting in my head and then losing track as you begin to concentrate on my sweet spot and every slap sends vibrations deep into my cunt. I have never been so close to coming from a spanking before, and when you stop so abruptly I cry out in protest.

You maneuver past my legs and out from under me. You are behind me and your cock is out of your pants, the head pressing against the opening of my pussy and then filling me up. Your hands are pressing me face-first into the couch, holding my wrists together at the small of my back. I am already on the verge of coming, and although I don't know you yet, don't know your body and the signs that would herald your approaching orgasm, I am guessing by the way you are frantically thrusting inside me that you are close too.

I am about to ask you for permission to come when you growl out, "Come for me, baby, come on, give it to me," and I am undone. I am tumbling over. I am screaming and spurting and messy and burst open and I am whole.

LATE SHOW

Lisabet Sarai

"Haley's back."

Suzy might as well have stuck my finger in an electric socket. I forced myself to breathe.

"Mama?"

JJ sensed my sudden shock. I loosened my death grip on his pajama top.

"It's okay, hon. Now the bottoms…" Wiping my sweaty palms on my skirt, I helped my son wriggle into the loose cotton garment.

"You sure?" I flung the deliberately casual question over my shoulder at my friend, amazed that my voice didn't shake.

"Saw her at Kroger, buying a six-pack. Same old Haley."

"Yeah, I guess." *How did she look?* I wanted to ask. *Does she still have that swagger, as if she owned the world and just let the rest of us live here? Did you talk to her?*

Did she mention me?

I changed the subject instead. "Thanks so much for helping

me out, Suze. I owe you." Normally Jack's mother took care of JJ when I had night shifts, but she had her bridge club on Saturdays, so I had to adapt.

"No problem. We'll have a great time, won't we, JJ? Want to watch *Shrek* again?"

The boy let out a whoop and streaked into the living room. Suzy grinned. "Wish I had a five-year-old's energy!"

I gave her a hug. "We're not cheerleaders anymore, but we're doing okay." After checking my makeup, perhaps a bit more critically than usual, I stuck my phone in my skirt pocket and headed for the door. On the way out I ruffled JJ's straw-blond curls. "Bedtime no later than seven thirty, young man."

"Okay, Mama." He was already fiddling with the video remote.

"I should be back by midnight, if not before."

"Have a good evening." Suzy plumped herself down onto the couch next to JJ. "Eat some popcorn for me. I'm still on that diet."

"Come on, you know I can't stand the stuff! After four years working for Mr. Parsons..."

"Just pulling your leg, girl. See you later."

The sun was just sinking behind Broad Hill. There was plenty of time to walk. I often did, except in winter, since the theater was barely a mile from the little house I'd rented after Jack left. The twenty-minute stroll gave me a chance to clear my mind, to recover from the constant bombardment of my darling son's requests and needs.

Tonight, though, my thoughts spun like the Tilt-A-Whirl at the county fair.

Haley. Oh god help me. Just hearing her name was enough to open the floodgates of memory. Haley in loose shorts and a tight top, brandishing her field-hockey stick like a weapon as she sprinted across the athletic field. Haley lounging in the swing on my dad's front porch, with a cigarette dangling from her tempting lips and a challenge in her hazel eyes. Haley in the dark—silky skin over solid muscle, nimble and knowing fingers, brazen tongue, voice like warm honey pouring into my innocent ears.

Heat captured during the long July day shimmered up from sidewalks. I couldn't blame the season, though, for the wetness under my arms and between my legs. My pulse hammered in my temples. I wished I'd worn a heavier blouse, one that would better conceal my shamefully swollen nipples.

Remembering Haley always had this effect on me. I tried not to do it too often.

Get hold of yourself, girl. You can't go to work like this.

Breathe in, slow, deep. Breathe out. Focus on the sounds and smells of the sultry summer dusk—kids shrieking as they chase each other through lawn sprinklers, the jingle from an ice-cream truck, hotdogs on the grill, fresh-cut grass. Forget about her lean thighs, her throaty laugh, her fuck-the-world attitude.

She's probably forgotten me, after ten years. The thought was an icy blade turning in my chest, but I didn't really believe it. From that first day, when she'd offered me a joint and I'd refused, we'd had this weird connection. If she walked into a room, I'd know it, even if I couldn't see her. I'd start to stammer and sweat, transformed in an instant from the prom queen to a nervous dork. Chemistry, she called it. Even then, I'd known it was just lust. That didn't mean I could resist.

Haley had left town the night of my engagement party. It had been way past midnight when she'd shimmied up the rose trellis and swung one slim leg over my windowsill. Taking off my makeup, high on champagne and rosy visions of my future with Granville's star quarterback, I'd felt her presence before she spoke.

"I can't take any more, Di. I'm getting out."

Her short-chopped locks stuck out at all angles. Oil stains spotted her jeans. Under her battered leather jacket, she wore a white T-shirt, sheer enough to reveal the dusky surround of her pert nipples. Her eyes sparkled like chips of topaz. Her lips were compressed into a scowl I ached to kiss away.

"Haley, I'm sorry." When I reached for her, she twisted out of my grasp.

"No, you're not—not really. You got what you wanted, right? A good-looking guy whose family has plenty of dough. A catch—that's what everyone's saying. Position. Respectability. Christ, six months after you're married you'll probably join the Garden Club!"

"It's not like that..."

"Isn't it? Why else did you pick him over me? It can't be the sex. I'll bet my last buck he can't drive you crazy the way I do..."

She'd swept me into a blistering kiss that sent rivulets of need flowing through me. While her tongue probed my mouth, her brazen fingers parted my robe and took possession of my weeping cunt. I melted in her arms, letting her take me places I'd never known existed before she'd entered my life. Implacable, diabolical, she had brought me to the very edge. Then she'd pushed me away.

My disappointed moan earned me a bitter laugh. "Just wanted to remind you what you're missing."

Oh god! How could she be so cruel?

"Haley, please—don't go. We—we can still—um..."

"Still what? Be friends? Be lovers? Don't kid yourself, girl. You won't dare sneak out to meet me once you're someone's wife. Anyway, I'm not gonna hang around for Jack Harrison's leavings. I'm taking off tonight, with or without you."

"Huh?"

She lowered her eyelids and gave me a sly, seductive smile. "You could come, too, you know. Throw a few things in a bag, hop on the back of my bike and we're out of here. Off to places bigger and better than this shitty town. Places where nobody knows or cares who we are or what we do." She brushed my blonde curls, mussed from our recent clinch, back into place. "Think how great it will be, Di. Freedom!"

Even her most casual touch sent me into a frenzy. I wanted to sink to my knees and press my lips to her crotch in worship, to spread myself naked upon the bed and have her feast on me, to confess that Jack's kisses left me cold compared to hers.

It would be so easy to say yes. Why not do what I wanted for once instead of what everyone else wanted me to do?

But everything was so settled—the newspaper announcements, the church and the hall already booked for September, the dress commissioned, the guest list half-finalized by Jack's mother and mine. It was too late to back out now. Wasn't it?

She'd seen my answer in my eyes before I stammered it out. Without a word—without saying good-bye—she'd exited through the window and climbed back to the street level. The stuttering motor of her battered old bike faded into silence.

I threw myself facedown on the bed, grinding my fingers into my pussy in search of what she'd offered and then withdrawn. I didn't find it.

After that, all I had was rumors and gossip. Every so often, her name would come up in conversation. Haley'd done time in the state pen, someone said, for armed robbery. Haley had made a fortune gambling in Vegas. She was down in Texas, riding the rodeo. She'd moved to Alaska to work as a lumberjack.

All it took was the mention of her name. In an instant I'd be back in that thrilling, terrifying summer of secret fire.

That familiar fever racked me once again as I arrived at the Starlight Cinema. She was close by. My body still knew.

"'Evening, Diane." My balding, bespectacled boss emerged from the glassed-in ticket booth to hand me the theater keys. "Matinee was pretty slow. Hope tonight's better."

"Should be, I'd think." I dragged my mind back to the present. I had a job to do. "People want to get out of this heat."

"They can do that at the multiplex off the Interstate." His brow furrowed. "I don't know why I don't just throw in the towel. Sell the place and retire."

"The town would be poorer if you did, Mr. Parsons."

"I'm worn out, to be honest. And who's going to keep the place going once I'm gone. You?"

"Maybe." I'd actually thought about it. After working as his manager for four years, I certainly knew the business. I didn't have much savings of my own but I figured I could get Jack's mother to front the money. Play on her guilt and all. "Anyway, go home and have your dinner. I'll take over."

After a brief trip inside to greet Harvey, the projectionist, I took my place in the cramped booth, awaiting the first customers for the seven o'clock screening. Working on autopilot, I counted and recorded the till, oiled the ticket-dispensing machine and set out a stack of coupons for discounted soda and popcorn. All the while, images of Haley prowled through my mind.

I imagined her in boxers and a singlet, sprawled on the lumpy mattress at one of the motels on the edge of town, with the wheezing air con turned up full blast. She gripped a can of beer in one hand. The other cupped one small breast through the sweat-damp cotton, twisting the protruding nipple. I could practically hear her moan, like some lost soul, as her fingers burrowed into her shorts and found her clit. I remembered that little bullet, so stiff and so sensitive—the only shy thing about her. She'd taught me how to coax it from its shelter with my tongue, how to make it swell and harden, how to lap harder as she clamped her thighs down around my ears and near-drowned me in her aromatic juices.

My own clit throbbed inside my damp underwear. My breasts felt meaty and tender, ready to burst at a touch like over-ripe fruit. An ominous heaviness hung in the night air, a barely palpable vibration, like distant thunder drawing nearer. Haley was coming.

A few customers arrived. I smiled, made small talk, dispensed tickets. All the while, my mind swung between longing and terror and my body melted into a puddle of need.

At seven thirty, after serving the stragglers, I cracked open my novel and tried to lose myself in the plot. Every so often a bolt of knowledge sizzled through, dragging me back to the present. Haley was on her way.

Eight o'clock. Eight thirty. The early show let out. I took a bathroom break and was mortified to discover I was thoroughly drenched. A trace of pussy scent clung to my fingers, even after I'd washed twice.

I sold a handful of tickets for the nine o'clock screening. I'd grown accustomed to the aching that gripped my pelvis and the pressure of my nipples against the wilting cotton of my blouse. Once I was sure no one else was coming, I leaned back and closed my eyes.

Exhausted by the tension of waiting, I must have dozed. Thunder woke me, a roar that made my belly clench. I opened my eyes in time to see a huge Harley execute a U-turn in the middle of Main Street, then pull up to the curb in front of the Starlight.

A lean figure dismounted the black-and-chrome monster. The driver peeled off black gloves that looked like leather and stuffed them in a back pocket, then removed the shiny black helmet and ran her fingers through her short, chestnut locks.

Long before I saw her face, I knew who it was.

"Hey, Di! Heard you worked here." She sauntered up to the booth and grinned at me through the glass. "How're ya doin'?"

I stared at her, paralyzed and dumb with lust. Heat rippled through me. My earlobes, my nipples, my clit, all felt like they'd burst into flames at any moment.

"Ah—um—hello...um...hi, Haley." I was eighteen again, tongue-tied, overwhelmed, marveling at her effortless, androgynous beauty. "Um—welcome back."

"I'm just passin' through—on my way to L.A., got a job waiting—but I had to stop by to look up an old friend..."

Her voice went low when she said that word. She meant something else. A chill skittered up my spine. "Wasn't sure you'd still be here, though, stuck in this dumpy little town. Weren't you headed to college?"

"Yeah, well..." I shrugged, a splinter of regret piercing the bubble of desire. "Jack didn't want me to go. You see, he was just starting his business, and he told me he needed my help..."

"Ah, yes. Jack." Haley's lips twisted like she'd eaten something sour. "And how is Jack?" Her fists clenched at the sides of her designer jeans. I almost expected her to spit.

My cheeks were on fire. "Um...Jack's gone. Took off with his secretary, nearly five years ago. I guess he's somewhere on the West Coast. He sends us a check every now and again—when he remembers."

"Bastard." Haley swept her fingers through her hair, pushing it off her forehead. I remembered the gesture. "What do you mean, us?"

"Me and my son. Jack Junior." Could I really be sorry about

my choices, given my baby? At that moment, though, may God forgive me, I wished he'd never been born.

Haley's expression softened. "You poor girl." She tugged open the door of the ticket booth. "You need a hug."

Her scent hadn't changed—tobacco and leather, old-fashioned lavender and good honest sweat. Like a trained dog, I began to salivate, new wetness flowing everywhere. When she leaned in, reaching for me, though, I shrank away. It was too dangerous. If she touched me, I was lost.

"No—Haley, there's no room in here—Mr. Parsons...the customers..."

She paused, her gaze raking over my trembling body before returning to my face. "After ten years, Di, you still gonna shut me out?"

We hung there in silence, mere inches between us. Close up, I could see the past decade in her face: some lines at the corners of her eyes, a hard set to her mouth, a half-inch scar along her right cheekbone. Then she smiled and the years vanished. Once more she was the bad girl, the school rebel, the one who'd cornered me behind the diner and dared me to kiss her.

"Never mind. I can wait till you get off work."

She strolled back to straddle her bike and lit a cigarette. I couldn't take my eyes off her, and she knew it.

For the next hour, she ignored me, or at least she pretended to. I sat in the ticket booth, squirming in my wet underwear, watching her chain-smoke, imagining those blunt, competent fingers molding my flesh.

The show let out. People wandered out of the theater, chattering about the movie, and disappeared into the balmy darkness. Harvey killed the lights on the marquee. "You want me to lock up inside?" he called out through the door.

"No, that's okay. I'll take care of it. You can go home."

He stepped out into the street. Noticing Haley, he gave her a friendly nod. "Good evening, miss. Nice bike."

"Thanks. I'm here to take Diane for a ride."

"Lucky lady." He waved and headed for his VW Beetle. "See you tomorrow, then."

The grumble of his vehicle died away as he rounded the corner onto Maple. Silence settled over the empty street. Still perched on her motorcycle, Haley watched as I stowed the cash drawer and locked the ticket booth behind me.

I swallowed the lump rising in my throat and held out my hand. "Come on."

Her calloused palm felt dry and cool against my fevered skin. I led her through the lobby, lit only by the glowing Coke machine, then through the velvet curtains into the dim auditorium.

I'd been thinking of heading for Mr. Parson's office, behind the screen. Haley didn't give me the chance. She yanked me to a stop, then swung me around to face her. One arm encircled my waist and pulled me into a tight embrace, compressing my full breasts against her smaller ones and striking sparks from my nipples. With her other hand, she fisted my hair and dragged my mouth to hers.

We went from zero to sixty in seconds. She forced her tongue between my lips, savage and hungry. I let her take me, drinking in the mingled flavors of smokes, beer and mint toothpaste. Meanwhile she grabbed my ass and ground her crotch against mine. Fierce bolts of pleasure shot through the heaviness coiling in my cunt.

I clawed at her shirt, desperate for her skin. She released me long enough to pull the garment over her head and toss it aside. She'd never worn a bra as a teenager; she hadn't changed. The girlish swellings still featured coffee-colored areolae the size of silver dollars. I dove for her sweet nipples, sucking hard the way she liked. If you had asked me what turned Haley on, I might not have been able to tell you, but my body remembered how to make her moan.

Each pull of suction tugged at my clit. Her nipple lengthened and swelled in response to my worship. The crinkled surround teased my lips. I circled the nub with my tongue, then paused to breathe, thinking I'd switch to the other side.

Haley shoved me backward. I stumbled, landing on my ass. She was on me in an instant, straddling my thighs, tearing open my blouse, tugging down my bra and burying her face between my breasts. She licked along the valley between them while pinching both tips. It hurt, but that's what I wanted—what I needed. The pain burned away all those empty years of wanting.

Her bare breasts grazed my belly. I arched up, craving more contact. Haley giggled and pulled away. When she flipped up my skirt and mouthed the soaked crotch of my panties, I almost came, from the mere thought of what she was about to do. She ran her tongue back and forth along the cotton-covered groove, making me squirm. "You want more, baby?" she teased. "Let's just get these off, and I'll give you what you want."

She flipped open a knife—where had that come from?—and slid the blade under the waistband of my panties, near my hip. "Don't move..." One flick of her wrist and the fabric yielded. She dragged the damp rag out of the way. Her warm breath fluttered over my exposed pussy. I lay back on the sticky floor, letting her do what she did so well.

A rough finger wriggled into my hole. Another digit grazed my clit.

"Oh god...Haley...please...!"

"You're so juicy, Di. But then you always were. Do you taste as sweet as ever?"

She sought the answer for herself, sweeping her tongue along my cleft from back to front, ending with a flick to the bead at the apex. I teetered on the edge of climax, the tension of the evening's wait knotting deep inside. When she pursed her lips around my clit and prodded it with her tongue, the strands snapped apart and I flew free, into a place of quivering bliss.

Haley continued making a meal of my cunt as I recovered. I rose quickly toward another crisis. But I didn't want to come alone.

"Wait—wait a minute! Don't be so greedy! I want to taste you, too."

"Oh yeah?" Her hands clamped down on my thighs, holding me to the floor. Her strength astonished and aroused me. She burrowed in my cunt for a few more minutes before continuing. "You remember how to eat pussy?"

"Like it was yesterday, Haley. Come on—please?"

"Since you ask so nice..."

Rolling away from me, she unzipped her jeans and worked them down over her hips to her knees. She wore nothing underneath. An earthy scent rose from the reddish tangles hiding her cunt. "Too hard to get these damn things off."

"I don't care. C'mere." I maneuvered my body till my face was opposite her pussy. Reaching behind her, I clasped her rear cheeks and drew her closer. Then I buried my nose in her fur and breathed her in.

Memory flooded back—that hot August night, stretched out together on a blanket atop Broad Hill, gloriously naked. The prickly scent of dry grass had mingled with the ripe, oceany aroma of women in heat as I'd knelt between Haley's knees for the very first time. I made her come twice. How proud I'd been! Afterward, we'd sprawled under the stars, limbs entangled, giddily caressing each other, drunk on our audacity.

Using my fingers to part her curls, I licked along her tender inner lips. My tongue gathered her tangy juices, making her wetter still. Her clit peeked out from its hood. I circled the bud, tempting it into view. When it finally emerged, I rewarded its boldness by suckling it.

Haley squirmed and strained, unable to part her legs much because of her confining jeans. I sucked harder, pausing every so often to nibble on her labia or poke my tongue into her channel. She was close—I remembered the signs—moaning and thrashing about so much that I had difficulty staying in control. Then she hoisted my leg over her shoulder to open me and dove into my muff. At that point, I lost control entirely.

It didn't seem to matter. Instinct took over. We knew each other on an animal level—we always had. We let the animals come out to play.

Time stood still. Only pleasure remained. And though I couldn't see Haley's face or hear her voice—our mouths were full—I knew exactly what she felt, what she wanted. The old magic seized us. We climbed toward orgasm together. We exploded at the same instant. Afterward, we lay sated and drained on the floor, wreathed in the odors of sex, sweat and stale popcorn.

The shrill call of my phone broke the spell. I groped in my skirt. The caller gave up before I found the device. I squinted at the display.

"Damn! Suzy!"

"Cute little Suzy Roberts?" Haley's voice was still languid with sex.

"Yeah. She's babysitting for me... Oh, shit! It's twelve thirty already." I didn't want to talk to Suze. I sent her a quick text, telling her I was fine and that I'd be back soon. Then I tried to button the ruins of my blouse. "I've got to get home."

Haley was on her feet, pulling her tight jeans up over her obviously damp thighs. "I'll give you a lift."

I fumbled for the theater keys. "No, you go ahead. I have to lock up all the exits."

She crossed her arms over her chest. "I can wait. Haven't got anyplace else I've gotta be..."

Her eyes followed me as I locked and tested each of the doors. I felt the heat in her gaze. She wanted more. And I...?

What I wanted didn't matter. I'd already made a terrible mistake.

The bike's engine was growling by the time I'd finished securing the main theater doors. "Climb on, baby. You wear the helmet. Fourteen-twenty-two Spring Ave, right?"

She'd done her homework. If I hadn't been working tonight, would she have shown up at the house?

The powerful cycle whipped around the corner and raced through the shadowy streets. I hung on for dear life, my arms around Haley's waist, my chest pressed against her warm back. I tried to ignore the effects of her closeness. I shut out the quivering pleasure set up by the engine's vibrations between my splayed thighs. *Enough sex tonight,* I told myself. *Enough.*

I couldn't see much, but after five minutes I knew we were going in the wrong direction. For one thing, we were climbing.

"Hey!" I yelled. The wind whisked my voice away. "Where are you taking me?" I pounded my fists against Haley's back. She paid no attention whatsoever. She might have been made of granite.

When the engine died, I snatched off the helmet. "What do you think you're doing? You think this is funny?"

Haley shook her head. "Not funny at all, Di." Something in her tone froze my indignation.

I looked around. "Broad Hill. I haven't been up here since..."

The town stretched below us like a set of toys, glittering and unreal.

"Yeah. Me neither." She stepped toward me.

"Haley, please…no." When she gathered me into her arms, though, I didn't fight—not her at least. I only fought myself. Her kiss was gentle as mist.

"I'm leaving tomorrow, Di. Come with me."

Oh god. Her scent. Her voice. The flow of hard muscle under her sun-bronzed skin.

"I can't. You know I can't. I have a child, Haley…"

Her hands wandered over my curves, waking pleasure everywhere they touched. "We're good together, Di. We always were."

"Yes, but…"

"You made the wrong choice last time. Not everyone gets a second chance. Choose me, baby. I swear I'll make you happy."

She cupped my pubis through my skirt, waking echoes of orgasms, recent and remembered.

"You deserve this, Di, after all the shit he put you through." With a simple tweak of my nipple, she rekindled the fever.

She was right. I deserved better. I'd had better and I'd thrown it away for social status and acceptability. I'd thought that Haley was just a fling. I was so, so wrong.

But now? I wanted her. I wanted to go with her, to be with her. I didn't care what the world thought. But more than my life was at stake now. I had to consider JJ.

"I can't leave my boy."

"Let Jack's mother keep him. She's earned the right. Or— what the hell—bring him along. I'm not much for kids, but if he's your flesh and blood, Di, I'm sure I can deal."

"And tear him away from his roots? His family? His friends? Life on the road—with someone like you—that's not any kind of life for a child."

"Someone like me?" I heard ten years of pain in her voice. She took a step backward, releasing her hold. I mourned the loss.

"You haven't changed, Di. You're still the same stuck-up little priss who's all worried about what other people are gonna think."

"No, it's not that, really..."

"Let me point out that you're not the head of the cheerleading squad anymore. You're no debutante. You're a single mom stuck in a dead-end job in a nowhere town. There ain't no fairy-tale prince coming to rescue you. If you stay, you'll just get old, lonely and bitter."

Her words stung. I didn't want the future she painted for me here in Granville. Still, I couldn't imagine a future that included her and my child, too. "It's too late, Haley. We can't rewrite the past."

"You're just making excuses. You're scared, Di. Scared to leave your familiar life, even though you hate it. Scared to show the world you love another woman."

I tried to picture a life with Haley. I could imagine the sex, vividly. But the rest? Would she ever settle? And what about JJ, forced to grow up with two mommies?

She read me, as she always could. "You won't come with me then?" Her voice was flat, dead.

"I can't. Try to understand."

"You're a fool, Diane Stone." She used my maiden name. Mounting her beast, she picked up the helmet and kicked the engine to life. "We won't meet again."

"Don't go! Don't leave me here..." The cycle swung in a wide arc. My chest felt ready to burst from the pain. I couldn't live without this woman.

A star winked above our heads. Something shifted in my

desperate mind. All at once, the impossible became possible. "Wait!" I screamed. "Turn that damn thing off for a minute."

"What? Change your mind?"

"You really think we can bring JJ with us?"

"If he's your son, I'll love him like my own."

Two mommies. But what the hell—that was twice as good as none.

I sucked the balmy night air into my lungs and summoned my courage. That first kiss behind the Brass Kettle had been tough, too, but worth it, in the end. "I'll come then. We'll come."

Haley brushed her short hair away from her face, scratched her head, gazed up at the sky arching over us. Finally she shrugged and gave me one of those knowing grins that turn me to mush.

"Hop on, Di. Let's go home and pick up our kid."

NAMING IT

Jean Roberta

"No." Deirdre looked especially waiflike as she shook her head, causing her golden-brown locks to part around her small, pink ears.

Tam (named Tammy-Lynne at birth) was amused. "Deirdre of the Sorrows," she sighed. "Do you plan to grieve for your lost love forever?" Tam wrapped one strong arm around Deirdre's thin shoulders, and soon found herself clutching the air.

"Fuck off!" Deirdre's eyes were the color of a storm at sea. "I'm not like you. I can't just hop on the next one that comes along. Paulie asked me to move in with her and I said yes. Do you know what a big commitment that was? I thought I could trust her. And then—" Deirdre took a deep breath and wiped her eyes. "Shit."

"Some butches be crazy," Tam said agreeably. "Getting it on with Sherry in a public washroom was not the best way for her to show you how much she wanted to share her life with you. 'Specially when you were there in the bar, drinking. As my mom says, what goes in must come out. I wonder how much time Paulie thought she had before you would need to use the facilities."

Tam fought down the urge to burst out laughing. The scene in the bar the night before had been like a fireworks display. Deirdre had made no effort to be discreet when she realized what Paulie and Sherry were doing in a crowded cubicle. The sound of Deirdre's fists banging on the metal door had reverberated through the bar like a bass line, with the screech of Deirdre's outraged voice as the melody. Everyone in the lesbian bar and gossip center had been given a topic of conversation for a week.

As a singer-songwriter, Tam enjoyed watching a certain amount of drama. It was inspiring.

She didn't blame Murphy, the bouncer, for throwing them all out on the street. Murphy was paid to keep trouble out of the bar, and she had been a deadpan professional. The three troublemakers had landed on that square in a board game that says MISS A TURN. Tam was simply a hanger-on who chose to leave with them. As the coolest head in the group, she felt that her presence was needed.

Deirdre had been like a porcelain vase full of dynamite that seemed likely to blow apart. Tam knew that most of that rage was based on hurt, fear and self-contempt. Even so, the scene had been sexy as hell.

Tam would have liked to defend Deirdre from one of the other dykes, if necessary. Of course, that could only happen if one of them threw the first punch. Tam had mastered enough self-defense moves to know that they should only be used as a last resort; some moves could kill. She wouldn't admit, even to herself, that she wanted to find out how deadly her fists could be.

Today Deirdre was hungover from an excess of emotion, not

an excess of booze. Tam knew that two drinks per night were her limit. She sat curled up on her sofa, her bare feet in Tam's lap. They had known each other since they were both in elementary school, and they had comforted each other through many disappointments.

"I don't—" Deirdre started.

"I don't mean—" said Tam. She stopped, not wanting Deirdre to feel silenced.

"You first," said Deirdre. This was awkward. Tam reflected that chivalry was sometimes hard to practice in the real world. She liked to think of herself as a gentleman.

Tam started again. "I don't mean you should rush out and find someone else right away. I know it takes time. I just think you need to stay away from her until you feel stronger, and you need to think about your future, that's all. That's all I said."

"That's not all you said." Deirdre's memory seemed remarkably clear under the circumstances. Her small, firm breasts still rose and fell with her breath in a way that made it hard for a listener to focus on her words. "Tam, I know you mean well. I'm really glad you were there. I don't know what I would have done if—but you made it sound as if you thought I was, like—"

Tam waited a beat, then jumped in. "Like Paulie?"

"Yes. A player. Someone who plays all the time and doesn't give a shit. Someone who promises what they don't mean. I can't do that." Tears welled up in Deirdre's eyes. "Jesus, Tam, do you think I'm a complete fool?"

This was clearly a time for diplomacy, but it was also a good time to seize the moment. Tam gathered Deirdre into her arms and rocked her. "Honey," she said into the fine, wavy, honey-colored hair that grazed Deirdre's shoulders. "Paulie's the fool, not you. She's the one who lost out."

To Tam's delight, Deirdre didn't slither away, as she usually did. "Thank you," she said, nestled against Tam's collarbone. "For not saying you told me so. I know you thought I should go slow, and I didn't. I wanted a home and a serious relationship, you know? We're not kids anymore."

While Tam was still gathering her thoughts, Deirdre shifted her position so she could look her old friend in the eyes. "Did you call me honey?"

Tam saw her dark eyes and strong features reflected in the troubled gray pools of Deirdre's. "I did, and I could call you other things too: sweet thing, baby, angel-face."

Something rippled through Deirdre's supple body. "Always joking, that's you," she said. "That's why we could never really be an item, even though you're my best friend. Sometimes I wish—"

Deirdre's phone rang for the sixth time that morning. She glanced at it, saw the name PAULIE DIDDLE once again, and made a visible effort to ignore the sound.

"Good girl," said Tam. She tightened her embrace and kissed Deirdre on the lips before she could pull away.

"Ummph," said Deirdre. Tam held her close and slipped the tip of her tongue between Deirdre's lips.

Deirdre broke the kiss. "What the fuck, Tam?" she asked. Tam knew how Deirdre sounded when she was really angry, and this question had a different tone. She was curious, even intrigued.

"What do you think, baby?" responded Tam the seducer. "Let's try it."

"You're my friend, Tam," said Deirdre, as though explaining the incest taboo. "Who will I turn to if you let me down?"

"I won't, honey." Tam pulled Deirdre onto her lap, and the lightweight woman settled herself as gracefully as a cat.

Whatever might happen, Tam knew she would get at least

one new song out of this episode. A few bluesy notes began to form a pattern in her mind.

"You don't have to feel sorry for me, Tam," the lap-rider was sniffing. "I'll be okay."

Tam lovingly kneaded Deirdre's backbone, one vertebra at a time. "Maybe you will," said Tam, aiming for a tone that was halfway between promise and threat. "I want to take advantage of you." Deirdre shivered under her hands. "I don't host parties for charity," Tam growled.

Deirdre wavered, sighed and moaned. Her eyes were wet. She seemed to be arguing silently with herself. "What the hell?" she asked herself aloud. "Oh, Tam." She pulled Tam's face to hers for a fierce kiss. Tongue met tongue in Deirdre's mouth.

After a few delicious moments, Tam tugged at Deirdre's T-shirt, and the wearer leaned back to pull the fabric up over her head. Deirdre then unhooked her bra, releasing her breasts into Tam's eager hands. Deirdre's nipples were like hard, pink berries.

For some reason, Tam's eyes fell on one of Deirdre's textbooks, splayed open on the coffee table. Tam hadn't taken Deirdre's ambition seriously enough when she had applied to get into law school, but now Deirdre was in her second year and doing well. Even as a child, Deirdre had always risen to a challenge.

"You too," she murmured, as though she wanted Tam to know she wouldn't accept any stone-butch behavior. Tam was soon naked to the waist, her full breasts bouncing a little as Deirdre felt, then squeezed them. "Bodacious," she snickered.

Tam couldn't help turning red. What kind of lover did Deirdre want her to be, and did the sight of her womanly boobs clash with Deirdre's fantasies? Apparently not. Deirdre didn't seem at all disappointed.

Two pairs of jeans and panties were the next things to go. The emergence of Deirdre's lithe, pale hips and her triangle of light-brown hair lit a fire in Tam's own crotch. She wanted to explore the treasure-trove that Paulie had lost because of her own stupid greed.

While holding Deirdre on her lap, Tam managed to slide two fingers inside a wet opening to tickle Deirdre's clit. "I need you to lie down," Tam ordered, hoping her girl was horny enough not to rebel against a bossy command.

"Oh, Tam," moaned Deirdre, scrambling into position. She was a pit of need, a hotbed of molten lava. Tam found her way in with questioning fingers that soon found answers. Tam could hardly believe that Deirdre wanted this, needed to be fucked by Tam, of all people, after so many jokes and evasions.

Tam lowered her mouth to Deirdre's dark-pink inner lips and spread them slightly with one hand to expose her swollen clit. The secret, salty taste of Deirdre's juice was a reward in itself. Tam stroked and circled and plunged far enough in to feel the slight dent of Deirdre's cervix, the entrance to her womb.

Deirdre's rising moans let Tam know she was on the right track. Tam needed to find the exact right spots inside a hungry cunt that needed to be touched, gently or roughly, to unleash Deirdre's considerable energy. Tam knew she wanted to let go, to let it all out.

Tam found ridges inside Deirdre, and scratched them experimentally. She prodded a spongy place and felt the slickness shift and move. "Ohhh," yelled Deirdre. "Don't—stop!" Tam kept going as Deirdre's muscles squeezed around her fingers and wetness poured out of her.

When Deirdre seemed somewhat recovered, Tam pressed her palm against her girl's slit, enjoying the wet warmth and the hot woman-smell that floated up to her nose. The dazed look on Deirdre's face almost moved Tam to tears, and she slid down to wrap Deirdre in her arms.

For a few minutes, both women seemed perfectly content. Even the persistent tingle in Tam's cunt was enjoyable.

Tam thought of her collection of dicks in various colors, sizes and materials. She wished she had thought of bringing one with her, but then she wondered about Deirdre's possible reaction. Were fake penises Politically Incorrect in her philosophy? Were they acceptable if they didn't look much like anything that grew on a human male, or any other mammal? How did Deirdre feel about butt plugs? Bondage? Role-play? Tam was aghast that she and Deirdre had never discussed such a broad and diverse topic.

Deirdre moved. "Heh," she snickered, and reached down to find Tam's clit.

"You don't have to—" started Tam. Then she couldn't finish her sentence. *You don't have to pay me back? You don't have to feel sorry for me?* Tam remembered how insulted she felt when Deirdre had told her she didn't "have to."

Deirdre was swift and skillful, and Tam was already near the point of an explosion. Deirdre tormented Tam's clit by squeezing and rolling it until Tam felt her whole cunt erupting in spasms.

Somehow the two women shifted into a comfortable side-by-side position. "Honey," sighed Tam, "it was better than I ever expected." Impulsively she added, "I love you."

"No you don't," came the response. Deirdre's voice was soothing, but her words hurt like needles. "You love me as a friend and that's good, but we can't afford to get confused about what's going on."

Tam stared at her, eye to eye. "Baby, we're not confused. We just figured out what we really mean to each other."

The phone rang. "Jesus. Can't you put her on hold?" Tam wanted to grab a knife out of a drawer in Deirdre's kitchen, run to Paulie's house and threaten to turn her into hamburger.

Deirdre sat up. "Don't worry, Tam. I'll do something better. I can report her to the phone company for harassment. I'd like to get a restraining order against her, but first she has to do something worse than phoning me fifty times a day. I think that could be arranged."

Tam felt chilled to the bone. Deirdre was already becoming the Queen of Torts, and she didn't want protection. Worst of all, she was thinking too much about Paulie.

Tam made things worse. "Maybe if I stay with you for a few days—" She stopped when she saw the look on Deirdre's face.

"Oh, Tam. No way. Look, I'm really glad you, I mean we, um, you gave me what I needed. I really needed it and I'm grateful. Thank you. But we can't afford to ruin our friendship."

Tam was speechless for a second. "*Ruin* it?" she shot back. "Deirdre, we need to take it to the next level."

Deirdre left the sofa with amazing speed, and put her clothes back on like a knight putting on armor. "Seriously, Tam. You know I'm right. I don't think we should see each other for about a month."

Tam felt desperate. She knew too well how Deirdre would react if pushed. "How about a week?" she bargained. "Not a month. And why don't we meet in a coffee shop, maybe Java's, to talk about our relationship. Meanwhile, if you need me for anything..."

"I'll call you," Deirdre promised unconvincingly. "Okay, next Sunday at Java's. At noon."

"I'll be counting the minutes," said Tam. "Okay, okay. I'm leaving. But please be there, Deirdre. Please."

"I will. Take care, Tam." The honest suitor was left to scramble off the sofa, take her clothes to the bathroom, make herself presentable and leave as quickly as possible. It was not what she wanted to do, but she had the sense to know that lingering would be counterproductive.

The week dragged by with the excruciating slowness of dripping water wearing away the enamel in a sink. Tam couldn't stop thinking about Deirdre, and she channeled her anxiety into a song about the scene in the bar, a lesbian version of the shoot-out at the O.K. Corral. Every day when she came home from her job at the music store, she took a beer out of the fridge, pulled out her guitar and strummed some chords. None of the notes really jelled into a satisfying melody, but she told herself that disappointment and despair were fuel for her art.

At last Sunday arrived. Tam showered and dressed to the sound of church bells, and wondered how many churchgoers really gained relief by confiding their troubles to the Lord. She wasn't a believer, and neither was Deirdre. Their escape from the Christianity of their families was one the things they had in common.

Thanks to Whomever, Java's was half-empty and Deirdre sat alone at a table. She was wearing a favorite blue blouse that set off her blue-gray eyes, and Tam pondered her wardrobe choice. Why was Deirdre determined to look adorable?

Deirdre didn't stand up, but she gave Tam an encouraging look. "Hi."

"Hi," answered Tam. "I need a mocha latte for this. Can I get you anything?"

"No, I have a cappuccino and a lemon square. I'm good."

You're excellent, thought Tam, *but you don't believe it. That's the root of your problems.*

Tam returned to the table, and Deirdre looked her in the eyes. "So?" asked Tam.

"So Paulie agreed to leave me alone after I warned her about legal consequences."

Tam tried to keep the smile off her face, but couldn't. "Good girl."

"You know me," said Deirdre. "Tam, I—couldn't stop thinking about last week. You know."

"Oh, I know. Me too." Tam resisted the impulse to reach across the table to kiss her beloved.

"I think we should agree on some rules." Deirdre actually reached for Tam's hand as she was about to grasp her coffee cup.

"Rules?" Tam felt as if she had been handed a surprise package that just might be a bomb.

"Our relationship has changed. We can't go back now. We need to name it for what it is."

Tam felt as if her smile would split her face. "A love that was meant to be?"

Deirdre looked thoughtful. "Lust and friendship? A hot-crotch conspiracy? I don't know. You could write a song about it."

"I'm working on it, my dear. And I'll tell the whole world it's about you."

Deirdre laughed on a sigh. "Tam, control yourself."

Tam took a deep breath. "Deirdre, how do you feel about toys? You know."

Deirdre gave her a wicked grin. "Sex toys? I love them."

"Seriously? You never said so."

"You never asked," replied the vixen. "So I never showed you mine." Tam felt light-headed. Deirdre went on: "We need some rules so we don't get hurt. I just want us to go slow. No moving in together for at least six months, and I think, I mean, we should promise not to date anyone else until we really know what we want to do. Tam."

"Honey, I don't want anyone but you. I swear I'll be faithful to you. If either of us ever wants to be with someone else, she should tell the other first."

Deirdre looked relieved. "Exactly." She looked down, then looked Tam in the eyes. "Tam. Did I ever tell you you're my hero?"

"You're telling me now." Tam held Deirdre's hand, hoping her touch would convey everything she wanted to say. "I'll try to live up to that." Tam imagined Deirdre naked, waiting for her in a real bed after brilliantly defending a client in court. Tam knew her woman was a firecracker, and she felt profoundly lucky.

"Tam." Deirdre looked dewy-eyed, as though she were fighting off tears. "I didn't see what was right in front of me. I'm sorry."

"Don't be, honey." Tam felt supremely confident, at least in the moment. "We're here now, and we both know what we want. One day at a time, right?"

That was the phrase Deirdre was planning to use. "You got it."

MY VISIT TO SUE ANNE

Anna Watson

I wasn't the youngest guy at Boys' Night Out, but I was definitely the least experienced. You should have heard the raunchy way those guys talked! If everything they said was true there wasn't a femme within the whole state of Massachusetts who hadn't been despoiled by Clem or Liz or Aiden or the half dozen other butches and transmen who showed up every Sunday afternoon at the VFW. If you believed their boasts, then they'd had girls in alleyways, bathrooms, up against cars and vans, in the beds of pickup trucks, outside by the reservoir, inside in hot tubs, and don't even get them started on positions and orifices, not that they needed any encouragement, because, ducky luv, they'd been *everywhere*. Actually, I did tend to encourage them, because as long as they were talking about their own prowess, they kept their mucky paws off of my own private business. They sure did get a kick out of the fact that I was going through a particularly arid dry spell, though. They had very clever, subtle ongoing jokes about it, often remarking that I must have an invisible

"Femme-away" force field around me, or a big No FEMMES circle slash emblazoned on my forehead. Or on my dick, according to Liz, and then she about ruptured herself laughing. Hardy har har.

I acted like none of it bothered me, like I was just fine taking a joke. I would drink my Bud Light and stay long enough to get a good dose of masculine bonding, then hie me back to the stacks, to *the very carrel* in which Aiden claimed he took a femme named Michelle doggie-style, but which was now as celibate as a church with only my tidy stacks of books and papers for excitement.

This extremely sorry state of affairs had been going on so long that I was more or less used to it, and barely noticed (so I told myself) one afternoon when the teasing was particularly raucous, probably for the benefit of a new guy, Charley, a young butch heavily invested in longboarding. After putting up with the manly joshing for about as long as I could take, I made my excuses—as always, they had to do with getting back to my research—and left them. I was anxious to get home, actually, divest myself of my dick (I always made a point of packing to Boys' Night, my butch armor) and get in a hot bath. So anxious, in fact, that I didn't notice Charley leaving as well, but when I got to my car, he was standing there, holding his board.

"Can I get a ride?"

"Sure, saddle up." I assumed he was too tipsy to longboard and didn't think much of it. When I pulled up in front of the grotty three-family where he lived with probably umpteen roommates, I expected him to quickly hop out with a lackadaisical, "Thanks, bro!" but he tarried.

"Del," he began. Yes, my name is Delilah. Shut up.

"Huh?" I had a paper due and was still mentally tracking down some articles.

"Why don't you go see Sue Anne?"

"Who?"

"You know. Sue Anne. The Femme?"

He actually said it that way, with a capitol *F.* I shook my head, thinking, *Heck, son, this is Lesbianville, USA, and there are a whole slew of femmes out here, and probably even a few Femmes as well, just ask them.* Sue Anne wasn't ringing a bell, except...

"You mean that old gal who hangs out at Diva's sometimes?" I didn't know her to speak to, but was vaguely aware that she was a local character, probably about a hundred years old and still stepping out, who dressed like it was the 1940s and got young studs to buy her Tom Collinses and light her ciggies.

"Yeah, that's her."

"What do you mean, go see her? Why should I?" Actually, now that he mentioned it, it didn't sound like such a bad idea. She might have something for me, especially if she was from the Midwest. I was working on my PhD in queer studies and my thesis was on the nascent queer liberation movement, concentrating on what our poor, misguided brothers and sisters on the coasts refer to as "flyover country." Sue Anne was definitely old enough to remember when Phyllis and the other Del started Daughters of Bilitis and the effect that had on lesbians all over America; she might even have a scrapbook or something that could be useful. This was brilliant! I didn't know why I hadn't thought of it before, except that I'm definitely more comfortable with books and websites than with people. Charley was looking at me expectantly, so I grinned and clapped him on the shoulder.

"That's a great idea!" I said. "I'll definitely give her a shout."

"You should." Now he did get out, trying not to bump

into anything with his board. "You know she's famous in L.A.? That's where she used to live."

I nodded, still grinning, but I'd already abandoned the idea of talking with her. L.A. was no use to me. If only she'd been from somewhere like Saint Louis! That would have been interesting. Which reminded me that I needed to track down a copy of Claude Harland's amazing autobiography because there was a quote I needed, and so I drove off, putting the whole slightly odd conversation behind me.

Every once in a while, when I got into such a state of unbearable need that I couldn't beat it back (excuse me) with study and more study, research and more research, I let one of the guys fix me up with a date. Those guys all had lots of femme friends, some of whom purported to think I was cute, and I was slowly disappointing the lot of them. We would go on one date, and I might even be allowed to give them a peck on the cheek, but then they wouldn't return my calls and I would hear why at the VFW later. Michelle thought I was too serious (and probably disapproved of the boring manner in which I was using "her" carrel); Jenny thought my sense of humor was weird and that my laugh was too high-pitched; Barb got grossed out when I started talking about my childhood habit of attempting to insert pennies into my nostrils alone at night in my bed, just to see if I could (it's true that I don't get out much and perhaps this wasn't the best memory to share over tiramisu, but we were discussing the fact that they're always saying they're going to stop making pennies and then they don't—I didn't just bring it up completely randomly!); Esther said I wasn't butch enough for her, and then, right after that below-the-belt blow, Marilee let me know loudly and in no uncertain terms that I didn't have what it would take to get her crawling naked across the kitchen floor to worship my shiny boots (it's true, I was wearing espadrilles) before we'd even gotten to the restaurant. I'm sure passersby on the sidewalk will remember the astonished look on my face as I watched her stalk off.

It had taken me some time to get back in the mood after Marilee, but here I was, about to meet Sarah, hope springing eternal in the butchly chest. I was wearing what I fondly believed was a presentable outfit because it was all I ever wore, despite the best efforts of my more dapper brothers: jeans, a polo button-down and, since it was winter, a pair of hiking boots. I picked her up and knew, just as soon as she got in the car, that it wouldn't work out. Not that she wasn't nice, because she was, but she just didn't do anything for me. At all. The rest of my dates had been much more my style, but sadly, Sarah was not ringing my bell, despite her trim figure, whimsical manicure (little Betty Boops on her long nails) and her cheerful demeanor. I made it through dinner—just barely—without cracking out in huge yawns, and took her home as soon as it was nominally polite. I couldn't even bring myself to give her a peck on the cheek, although I believe she was hoping for one. It was Clem who had set us up, and it was Clem I called in despair. I had just about had it.

He answered on the first ring. "No go with Sarah?"

"No go, no go, no go!" Forgive me if I was whining. A guy can take only so much, even a mild-mannered, usually decorous guy such as myself, and it had been over a year since I'd been on the receiving end of any intimate affection.

"Well, dude, I don't know what to tell you. What the hell. Sarah's a nice girl, and she's seriously hot. I fucked her…"

"I know, I know!" I didn't want to hear about the suspension bridge over the gorge again, the spray from the waterfall, all that. "She just didn't do it for me."

"Well, no arguing with that. Okay, let me think. Denise is out, she's about to get married, Carla, no, she's got that whole abstinence thing going on with her Master, and Miou-Miou suddenly turned butch—I can't even think about that—okay, wait, give me a minute. Wait. Okay, dude, I've got it! At this point, you just need some relief, right? I mean, I know you're looking for the girl you can marry and take home to mama, but at this point getting your rocks off is really more of a priority, am I right?"

Much as I hated to admit it, he was right. "That would be just the ticket," I said in a small voice.

"Okay, then, I've got it! You have to go see Sue Anne. Of course! Why the fuck didn't we think of her before?"

"Who?" Then I remembered. "The aged crone from Diva's? What is it with her?"

"Okay, it's a little bit kinky, a little bit twisted, but it's a good option in your desperate situation—trust me!"

"Clem, I'm desperate, but not that desperate! I mean, *Harold and Maude* is a cute film and everything, but…"

Clem was chuckling, but there was something grave in his voice when he said, "No. Trust me, man. Go see her."

He gave me all the information, address, phone number, the best time to call since she didn't have a cell, just a landline, and he wasn't even sure she had voice mail. I didn't write it down. I thought he was kidding. But the next Boys' Night Out, everyone asked me about my visit, and when I just laughed and shrugged it off, they all got really serious.

"Dude, you are going to dry up and blow away if you don't get laid," said Liz, resting her hand on the bulge at the front of her jeans. "Your pecker is going to self-combust."

The other guys were nodding.

"It's not healthy," said Aiden.

"Not healthy at all," agreed Clem. "Don't wait forever, man. We've all been there!"

"Been where? In your grandmother's underpants?" I'm usually not that sharp with the fellas, but I had had about enough of them, too. Everything was irritating and unpleasant. I finished my beer and left, since even if no one else would, the library always welcomed me with open arms. Once again, Charley was waiting by my car. I didn't say anything, just unlocked the doors and he got in.

"Drive," he said. "I already called her. She's expecting you."

Sue Anne lived in a bungalow in a quiet neighborhood in Easthampton with an amazing view of Mount Tom. Not that I was paying too much attention, since I was devoting most of my energy to being nervous and angry, but it was hard to miss: the gorgeous vista, dusted with snow, soaring up and up, the stern mountain glare. A person could feel very small at the bottom of that big hill.

I parked in the driveway and we got out. The door to the bungalow opened, but I couldn't see anyone. Charley walked up the path with me, then turned and got on his board, grinning and waving as he pushed off. Probably the guys had told him he had to make sure I went in. Bastards! Sighing, I turned to greet my hostess. Only there was no one there.

Curious now as well as frustrated and embarrassed, I went in. I could smell clove cigarettes with a faint, comforting under-aroma of dog. The door opened right onto the living room, which was cozy and a little messy, newspapers scattered here and there, a fire in the fireplace and an old lab mix thumping his tail at me from his basket. I stroked his head, calling out, "Hello?"

"Yes, dear. Come right on back! Make sure you close the door behind you."

That voice! Was that Sue Anne? I realized I'd never heard

her speak, never gotten close enough to her in the club. From her voice, you couldn't tell she was a granny. From her voice, you would think that she was a sultry young thing, all big eyes and heaving bosom, waiting for you wearing a wisp of nothing, a scrap of lace you could pluck from her, exposing her rosy skin, her ripe limbs and willing cunt. I actually said *cunt* like that in my head, and I am not generally one to use crude words. It was her voice that did it, her voice that would have made even the world's most proper gentleman begin to sweat and swear. I walked through the dim hallway to the back of the bungalow, and I am not joking when I say that I was leading with my cock.

This was strange and getting stranger. The bedroom was almost completely dark. The pungent smell of cloves was stronger, fresher. She must have just put one out.

"Oh, what a sweet boy they've sent me this time," came that voice. I could see her silhouette where she sat in an armchair under the window, which was covered with a room-darkening shade. The eensiest bit of daylight crept in around the sides, but not enough for me to see her face. Funny, as I stood there, swaying slightly, I couldn't quite remember what she looked like, and as she murmured on and on about what a nice boy I was, how handsome, how kind it was of me to come and see her, a lonely girl on a lonely winter afternoon, I could see only the image her voice had conjured up for me, of that luscious someone, a femme made of pliant and willing flesh, all for me.

"Come in," said Sue Anne. "Do come in."

I crossed over the threshold and without being told to, went and sat on the bed. It was so dark that even close up I couldn't quite make out her features. She continued speaking softly, telling me how much she liked a young man such as myself, a polite young fellow, she could tell, not like some of the rascals out there. From her mischievous tone, though, I could tell that she liked the rascals, liked them just as much as us politer guys. This was a femme who liked butches in all flavors, however they came to her.

"Why don't you get comfortable—Del, was it? A lovely, old-fashioned name. Take off your boots, honey, so they don't mar the coverlet. Lie back, that's right, make yourself completely at home."

Maybe the clove smoke was going to my head, but I did as I was instructed, stretching out dreamily on the bed, my head propped up by soft, yielding pillows.

"Now Del," said Sue Anne, leaning forward. "The boys say you have a little problem. Do you want to tell me about it?"

Oh god, that voice! It made me want to spill, to dive into the warmth it created in the room, to wallow in the honey liquid, the smooth lilting hollows. I didn't know her, she was old, she was old enough to be my grandmother, but that question split me open. I cleared my throat and heard myself begin to speak, the details of my pitiful little story flowing out of my mouth. I told her about Michelle and Jenny, Barb and Marilee, playing to her deep, throaty chuckle, becoming more and more witty as I progressed, my word choice making her hum with approval, my commentary incisive and to the point. I didn't hesitate to tell her how horny I was, day in and day out, and what a disappointment my last date, poor Sarah, had been. I'd never had such an attentive listener, never felt so at ease discussing such personal business. Femme magic, that's what it was, a pure distillate of Sue Anne's long, long history with butches from every walk of life. It was a balm, it was an elixir, it was a gift. It was an incredible turn-on.

Given all that I was saying, given how she was listening with such generosity, it didn't seem strange when she got up from the chair and came over to the bed. It didn't seem strange at all that she would lean over me, begin to stroke my hair, pass her hands down the sides of my face, grasp my shoulders and arms, trace circles on my belly. She hesitated briefly over my chest, and when I nodded, she sighed happily as she began lightly twisting my nipples, all the time encouraging me to continue talking. The nipple twisting made it hard to concentrate, but I tried to keep telling her about my high school girlfriend and her obsession with avocados—she seemed so interested!—until I lost all ability to talk when she began unbuckling my belt.

"Oh, there he is, so handsome and firm!" she murmured, reaching into my boxers. "He's been such a brave soldier, and now he must get a little relief." She gave me a tug, a light slap, then settled into a delicious rhythm, a firm handling that had me vocalizing again, although not in words and no longer particularly witty. It felt so good, god, it was exactly right, and it was building, building, and this was exactly what I'd been needing, except...

"Sue Anne!" I gasped out. "I need to see you better!"

She chuckled and tut-tutted, and asked me if I was sure, but didn't stop me as I flailed about, finally making contact with the bottom of the shade and sending it ratcheting up. The setting sun came streaming right into the room. For a moment I couldn't see and had to close my eyes. When I opened them, there she was, sitting on the bed, half turned toward me, her hand on my dick, her smiling eyes, the red lipstick on her mouth.

"Some boys don't like to see me," she said. "I don't mind. I was the same way when I was young."

"Fuck them!" I was thrusting into her hand, grabbing for her waist, my gaze locked with hers. "Why don't you put that cocksucking lipstick to some good use?" Those words came out of my own mouth! I heaved myself up, swung my legs over the side of the bed, and helped her down onto her knees, right where I wanted her.

"Oh, sweet boy, sweet kid," she crooned before fastening that gorgeous mouth onto my dick and giving it to me good. I didn't think, then, about old or young, just knotted my fists into the coverlet and pumped until I was coming, shooting my load, gasping with such a profound sense of release that I felt a rush of tears. Sue Anne licked her way off my dick and looked up at me. In the light, even in my post-come daze, I could see how old she was. I could see that she had a slight tremor, that her eyes were sunken in their sockets, her cheeks were wrinkled, her lips—the lipstick now smeared all over my cock—were thin and pale. But she was smiling so damn pretty, and had the cutest, smug look on her face, a look that said she knew exactly how I was feeling and what she had done for me. It was the sexiest look I'd ever seen in my life, and I was hard again in an instant. She laughed, and took me back into her mouth.

I told her afterward, and it was true, that our fucking that afternoon was transcendent. I wanted more, but she wouldn't let me. "I'm a one-time-only kind of girl," she told me over the phone, me practically coming all over the place hearing her amazing voice again. "Besides, didn't anybody tell you about Buddy? She just doesn't like it if the baby boys keep coming around, and I wouldn't want to hurt my Buddy. She and I have it all worked out, and honey, you got yours and you got to move along. I primed your pump, baby bird, and now it's up to you."

I was upset at the time, even drove by her house once or twice until I made eye contact with Buddy and decided to hightail it back to Northampton. She was right, though. Something inside me had been turned on (pardon me) and it wasn't more than a month later that I met Sharon. You can see us dancing at Diva's, and she doesn't mind, doesn't mind a bit when we take a break and I order a Tom Collins, buff up the lighter I keep solely for nights like these, muscle past all those poseurs surrounding my Sue Anne, offer her her favorite drink, and, with oh, so much reverence, put a flame to the tip of her clove.

GIRLZ IN THE MIST

Cammy May Hunnicutt

I only went there once.

But I'm really glad I did.

Maybe just to know it's there, even if it's not quite for me.

A magic world that just wraps you up and does away with you, until there's nothing left but a throb and a glow.

Never-never land.

No boys allowed.

Luz invited me to come with her but was pretty vague on where we were going. Somewhere over in Hollywood, about halfway for both of us, so we met up at the Denny's on Gower and took my car to this "spa." I took one look and said, "This is the cool place you want me to see, bitch? It's a gay bath house."

She gave me a coy smile and said, "Not on Wednesday nights it's not, *puta*. Park over there. You're going to like this. Or your money back."

"Money?" Hadn't mentioned that.

"Your turn to treat."

Great.

We went on in and all I saw was women. So it must have been Wednesday. This very severe gal in her forties gave us towels and little bracelets with locker keys. She looked right through me, but gave Luz a kind of constipated smile, so I guessed my friend was a repeat customer.

The locker room was nothing special. No posters of pride parades or Orlando Bloom with his loaf hanging out or anything. Strip down, lock it up, head for the steam room. You had to walk through a shower to get there and Luz turned it on, adjusted it to nice and warm and started scrubbing up. Looking at me, smiling, flaunting her body.

Which was darned flaunt-friendly, let me tell you for true. She's over six feet of lean, mean athlete, my usual partner for highly competitive beach volleyball. Honed legs and stomach of a fighter—with a couple of knife scars to back it up. Strong, hard breasts with nipples like black olives. Burnt butterscotch Latina-tone skin with creamy caramel inside the tiny bikini tan lines. Face like a *barrio* street angel, big black eyes under no-nonsense Frida Kahlo eyebrows, nipple-length hair so black the highlights are almost blue, like those neon lowrider paint jobs. She didn't make a move to touch me, and I didn't either. We'd done some major touching on other occasions but don't mix it up all that often. A very special friendship that rests on some delicate spacing. For one thing, she was born as lesbian as it gets, and I don't see myself that way. Just like to fool around with pretty women now and again. For another thing, we're neither one of us the type for long-term hookups.

She said, "Wet down your hair, *guera*." She just loved my hair. She'd told me all Latina chicks secretly yearn to be blondes, have blonde babies. I put my head under the spray and shook it out and she smiled, reached over to kind of smooth it down and jerked her head at the tiled passage to the steam.

My first impression was that I was swimming through light. The room—rooms, actually, a little labyrinth of tiled chambers— was full of steam. Duh. And lit by dim, buttery, industrial-style lights on the walls. The light just flowed around in the steam, reflecting off itself. It was like being in a dust storm of warm, moist light. With a faint smell of eucalyptus and something else. Maybe sage. The body-temperature fog muffled sound. It felt like a silent underwater world with only a faint hiss in the background, like a radio that had lost its signal. I padded along, wading in luminous vapor. Luz strode through readily, heading somewhere in the small rooms and corridors. I felt, rather than saw, that there were other people in there with us. They were shadows on the multilevel benches around us. An inventory of dark ghosts stocked on shelves.

Visibility into the cottony white sheen was pretty limited and seemed to vary with which direction you were looking. It was a sort of culture medium gel, warm and moist as an orifice, full of female bodies moving lazily around. I couldn't tell how big it was, how many people were there, what they really looked like. It was a diaphanous veil that I was imbedded in like a gold fish in a white sea. People were talking, but it was a dull hum with no words. I heard moaning, but it seemed stylized, like a loop of an Enya video. The light shook and shimmered as dark silhouettes moved around me. A face would emerge, or a lovely pair of breasts topped only by a mop of wet hair instead of a face. An outline of two women hugging, full asses emerging and sinking into the fog. A big, really ugly woman stood right in front of me, then turned and disappeared, her flaccid butt hanging in my vision like the Cheshire smile. Wonderland, I was thinking. The Cave of the Lost Girls.

I asked Luz, "Who are these people? Some sort of lesbo jamboree?"

"You don't know shit about lesbos, *gringa*. Believe me."

"And you should think I should know more? That's why you brought me here?"

"I brought you here because they're going to take one look at you—sweet little blonde lingerie model—and lick their lips and vote me president of the Dykes with Two Strikes Club."

Oh, goddamn it. I said, "Luuuuucy..." but she interrupted me.

"Now, see..." She leaned down from behind me with her head right on my shoulder. "You gotta know more about who you are or you'll never find out who you aren't."

"Who said that? Schopenhauer?"

I felt her shrug instead of seeing it. "It's tagged on an overpass in Echo Park."

She put her hands on my waist, spanning the top of my hips, and said, "They're freedom fighters, *'mana*. Guerrillas in the mist."

"Freedom from what?"

"Not 'from what.' 'To what.' You're going to find out."

She started moving away from me, leaving me standing in the void. I asked her what I was supposed to do.

"Just stand there," she said. "See what you get. What does that take? You're Little Miss Gutz Girl and all that; just hang." She started moving away, dissolving into the fog. Her voice had a kind of bottom-of-the-well hollow sound even just a yard or two away, telling me, "Hey, I brought you here, *guapa*. I got your back. And your ass."

I watched her fading into the white wall, stopping in front of a woman with skin so pale I could only pick her out from the mist because she had really vivid red hair. I could see a sort of slow-mo, unfocused ballet as Luz moved around her, checking her out, looming over her. Luz can look pretty intimidating close-up like that with her strong features, laser gaze, big brown combat-ready body, tats and scars. Lil Red was getting that weak-in-the-knees look. I knew the feeling: getting Luz's full attention is like standing in front of a cannon and wondering when it's going to go off.

Suddenly I saw the blatantly false red hair fly up into the pale air and fade away from my sight. Luz's favored pickup technique, commonly known as the Fireman's Carry. Believe me, it makes a statement. I was betting that henna hair would be hanging upside down, tossing around as her invisible face plowed between Luz's taut thighs, her own legs resting on wide shoulders and kicking as she got mopped out.

But also betting that even in the middle of scarfing her favorite flavor—raspberry red—Luz would be aware of me, watching my bare back. The gang-girl way she's wired. I relaxed and just stood there in the middle of Dr. Sappho's Pandemonium Shadow Show, waiting it out. I'm small, but major tough, nobody to mess with. But being naked and presenting is a little different situation. Like, do you find out where the lines are drawn before they've moved in on you?

It came fitfully, hands reaching out from the mist to stroke me, hands on my back and ass, weaving into my wet hair. I stood still, not knowing where the next touch would come from. It didn't feel like getting cruised by a wolf pack, though, more like wearing a gauze blindfold while a new lover discovered, explored and started to torment.

Women appeared out of the fog, not just passing by but step-ping in to confront me, to check me out. I just stood there as eyes resolved out of the whiteout and looked into mine, boldly scanned my body. One husky black woman in her forties smiled at me and I smiled back. I felt a soft, almost tentative, hand on my shoulder blades, but didn't move. It slid slowly down the curve of my back, caressed my asscheeks, then was gone. I didn't react or turn around. Just the feeling I got, how I should play it. A slim white girl with small tits and pale eyes materialized out of the shining mist and cupped my breasts, holding them, massaging them slightly, not meeting my eyes but staring at my nipples as if hypnotized. At the same time I felt the arch of a foot caress the inside of my calf and slowly slide up my thighs. When it touched my pussy, it sort of moved back and forth, then slid back down. Immediately I felt two hands roughly grab my buttocks and start squeezing and grinding them. In the process fingers slid along the rails of my pussy. Which was getting a little warm and moist, but that also faded into the air around me. The whole place was moist and warm and sexually charged. The air itself was moving around on me and into me. I shifted my stance: feet farther apart, my hands on my hips, my tits arched up into the nebulous glow.

A short Chicana or Filipina girl moved in from my flank, straddling my hip to press her belly against my pelvic bone and stroke me with her hands, front and rear, then grab me by the notch of my crotch. She sunk her fingers into my pussy and started sliding hers up and down my leg. I didn't move.

The black woman was back, still smiling. Until she took one of my nipples between her lips and started jerking her head back and forth, worrying my tit like a dog with a bone. She licked and slobbered on my nipple, drooling a stream down to my ribs. Then slowly, her lips left off with the nipple and started a long, slow slide down my torso. She reached behind me as she landed on the floor on her knees, kissing my mound. The other girl still had the fore/aft grip there, but she kissed me steadily and sloppily anywhere she could make contact. Another pair of hands came in under my armpits, dragging the thumbs along the shaved strip there, and grabbing both tits for a series of squeezes, my nips slipping between the fingers.

A tall ash blonde with a thick, waist-length Scandinavian braid moved up behind the black woman loving up my crotch, straddling across her shoulders as she took my face in her hands and started moving her lips around on it. Licking inside my ears, sucking on my nose, teasing a tongue between my lips. She leaned into me, pressing the squeezing hands harder onto my boobs. An unseen woman embraced me from my other side, her hand sliding down the crack of my ass and a long-nailed finger, slick with some sort of lube that had a wintergreen tang to it, delicately inserting itself into my anus. Another pair of hands slipped up my inner thighs and buried a pair of thumbs all the way into my pussy, where they twiddled and danced to a different drum.

I was surrounded by women, all touching me, pressing against me, handling and possessing me. The insertions and caresses were building up a fire in my loins, as they say, the sheer strangeness and "strangerness" of it making it that much more exciting. I was allowing unknown, even unseen, people to take liberties with me that I would have denied a lot of lovers. I was tolerating my own violation, erasing something individual about myself. And I had the help of many willing hands.

I was getting light-headed, but realized I was being turned, rotated around my spine. My feet had left the floor. I spread my arms wide and tossed my head back, my hair falling onto the heads of my idolaters. I rotated and rose, my own personal *cirque du soleil* crucifixion. I hung at shoulder height in the depthless fog, my legs spread wide. I felt lips on my labia, a tongue exploring my vulva. There were two fingers socketing in and out of my asshole. There must have been six hands on my breasts, four

...re squeezing my buttocks. God knows how many more all over me, supporting me, but sliding around like snakes or otters. It was like having a barrel of hands and lips poured all over me, like hanging under a shower tap of liquid flesh.

I was really starting to feel it by then, hyperventilating a little. My pussy was like some sort of freeway for random transient traffic; my tits were slick with pressure and pleasure. I was lying on my back, but being carried around, sort of tossing on waves of avid women. I saw a henna head buried between my thighs, felt the sucking on my clit, and thought, *Why you little slut, jumping from Luz to me.*

The silliness of that one hit me, and I started laughing. I laughed twice, then the first orgasm hit me like a slap in the face. All that tactile hustling just soared up and blew me out. I went limp on dozens of hands, my head flopping back and my eyes rolling shut. I vocalized something, but don't know what. It got torn away by the mist, by the seething jungle of hands and fingers and lips.

I was lying on a bench. Or more like a blanket of moving hands tossed over a bench. I'd look up toward the light and see only a moving crowd of bodies and backlit faces around me, feeling nothing but a universal generic caress all over. There was a pair of hands cupping my throat, another holding my feet up while several sets of lips massaged my inner thighs, sucked at my twat. There were lips running around all over my torso and tits. I was straddled again and again, wet pussies pressed to me and wiping me down. I came again.

And again. And so on.

And on.

I was rotated onto my stomach, cocked into an ass-up position, and the slick stream of meat flowed over my rear-access profile. My ass was buffed to a sheen, my pussy pummeled and fisted, my asshole tickled and tortured, both holes simultaneously and serially invaded.

But nobody sat on my face. Nobody stuck anything in my mouth but a kiss. It was like I was meat for them all, but they didn't make me really participate. I don't know if there were some sort of bylaws for the Steamdyke Club, or if it was just some tribal pack consciousness. Later I was grateful for that because eating pussy wasn't something I'd done and it didn't particularly appeal to me. I would have, though. I was slapping my lips on anything that came into range, sucking at tongues and lips and tits. I was also lunging my pussy up into whatever might be up on it, in between periods of total semi-pass-out passivity when another wave of orgasms blew me away. I was being reduced as if I'd jumped into a blender, souped down to undifferentiated response jerks, waves of sensation rolling over me from all directions, making little peaks and valleys where they met each other. I was hamburger being patted into shape, out of my mind from a continuous throb of uncounted orgasms, cumming my soul out, my self completely lost in the uncontrollable flash flood of stimuli. There was no longer any question of orgasms, plural. I was aglow with one solid dark sheet of oblivion, one single pulsing gasp. What I'm saying: I totally lost it. And some of what I lost, I think, was gone for good. Good riddance, I guess.

I felt a pair of lips on mine and slowly realized there were just those two lips, very firm but gentle. An enchanted wake-up kiss from Neverland. I didn't open my eyes, but came to realize the lips belonged to Luz. I was lying on my back on a bench; somebody had draped a big towel over me and it was soaked. I was devastated. No question about talking. I lay there and attempted making a fist or opening my eyes. I still throbbed inside, felt scrubbed out and sandblasted. They chewed me up and left me torn down for rebuild. And Luz had come to scrape me up and take me out. When I started responding to her kiss, she put an arm under my shoulders and one under my knees and picked me up like a baby. Strong six-footer versus ninety-eight-pound petite, not a strain. She carried me out through the shifting gleam and held me up to the shower, sluicing me with hot water, then cool. She laid me on a wooden bench by the lockers and got me into most of my clothes.

I walked out to the front on Jell-O legs, stepping very careful; owl eyed and quivery as a fawn. I'd have been better off crawling, but Luz was there at my elbow, steadying me and chuckling. The front-desk woman was a Mexican-Indian-looking gal in her midthirties, stocky and busty. I sort of recognized her face, but lord knows what she was doing the last time I saw her. I gave her a dazed smile and said, "Thank you."

She gave me a big grin and said, "*Al contrario, guera.*" Luz laughed and slapped her a high five. I stumbled out the door with whatever degree of dignity you might carry after you've been had by the house.

At the car Luz just slipped a hand in my purse and came out with my keys. She stacked me in the passenger seat and reclined it back a bit, then got in and fired it up, sitting there a minute listening to my well-tempered Camaro rumble and growl and fart. I leaned over and put my head on her shoulder, kind of snuggled up to her like a kid. I still felt empty inside. But not drained and bleak, more rinsed out. Rode hard and wet and ready for the stable. I said, "*Gracias*, Luz."

She turned and kissed me and said, "*De nalga, chula mia.*"

Turning out onto the street she said, "You're jumped-in now."

I was like, *Huh?* I said, "Initiated? Into what?"

"NBA," she said, laughing. "Nasty Bitches Anonymous. It's

good you came. And you played it just right. Didn't even embarrass me or nothing."

"Like I had a choice."

"You had a choice, Cammita. That's the whole point." She drove me home and walked me in, pushed me over on the bed, stripped me down and tucked me in. But didn't stay. I was asleep before she left the room. Took off with my car for three days, I might add, but had it washed before she brought it back.

I never went back, and she never invited me again. I don't think you get that treatment on a regular basis. What I figured: I'd seen an ultimate extreme. I don't see any possible way you could get any further sexual response than that, no further conclusion you could cum to. What the extremes in life are, they're like the white lines they draw around the places we play sports. You need to know where they are, but you don't play there, you play on center court, at the key, between the hash marks. I couldn't tell you what I found out in there, or what fell into place the next week or so. During which I was unusually quiet, almost meek. Zero interest in sex. Very pensive. But I knew it was important stuff to know, and did something to the way I walk in the world and what goes on in my head when I turn out the lights.

One more guerrilla. Moving silent and semi-visible through the mist.

KISS OF THE RAIN QUEEN

Fiona Zedde

Hasnaa, the chief's fifth most beautiful daughter, had been sold for rain.

She held her head high as she alighted from the luxurious palanquin, usually reserved to carry her father or one of his wives. She was at her new home now. The palace of the Rain Queen. Or, as her father called the woman, an imposter.

The Rain Queen's lands near the sea were lush, the greenest part of the great continent that Hasnaa had ever seen. Although the sun was bright in the sky, the very air smelled like rain, a seductive and wet scent she'd only experienced a few times in her father's village. As the men had carried her in the palanquin, she passed beautiful flowers and animals running wild on the Serengeti, tall trees, women dressed like warriors practicing their martial arts under the open sky.

Hasnaa stepped onto the soft and rich black dirt, her sandaled feet sinking in with the sound of a sigh. She furtively stretched her cramped body, not wanting the four manservants to see her weakness. After all, she had done nothing more than spend the thirteen-day journey swaying in her loneliness while the men carried her on their shoulders.

The four men, their bodies roped with muscle and their flesh moist with sweat, stood still while Hasnaa stared at what was to be her new home. Instead of the semicircle of huts with the chief's residence at its apex, the Rain Queen's home was a single large and ornate structure made of white stone, coral from the nearby sea, and spread out for nearly a *maili* like the petals of a sunflower. They had been welcomed through an unguarded archway into a large courtyard with neatly swept dirt.

The joined circle of buildings around the courtyard were low and white, beautiful with blooming flowers bursting from every doorway. The loveliness of the palace was strange. Even frightening. It was nothing like where she came from, her village of floating dust, men and boy children with their spears and animal skins. Here, there were only women. Girls playing hand games together on benches as they sang in a language Hasnaa had only heard in dreams from her long-dead mother's lips. Young babies resting on straw mats at their mothers' feet, laughing and content.

Behind her, her father's men shuffled their feet, waiting to be received by the Rain Queen and then dismissed. Hasnaa hid her own unease.

She kept her face tranquil and regal. Although the truth was that she was neither. The second born of her father's seed and twelfth favorite of twelve children, she had felt carried along on a tide of fear since her father told her she was to become the Rain Queen's bride. Many moons ago, that fear had become resignation. Only recently had it turned to anger.

Hasnaa had wanted children but because of this marriage to another woman, she wouldn't have any. Her hands clenched at her side. She breathed deeply and forced the anger back to its cage.

She shifted her body, preparing to wait for a long time while the sun caressed her neck and bare shoulders. Even the heat here was different. It did not burn. Instead, its touch was almost playful as it stroked the skin left bare by her skirt and *ciwaya* that covered her breasts, a new garment she had to wear as a recently married woman.

The men stopped moving. Their silence was as immediate as it was unexpected. Hasnaa felt a light brush of awareness at the back of her neck, felt more than saw her father's men twist around to see who had entered the compound. Without turning, she knew it was the woman she had married by proxy from hundreds of miles away.

Hasnaa forced herself to remain still at the sound of delicate footsteps behind her. She did not want the woman to know that she was afraid.

The queen spoke. "I accept the gift you have brought to me. Tell your chief I am well pleased."

She gave the ceremonial words that Hasnaa had been afraid would not come, nervous that the Rain Queen would dismiss her father's lie of a gift. "You may stay until the morning," the woman continued. "Be welcome to my food and hospitality. Drink, eat, and take word back to your chief."

Chief. Even in her father's absence, the woman was respectful to him. The chief of the Izana people was not so kindly disposed toward her. At every opportunity he had taken the chance to mock the Rain Queen and her power. He made sure to stress to Hasnaa over and over again that this woman was no true queen, that she was an imposter.

"Never bow your head to this woman," her father had told her many times as he scowled at the rainless skies. "She is not my queen, and she is certainly not yours."

In her village, the rains had been meager for the past two seasons. At first, her father had tried to call upon the rainmakers directly, paying the most renowned ones to stand in the center of the village and beseech the gods to make fertile what was barren and scorched from the high sun.

But there had been no rain. Her father believed only in the power of men. Everything came from the father to the son and to the next son and so forth. Women, for him, were to bear children and take pleasure from. The idea of sacrificing to a Rain Queen or even acknowledging that such a person was needed, galled him to spitting in the dirt.

He did the opposite of what the law stated: For favor from the Rain Queen, the regent with power over the waters, offer your most favored woman child and the bounty of the skies will be yours.

And so, because of this, he had sacrificed his least favorite child.

Behind her, the manservants drew a collective breath of relief and quickly gathered the palanquin and left in the direction the queen must have indicated. Light footsteps sounded again near Hasnaa and a scent of flowers touched her nose. The scent was both sweet and seductive.

The queen stepped forward. And Hasnaa gasped softly. From what her father said, she had expected a woman who carried herself like a man. She expected a tall and strong-boned warrior with the arrogant look of some chiefs. But the queen looked, simply, like a beautiful woman.

Nyandoro. The Rain Queen.

Although she had a man's name, she wore her femininity like a perfume.

She was dressed in a long tunic a brighter blue than any

sky, than any orchid, Hasnaa had ever seen. The fabric flowed from her shoulders, draping over her full-hipped body with a disturbing intimacy. A stack of delicate gold armlets rested just above her elbow.

The queen was delicate, no taller than Hasnaa's shoulders, with her round face, large cat's eyes, and full lips touched with a stroke of pink. There was no hair on her head to distract from the loveliness of her face. Her beauty was shocking.

"I expected you to be very ugly." Nyandoro's voice was amused.

With those few words, she let Hasnaa understand that she knew of her father's trickery. As she slowly circled Hasnaa again, the tunic swayed on her body, fluttering at her ankles and revealing bare feet. She wore gold rings on her toes.

"I am not the most beautiful, true." Hasnaa raised her chin, defiant. "But you cannot send me back. You've already accepted me as your bride." Despite her confident words, her knees shook. She did not want to go back to her father as a failure.

"I wouldn't dream of sending you back." The cat's eyes tore Hasnaa apart, lingering on her throat, her breasts beneath the fall of beads and the thin cloth. "You are already mine."

Something about the way she said the words made Hasnaa fear for her father's safety and for the rains he so desperately needed. But she refused to show that fear. "Will you make him suffer?"

"He has already created his own suffering." Nyandoro looked over her shoulder toward a darkened passageway. "Attend her."

Within moments, a flock of brightly dressed women flew from one of the entrances to tug Hasnaa away. One moment, she was in the presence of the Rain Queen and the next she was being swept down a brightly lit hallway and into a large suite of rooms.

It was all so quick: a flurry of sound and the scent of sun-warmed flesh. The women were covered from shoulder to ankle in soft cloths that brushed their bodies in a way that made Hasnaa agitated, made her palms itch and her mouth dry. There was a sensuality to their covered flesh that she, who had been raised in a village where the girls went with their breasts uncovered until engaged or married, had never experienced before.

"So pretty," she heard one of them say in the Ndebele language that had been her mother's. A language they did not know she spoke.

"She's not so nice as all that. Aneni is much prettier."

"But our wife does not want her." A lovely woman, like a warrior with her muscled arms and proud forehead, tugged off Hasnaa's beaded throat ornament. "She did not take her to bed after that first night, everyone knows that. Pretty means nothing to her."

Hasnaa shivered. The women plucked off her clothes without asking, tossing aside her Izana garments to leave her naked in the bright room. She twisted away from them but they effortlessly caught her, held her prisoner in their nest of scented female flesh. She smelled them, tasted her own unease behind her teeth. The women were not shy about staring at her body, assessing it and comparing it to theirs. One of them, a woman who had as many years as her long-dead mother would have, pinched Hasnaa's thighs. "So firm." She laughed.

Hasnaa tried again to back away from them, unused to such sensual play among women. They only laughed and touched her even more.

"Stop it." She clenched her fists. Her heart beat like a war drum in her chest.

But the women ignored her. Instead, they herded her toward the tub, a hollowed-out tree smoothed from many years of use.

She could smell the herbs that floated on the water's surface. Mint and sweet flowers. Hasnaa didn't want to dishonor herself, or her father. But she felt the fear rising up hard in her. A heavy thudding of pulse and heart and rising body stink that made her want to claw at them.

Three of the women pushed her toward the tub of water. They were so insistent, their femaleness so overwhelming. In desperation, she spun and turned away from them, dropping into a low warrior's crouch like her brothers had taught her.

"Leave me alone!" she shouted.

The other wives stopped and stared at her, obviously startled. One of them seemed as if she would cry at any moment.

"Our lady will be angry with us!" she gasped with a hand over her mouth.

The one who had pinched Hasnaa earlier stepped forward and spoke in her father's language. "We are here to bathe you."

Hasnaa shook her head as their hostility rolled over her like a cloud. One of the women darted forward and grabbed her. The others followed, pushing her toward the tub that was big enough to swallow her body. She shouted again for them to leave her alone.

She had already agreed to be the sacrifice, to allow her sisters to keep their lives and her father to keep his honor. But what did that leave for her? Was her life to be over as soon as she stepped into that tub? The women rushed at Hasnaa again but she twisted from them, her body slippery with the sweat of her fear. She cried out again, although she knew there was no one to help her. She had to save herself.

Hasnaa grabbed a stone jug that stood on a high pedestal nearby. She smashed it against the floor and swept up a shard of the pottery in her hands. The sharp edge cut into her flesh but, intent only on protecting herself, she barely winced at the pain.

She whirled with the weapon, panting, trying to keep all the women within her sight.

"What's going on in here?"

The wives froze, drawing a collective breath of surprise. The room fell abruptly silent. Hasnaa only heard the sound of her own frantic heartbeat. She panted in fear, her naked body dripping its sweat and the pottery shard clenched in her fist. The Rain Queen stood in the doorway of the small room. As if thawed at the same moment, the women fell to their knees. All except for the older woman who merely dropped her eyes to the floor.

"My queen."

Nyandoro stood in the doorway, patiently waiting for an explanation of the broken jug, the shouting, the young wife in tears.

It was the oldest wife who spoke, the one who had stayed on her feet. "She did not want to take her bath, my lady."

Nyandoro raised an eyebrow. "Is that true? You'd rather be dirty than have my wives bathe you?"

Hasnaa was frightened of the look in Nyandoro's eyes, a look that was strangely like her father's. Autocratic and displeased. She shook her head and backed away from the queen, jerking up the piece of smashed pottery. A part of her watched with horror as she held a weapon against her new wife.

Nyandoro's eyes turned to the hardest coral.

"Leave us."

The women rose to their feet and scattered from the room, a school of startled fish flowing around an immovable rock.

"Drop that immediately."

But Hasnaa shook her head again. Nyandoro made a sound of annoyance and undid the clasp on her bright tunic. Hasnaa watched, shocked, as the garment dropped away from the surprisingly muscled and spare body.

KISS OF THE RAIN QUEEN

Hasnaa was so preoccupied staring at Nyandoro, that she didn't notice the swift movement, her wife grabbing the improvised knife from her hand, until it was too late. Blood drops fell to the white stone floor.

"You've hurt yourself."

Nyandoro lifted Hasnaa's hand and examined it with clinical interest. The slashing wound, the blood welling up in her palm. Hasnaa fisted her hand and tried to pull away, but the queen's grip was firm around her wrist. For the first time, she felt the pain from the wound. It throbbed to the rhythm of her frantic heart.

She swallowed the angry words that wanted to rise to her lips. Instead, she tried for diplomacy. "I meant no insult, my lady."

"Yes, you did."

The queen carefully put the pottery shard on the floor near the tub. She turned over Hasnaa's clenched hand, straightened each finger until the raw wound in her palm was naked to both their eyes. The pain stung, slowly spreading deep into her hand and up her arm. Hasnaa bit her lip to keep from crying out. She wanted to clench her fingers tight again and push the queen away, but she could do nothing more than whimper in frustrated anger.

Nyandoro lifted a dark and wild gaze to Hasnaa's, seemingly searching for something behind her eyes. She brushed her fingers over the throbbing wound. A breath later, the pain was gone. The *wound* was gone.

Hasnaa jerked in astonishment. A shiver of alarm, of fear, began in the pit of her stomach. Her father always said Nyandoro was an imposter and that she had no real power. How then could she do this?

Nyandoro brushed her questioning look aside. "Come."

She walked up the two short steps and climbed into the tub. She gently guided Hasnaa into the water with her. Fear of the queen's revealed power quivered beneath her skin.

"You have nothing to fear from me," Nyandoro said. "Turn your back."

After a quick glance at the queen's impassive face, Hasnaa sank slowly into the water, its warmth caressing her legs, her thighs, the indentation of her waist, her breasts. She shuddered as the water covered her nipples, the wings of her collarbones. What had her father thrown her into?

From the corner of her eye, she saw her wife reach for the white cloth neatly folded on the side of the tub. She rubbed soap into it and the scent of mint and night orchids rose around them. Hasnaa heard the movement of the washing cloth in water, felt the wet ripple against her skin. She shivered.

"Are you afraid of water?" A whisper of breath stroked her ear.

"No."

"Are you afraid of me?"

Hasnaa forced herself not to look over her shoulder as she assessed the true motive of the queen's question. Then the soapy cloth touched her skin, inciting pleasure and unexpected… comfort. "Yes."

She flinched in shock as the queen playfully bit her shoulder. "If I wanted to kill you, I would have done it long before now. On your long journey, I had many opportunities."

Nyandoro soaped her body, moving the cloth slowly and thoroughly on Hasnaa's flesh. Over her throat, her breasts, her belly, between her legs. Hasnaa flushed with embarrassment and arousal. She cleared her throat and tried to focus on what they had been talking about. And on what she feared.

"What *are* you?" she breathed through the desire slipping into her body like poison. Self-preservation made her grip the edges of the tub, preparing to jump up and run—but to where?—if she had to.

Soap bubbles squelched from the cloth and slid over Hasnaa's shoulders. Nyandoro's sweet breath teased her skin. "I am your wife and your queen."

"Don't toy with me." The words snapped from her lips, unwise. Her body was a mass of conflicting emotions. Desire and fear. Arousal and trepidation.

For this, Hasnaa expected retaliation. But the queen only said, very mildly. "I wouldn't dream of it, wife."

"Then give me the answer I seek."

A thoughtful silence quivered around them before Nyandoro spoke again. "Yemaya, the mother goddess and the spirit of water herself, has condescended to use me as her instrument among those who show her proper worship."

Hasnaa sighed in understanding. Her mother, a woman of great passion and bravery, had shown the mother goddess proper worship with an altar containing sea shells, dried starfish and what she suddenly realized was coral from the deepest part of the sea. The coral from that altar looked like it could have been taken from any part of the Rain Queen's palace. Her mother had believed in magic. But her father had not.

"My mother...my mother loved Yemaya," Hasnaa said huskily, losing her voice to the awakening of her body. She felt her eyes falling shut to savor the sensation of Nyandoro's thorough care. Her grip on the tub's edge loosened and she licked her lips, drew a calming breath. "She died before I could know her. But my whole life, she has come to me in dreams. In her last years, she prayed to the goddess for a child from my father, but was killed by a jealous sister-wife the night I was born."

Even now, speaking about the circumstances of her mother's

death, a woman who had fought to give her life even as her own washed away, made tears prick Hasnaa's eyes.

"Yes," Nyandoro said. "I know."

The towel moved again over Hasnaa's breasts, the rough cloth brushing her nipples again and again. She thought she heard her wife's breathing deepen. Hasnaa shifted her thighs beneath the water, squeezed them together as she grew slippery with desire.

"I saw her courage in a dream," the queen continued. "And I saw you, Yemaya's gift to me. Your arrival here was as it should be."

The cleaning cloth fell away until it was just Nyandoro's bare hands on Hasnaa's breasts, lazily caressing the soft flesh, rolling the painfully hard nipples between her fingers. Against her wishes, Hasnaa's head fell back and her lips parted to release a sigh. Her wife's mouth pressed into her neck, a hot and wet suction.

"A dream?" Gods! What was happening to her? Desire had never ruled her like this before. Hasnaa licked her lips again. "Stop it…I can't think."

"Why think when you can feel like this?"

A firm tongue licked her throat. A hand floated from her breast to tease her beneath the water, lazily circling the seed of her desire. Molten pleasure twisted in her core, the sensation unlike anything she'd ever experienced. It tore apart whatever self-control she thought she had. It threw the fear away as if it had never been. But that was a lie.

Hasnaa bucked in Nyandoro's embrace. "Stop it!"

After a breathless pause, Nyandoro pulled her hands from her, then briefly heated the back of her neck with a kiss. "As you wish." She sighed. "Now let's finish here before I forget myself again."

Nyandoro finished bathing Hasnaa. Dried her body, oiled it,

then picked up a nearby tunic that was the deep green of fertile things.

The material was as thin as a sun cloud. It plainly showed the queen's form on the other side as she held it up. Hasnaa's face burned at the impropriety of Nyandoro dressing her, her hands skillfully twisting the cloth into the ceremonial tunic. How was she to act when a queen dressed her as efficiently as a servant?

"Very lovely." She used the word in Hasnaa's father's language that meant beautiful to the eye as well as to the taste. "I look forward to your flavoring on my tongue."

Hasnaa blushed again. Her thoughts cleared briefly as Nyandoro took a step back to admire her work with the cloth.

"Forgive me my resistance." Hasnaa allowed the truth to escape. "I *am* afraid, but I will not lie down and be ravaged by that fear."

Nyandoro smiled. "Ah, you *are* perfection. I'm going to enjoy making you mine in *every* way."

Hasnaa shivered, swept away by the abrupt vision of bodies, hers and Nyandoro's, moving together. Sweat. The queen's mouth wet with her juices and her eyes flaming with desire as she crawled from between Hasnaa's legs. Her nipples peaked beneath the thin cloth.

She looked away from Nyandoro dressing herself.

"Come with me." She signaled for Hasnaa to walk with her, a motion that chimed the dozen gold bangles on her upper arms.

Nyandoro took her to an indoor garden. A wide room filled with plants of all sorts, deep purple violets, leopard orchids with their unique spots, blue lilies, the flowers turned up to the sunlight falling through the open ceiling. Cool stone lay under their feet, the pieces fitting together like parts of a puzzle. Thunder rumbled overhead though the sun still shone brightly.

The very air smelled of impending rain and soft, growing

things. Hasnaa lifted her eyes to the open roof, the blue sky with a vast landscape of clouds. The sun's warm glow caressed her cheeks.

For a moment, she allowed herself the simple pleasure of it. Then the reality of her situation came back to her. She swallowed and looked away from the sun. "Will my village get rain?"

Nyandoro was glowing perfection under the bright light, her eyes effortlessly undressing Hasnaa.

"Will you give yourself to me?"

Hasnaa hesitated. Unless the queen died and left her a widow, she could not marry a man and bear children. She could only serve Nyandoro in whatever capacity the queen desired. Already she had been born female in her father's village and thus disposable. Would saying the words *I do give myself to you* take away any chance of a future beyond the queen? Would she be disposed of again?

"You are female, yes, but not disposable." Nyandoro touched her arm.

She shivered from the casual-seeming touch that sent a jolt of electricity through her body. She backed away. "Why ask questions when you already know the answers?"

Nyandoro chuckled. "I like how you defy me."

Then she pulled Hasnaa into her arms. Her mouth was gentle, an unexpected tenderness. Hasnaa shivered as if caught in a sudden storm, tremors of awareness skipping over her skin like tiny strikes of lightning. She gasped, a soft and surprised sound, which gave the queen the perfect opportunity to lick her parted lips. Hasnaa shivered again as moisture flooded between her legs. Her nipples tightened to the point of pain. The fear left her, leaving only anticipation in its wake. This time, she did not fight it.

Hasnaa whimpered. "What are you doing to me?"

"Bringing you the rains that you desire."

Her eyes fluttered closed as warm hands moved up her arms and damp kisses seared her throat, the line of her shoulder. She felt each caress *below* the flesh, deep inside her where she had never been touched before.

"Beautiful," Nyandoro murmured into her skin. "So beautiful."

She moaned against Hasnaa's throat, bit into her skin. The new tunic Hasnaa wore rested like a kiss on her sensitive flesh, the delicate material brushing her nipples with each touch.

"You are as lovely as in my dreams."

Hasnaa swayed to the delicate music of desire moving through her. Then she felt cool stone at the back of her knees. She turned her head and opened her heavy-lidded eyes to the sight of a wide piece of dark stone, high as a bed and polished to a smooth sheen. The stone platform seemed more like an altar than a bed, a place to worship and sacrifice rather than to simply rest.

Nyandoro gently pushed her back onto the stone bed. For a moment, Hasnaa saw herself through the queen's eyes. Her body stretched out on the marbled stone, wanton and ready for whatever was to come, her legs spread beneath the thin cloth and showing the lean length of them, the fullness of her thighs, the dark patch of hair shielding her pussy. A sudden hunger filled her, clutching hard at her belly.

Nyandoro roughly pulled off her tunic and dropped it on the floor, muttering something beneath her breath that Hasnaa did not hear. Thunder rolled through the sky and lightning burst alongside the sun. Hasnaa smelled rain. Above her, the queen was beyond beauty. Skin gleaming under the sunlight. The face of a goddess with her round cheeks and skin like the bark of a baobab tree. Her breasts were small and high. The nipples firm in the air, already hard and begging for a lover's mouth. A shiver of awareness moved through Hasnaa. Her body was damp and aching, yet her wife had yet to touch her.

"Are you still afraid, Hasnaa, beautiful one?"

She told her the truth. "No, my queen."

Nyandoro smiled with ferocious satisfaction before she kissed Hasnaa again. This time there was no hesitation to her touch. She swept her tongue deep in Hasnaa's mouth and brought the desire that had lain like a sleeping lioness between them roaring to life. It reared up and bit Hasnaa between her thighs. She whimpered as Nyandoro's tongue flicked inside her mouth, firm yet soft.

It began to rain. Light drops fell on her face, her cheeks, her arms. She moaned at the strangely erotic touches of water on her skin. Nyandoro caressed her breasts, touching her nipples delicately at first, then more firmly, building in strength to match the ferocity of her kisses. The desire beneath her skin was nearly unbearable.

It burned.

And it was the rain of the queen's touch that she needed to put out the flames.

Hasnaa cried out when the hot mouth covered her nipple.

Her hands flew to the back of Nyandoro's head. Raindrops, cool and fat, danced over her hands and arms, down the queen's head and the muscled line of her back that Hasnaa caressed with deepening hunger. Between her thighs was a forest of wet. A thick and greedy place that begged for Nyandoro's touch. She parted her legs.

"Please," she moaned. "Please touch me."

"Are you begging, my wife?" The amusement seared into her skin as she writhed beneath Nyandoro's touch, crying out for a relief from the heat and agitation inside her.

"Yes," she cried. "Yes!"

A hand touched her wet and aching pussy. She quivered, unable to stop herself from gasping her wife's name.

"You don't need rains from me, you already have your own."

Then Nyandoro gave her what she needed, a warm mouth on her pussy, fingers on the button to her pleasure, soft moans that vibrated inside Hasnaa like a song. The rains came harder. She felt them on her face, her lips, on her bare breasts. She blinked up into the bright sky, her lashes fluttering beneath the wetness as her lover used her mouth, licking and sucking and making her dance beneath the rain.

The waters poured over them from the sky, over Nyandoro's shoulders, the decadent rise of her buttocks as she pleasured Hasnaa with her mouth. Lightning flashed again, but this time it was inside her body, an arrow of sensation. Then she was crying out, her body shuddering violently in release.

Nyandoro looked up from between Hasnaa's legs, her lips wet with her desire. Hasnaa felt a moment of déjà vu, as if she'd experienced that moment before.

"Are you mine, wife?" Nyandoro's voice deepened. A rumbling drum of sound that seemed to come from the very center of the earth or the skies.

"You didn't answer me." The queen rose up, her eyes both pale and dark like rain clouds, eerily bright against her skin. "Are you mine?"

The fear rushed through Hasnaa again, obliterating her desire's satisfaction. She felt her mouth tremble, her eyes grow wide. It seemed then that the face she had worn for Hasnaa was not enough to contain the power that moved beneath her skin. That power elongated her chin then widened her mouth, stretched her cheeks, before resolving once again into the queen who had given her so much pleasure.

Hasnaa knew then that this was no mere "upstart woman" as her father had dismissively described the queen. She was even more than a chief. The favor of the goddess, Yemaya, rested in her heated gaze. Rain, the waters, pleasure. She was indeed the goddess's vessel and the bringer of life.

Nyandoro rose up from between Hasnaa's legs and slid her fingers through the damp and swollen folds of her pussy. Hasnaa gasped.

"My queen!"

Then it seemed like Nyandoro's hands were everywhere at once. Tugging on her nipples, fucking her tight wetness, digging into her hips. The fingers inside her were strong and persistent, pulling pleasure from Hasnaa until she was screaming and the rainwater poured into her mouth, into her eyes, blinding her. Pleasure consumed her, turning her into steam.

Then the queen vanished.

Nyandoro *became* the water touching her. Like the goddess Yemaya, she was everywhere and nowhere. Hasnaa felt her on every surface of her skin, beneath her bones, in her head, whispering shocking and profane things. Things that made Hasnaa's heart beat faster, her pussy get wetter. The water touched Hasnaa with its heaviness, stroking her from forehead to toes, rivulets of pleasure taking over her body. She was soaked with her desire.

She bucked beneath the heaviness of the water, helpless before the violent release wracking through her body. She panted at the end of it, squeezed her eyes tightly shut for long moments before opening them again. The queen lay over her, a woman again, her eyes cleared of the white storm clouds.

Nyandoro pulled her fingers from the damp quiver of Hasnaa's pussy. "Now, all your lands are wet."

She touched Hasnaa's belly with sticky fingers, swirling dampness over the feminine curve. Hasnaa felt the slightest sensation deep within her, a quickening of life. A child. She blinked in shock, staring up at Nyandoro with the knowledge of what had just happened between them. The queen smiled, a touch of arrogance in her look, the searing flame of unending desire. She got to her knees and spread her legs, showing off the lush abundance of her pussy, the hairs matted with her juices, the pebble of her pleasure large and firm.

"I've given you what you wanted, wife." Her dark eyes glittered through the rain still pouring from the open roof. "Now, reward me."

As Hasnaa levered herself up on trembling arms, she felt a new strength in her body, a fierceness and a hunger. A belonging. Her mouth watered to taste the queen and give her rains of her own to soak all her forests and sweep her completely away.

"It would be a pleasure, my queen."

She dipped her head to drink.

MURCIELAGO

Theda Hudson

Carina stands in the center of our living room. She wears these cream-colored capris embellished with gold and dark-brown embroidery. She has brown ballerina flats with tan knee-high socks with clocking up the sides. Her cocoa-lace Victoria's Secret bra peeks out from under a tan bolero jacket covered with brick-red and gold ribbon in a soutache pattern.

I've never seen it, so she must have gotten it when she went out to fill one of my innumerable prescriptions.

She pouts her lips. God I love her lips, full and red. I used to lick them, then French her deep, letting our tongues spar like we were sword fighting.

But I haven't for a year now. Now we just smooch like a couple of old grammas. She always does it three times. Like quantity makes up for quality. *Smooch, smooch, smooch.*

So Carina poses, lithe and tall like some kind of urban bull-fighter, with an espresso-colored beret set at a jaunty angle on her dark hair. I can smell the lavender body wash she uses. She holds a small sheet of purple latex to the side that she flaps back and forth lazily.

My belly is roiling, has been all day, but if I had taken an Ativan, I would have been muzzy, then out for the count. This is our night, and I'm not going to let anything take it away. She's getting back into the big time at her job, leaving for Saint Louis tomorrow to work on a project the rest of the week.

She tosses me a black cap. It has red satin devil's horns on it, but here, now, they are bull's horns.

Taking a deep, calming breath, in through my nose and out through my mouth, I tell myself I can ignore the nausea. I can. I will.

Oh god, I understand what she's doing. I do, and I want to cry, she is so great. The cap is a new part of the "if we can't do that, fuck it, let's do this and make it ours."

I leer at her and slowly pull off my rainbow fuzzy cap and lay it to the side. Without breaking eye contact, I slide it on and push myself up off the couch, putting my head down, and paw the tan carpet with my slippered foot.

"Murcielago, come to me," she croons in the exaggerated Spanish accent she made for this game, her brown eyes lazy and sultry as she cocks her head at me.

Last night she told me about this famous Spanish fighting bull named Murcielago that withstood something like twenty-four sword strikes. It sounded kind of like Marcy, my name. And my last name is Bulitana. She has made him the perfect metaphor for me in my battle with cancer.

And so I play along, snorting and weaving my head back and forth while she takes up the classic bullfighter's pose. Then I run at the little square of purple latex and turn just before I would crash into the TV.

Snorting and blowing, I stare at her with what I think are my dangerous eyes.

Carina waggles one eyebrow. I pass again and she flips the latex around with a sharp snap, twirls tightly on the balls of her feet, letting one hand run over my back, and gives me a smack on the ass.

I pirouette in front of the deep-green moleskin couch with the cushion that is now dipped from me living on it. Carina calls it Recovery Central. I call it comfy, especially with Morton, our little black and silver tabby, for company.

I'm not supposed to let him get on me since I'm immune-compromised, but try and stop him. Carina spends a lot of time brushing him in the mudroom and even got him to submit to bathing once a week. He knows by now that he can't lick me and that my comforter-covered lap is as close to cuddling as I can manage, so it's worked out.

Carina waves her little cape, teasing me, and I toss my head and charge, feeling the cool latex slip over me.

When her arms go around me, I give in and let her pull me up to face her. She nuzzles, not touching; she can't do that since the chemo is toxic, sort of like an über-bad poison ivy that you can get from anything I excrete.

But her warm breath, smelling of that wintergreen gum she chews all the time, puffing against my cheek, then my neck and over my shoulder feels wonderful.

"Ahh," I groan. The sensation travels all the way down my body, ending up in my pussy, which glows like an ember in a long-banked fire.

"You ready, my precious Murcielago? You ready for the real dance?" she murmurs in that Spanish accent now sounding incredibly sexy, all hoarse with desire, with love.

"Yes, Carina," I say, like Gomez Addams would say to Morticia. We went as that crazy couple for Halloween the month before I was diagnosed. She was so hot in that black dress, cut down to her navel, the long black wig shading her face as she looked up under her brows at me. I'd creamed that pin-striped suit before we got home. And then I creamed it again, my face buried in that V, my fingers buried in her cunt under the folds of that soft dress.

"Then come with me."

I follow her swaying ass to the bedroom and let her strip off the flannel jammies that I live in. You can't really tell I had cancer. Even though I've had tons of chemo and two surgeries, I don't look drawn, my color is good, and I wear a scarf or a knit cap most of the time. Not because I'm ashamed of being bald, but because it's too cold otherwise. Who knew hair made that much difference?

Carina pushes me back onto the shocking-green beach towel covering the bed's blue fuzzy coverlet. I put my hands behind my head and watch her slip the bolero off. Her skin is coffee with a dollop of cream and super smooth.

I like to touch her. I can if I make sure my hands are clean and dry. I like to wash them and then take the towel into the bedroom so I can make a big deal out of staring into her eyes while I meticulously dry my hands and fingers. She always shivers, knowing what I will do when I lay the towel down, and I love knowing that I can affect her like that even now.

Her tits are round and firm, with dusky areolae, and they jiggle when she lets her bra fall away. I can lick them if she showers when we're done. And I do. I lick and nuzzle and suckle like a hungry little baby.

She puts her arms out toward me and shakes her boobs like a stripper. I groan watching. Sometimes, she does it right in my face and I breathe in her musky fragrance.

I'm growing warm, which is nice. Sometimes I want to, but I just can't summon enough energy or desire through all the side effects of the stuff I take to offset the ups and downs of the drugs that are supposed to cure me.

But now, I want her. I want her close; I want her hands on me. And she knows. She shucks the flats, pulls off the socks and flips them away from her, then shimmies out of those bling-bling capris and the lime-green G-string, leaving the beret on. She lets me have a good look before she turns to the wooden icebox that doubles as a cupboard in the bedroom.

She pulls out a pair of purple latex gloves and holds them up, looking from them to me, lifting her chin and her eyebrows.

God, she is beautiful, and I love her so much in this moment. And I am totally grateful. I know how hard this has been for her. Not just the worry, but all the work.

There're all the innumerable doctor appointments and tests, cleaning my PIC line every day in the first months when I came home, then ordering all the prescriptions.

That would be enough for anyone, but the house has to be scrupulously clean, too, the kitchen immaculate. And the food I can eat when I have an appetite has to be washed and thoroughly cooked. It's hard work on top of her usual job.

I'm definitely warm now, a buzz rumbling in my pussy.

She climbs on the bed like a cat and pushes my legs apart, kneeling between them. Her skin is soft and smooth against my legs and I rub them against hers.

"Mmm," we say at the same time, then laugh.

She leans over me, her arms on either side of me, so close I can feel her heat. She chuffs her breath lightly over me, starting at my neck and working her way down. I can feel sweat start to build with its acrid chemical smell.

I feel embarrassed, but she's told me she doesn't care. She says she'd take any side effect if it meant I would live, that I'd beat the Big C.

"Breathe, Murcielago," she says. "Just be. Enjoy the moment. Be in it."

Early on, I would get upset when nothing would happen. "But it is happening," she insisted. "We're together, cuddling, touching, being together, and that is a gift right there."

When I was still in the hospital, I would see her face when she came back from the little kitchen and I'd know she'd been speaking to the other patients' families. She'd try to mask the horrors, the tragedies they'd shared, but I knew my Carina as well as I knew my own hands. My heart would beat faster, and I'd be afraid that I wouldn't survive.

But I knew had to, just so I could wash that fear away from her face. And I had. Not twenty-four cuts like the bull, but I'd given the Big C the finger at every turn.

She breathes over my pussy, and I lift up. Then she lays that square of purple latex on my mound and bends over it. I watch her extend her tongue out and lap delicately between my lips through it.

"Ahhh," I say, pushing up toward her like a crocus to the spring sun.

She chuckles low in her throat and pushes her tongue between my lips through the rubber. It feels weird, but dirty. Somehow the idea that we aren't supposed to be doing this, but she insists, and does it through the plastic is really exciting. Breaking rules is part of the allure, finding our own way is more of it, and I mentally flip the Big C the bird.

That gives me a twinge that plays alongside the buzz that her tongue creates, and I moan.

She sucks and nibbles and licks through the latex and everything tightens, growing warm in the well in my center, my sexual core. I could come wet and that excites and scares me all once.

I used to come wet prodigiously, a flood that would soak the towels we shoved under me. They are the best, most satisfying, most exhausting orgasms I've ever experienced. And Carina would take pride in making me come like that.

But now, it's just a deluge of toxic chemicals and some of it could get on her.

What a quandary.

She smacks my flank. "Stop thinking and just Be. In. The. Moment," she growls and goes back to work.

But how can I? Maybe if I just go for an orgasm and stop the flood. I can do that, although it's always dissatisfying. But I don't want to cause problems just to please myself. I need to consider Carina and any danger I could pose for her.

Which is another thing I hate about cancer. It takes the front seat all the time. Not just an elephant in the room, but a host of requirements, taboos, special considerations. I hate it. I hate me for having to give it such privilege.

"Do I have to smack you again?"

"No. No," I say and settle back in.

Carina buries her face in my cunt and attacks. I think about breaking rules, pushing the cancer to the backseat, and enjoy that idea, trying to let go. It works enough that I let go, feeling the warmth rising along with the pleasure.

She gets me up close to the edge. We haven't been here often, and it usually takes longer. Much longer, with no guarantee of success. Even with the Magic Wand, which used to be an immediate success.

I'm right up at the edge and push and push, trying to find a path, a tremor, a buzz that will let me get over the edge, with a waterfall or not.

Carina kneels up and smiles down at me. "Feels good, doesn't it?"

"Yeah. It does."

"This will be good, too." She waves the purple latex gloves at me and slips one on with a decisive *snap!*, grinning wickedly.

This is another part that gets me excited. When I was in the hospital, we started asking about sex. It was weird. No one wanted to talk about it, not the oncologists, not the nurses, not even the counselors. They all recommended complete abstention.

"So, I can have cancer," I said to my oncologist. "I can recover, but I can't enjoy the basic pleasures that come with life?"

He just shrugged. "Better to be safe," he said.

Finally, one nurse told us they all fear a pregnancy, which would likely have horrible defects from all the chemicals. When we mentioned that we were a lesbian couple, with no plans for kids, and perfectly capable of practicing outercourse, she shrugged. "Lawsuits."

So we read everything we could, talked to other patients in our respective circles, read blogs and figured out ways to enjoy ourselves. When my drug-laden body would cooperate. A bigger finger to the Big C and all the rules it and the medical establishment thought it could lay on us.

The other glove follows and Carina waggles her fingers at me and then makes a come-here motion with her middle finger and I groan as my body recognizes what that will do to me when she slips that busy finger into my cunt. I close my eyes and concentrate on the heat growing, filling my core, and try to hang on to that excitement.

When she gets to the bowl of my hips, she lifts her hands up, supporting herself with her belly muscles, and starts tracking her fingers over me—shoulders, arms, breasts. She gently moves the PIC line off my tit, letting it fall to the side. Then she pays special attention to my rosy nipples, which have risen up into hard little pegs.

I give over to her as she traces arcane lines over my belly, closing my eyes so I can enjoy her touch.

I hear the snick of the bottle and the flowery clean smell of the lube hits my nose. I open my eyes to see her tip the bottle of Caribbean-flavored lube toward me like she's making a toast.

She upends the bottle and she meets my eyes as a generous drop falls onto her finger. The late afternoon light peeking in around the blinds makes her finger shine.

She flips the cap back with a snap and lays the bottle aside. As her finger slides into my snatch, I close my eyes. The lube is cold and smooth and her latex-covered finger skates over my clit like she's going for the gold medal. My thighs tighten and my belly clenches. It feels good, whispers of pleasure coursing through my body. I try to encourage it, concentrating hard on pulling those little bits together into a whole cloth that I can wrap myself up in.

"Relax, Murcielago," Carina whispers. "Just be, enjoy it. You try too hard and get wound up."

Moaning in frustration, I take a breath, then another, let everything relax, drift. I just want this night to be wonderful, pleasurable, with a climax both of us can enjoy.

She slides over and over my clit, twirling, pirouetting grace-fully, ramping up, slowing down, pausing to pour a few more drops of lube over me. The cold meets the heat she's engen-dered and I gasp, leaping when she slides two fingers between my lips and up into my cunt. I bear down, squeezing, hugging her fingers, as she rubs the front of my cunt, stroking the pros-tate there.

I feel the upwelling and I know I could come, come wet, come hard. If everything will just cooperate. But what if it doesn't? Our evening will be a shambles, and Carina will cuddle me and whisper that it's okay.

But it won't be. The cancer and the chemo and all the shit I've been through to live will win.

"Stop thinking, Murcielago," Carina commands. "Stop fretting. Be in the moment, let it happen. We have all evening. I'm not going anywhere." She wiggles around between my thighs. "And neither are you."

I settle back down again and she reaches up to pinch my nipple. I whimper at the sharp pain, and then moan as it travels through my belly and pokes at the warm well of pleasure she's creating.

She runs a fingernail down my belly, and I can feel it through the rubber glove. She grasps my hip and traces the line of what she calls my bone-china before sliding down to join the other hand, her thumb ringing the doorbell, even as she pushes through the front door with her other fingers.

Ah, ah, I'm finding the rhythm more often than not and the warm feeling grows, rises. Then the feeling fades and I groan, feeling hot and sweaty and frustrated.

"You're working too hard, Murcielago. Let it come to you. Let me bring it to you."

I growl and roll my shoulders against the towel. This is not going to work. She's going to go tomorrow and I'll be left with this memory and the Big C will be hanging over it all.

Smack! She slaps the outside of my thigh and the shock of it makes me open my eyes, even as the sharp pain chases the trails of pleasure her fingers engender, pushing me surprisingly close to the edge.

"I'm serious, woman. You need to get out of your own way and just Be. In. The. Moment." Each word is punctuated by a smack and stroke on that little spot, that lovely little doorway to the secret well of gushing pleasure in me.

We stare at each other as she works to bring me up to that

climax, her eyes smoldering, her hands demanding. I am pulled up to the brink, the well filling, filling and then suddenly over-flowing.

"I'm coming, I'm coming," I shout. And I am, the muscles spasming in waves, crushing her fingers, my legs rigid, my toes curled tight with the strength of the orgasm. Then the hot gush of ejaculate begins, spurting, not like the flood I'm used to, but a definite stream that splashes over her latex-covered hands and wets the towel beneath me.

I am gasping for breath, my face and shoulders hot and flushed. She smiles and cocks her head. "That you are. That you are, my brave, brave Murcielago."

She lies down beside me and strokes me, her face snuggled into the space between my shoulder and my head. I pull her in and we cuddle.

Carina did it. She made me come. She pushed a finger right through the middle of the Big C and gave me back the heart of myself.

"Fuck cancer," I say, and she turns my head over to face her. She kisses me. *Smooch. Smooch. Smooch.*

Now, it doesn't seem like a gramma thing. Now it's our thing.

She lifts my strap-on and a condom from behind the pillows.

"Yeah," she says. "But I'd rather you fucked me."

"Oh, yeah," I say, reaching for it. "That's even better."

IN MY SKIN

Beth Wylde

I saw the flashing neon sign of Melissa's shop from over a mile away. The closer I got, the harder my foot pressed on the accelerator. Instead of slowing down, I flew past the exit, missing the turn while my heart hammered in fear. "Shit! I can do this. I can do this. I'm not a coward."

I repeated the phrase over and over again as I pulled an illegal U-turn at the next intersection and forced myself to go back. By the time I parked the car and stumbled to the sidewalk, my legs were shaking so badly I almost fell flat on my ass. My mantra wasn't working. I was scared shitless. I stopped a block from my destination and leaned back against the nondescript wall of a tiny convenience store, one of the hundreds that filled the city. I had to calm down. "For Christ's sake, Kendra. Get a grip on yourself. People do this every fucking day."

The laugh that escaped sounded slightly hysterical. Who was I trying to kid? Maybe some people visited tattoo parlors regularly, but I wasn't one of them. In fact, I had a bit of a phobia where needles were concerned. I couldn't even have blood drawn at my doctor's office without passing out. "This is going to be a freaking disaster."

I'd just put my hand on the doorknob when the flashing INK BY M sign overhead went out, like an omen of something sinister coming my way. Considering what I was about to do, the warning seemed pretty appropriate. I did my best to shrug off the negativity, sucked in a deep breath, and forced myself to open the door. All I really wanted to do was turn around and run away. Fast. "I'm not a coward. I'm not a coward."

I kept repeating my mantra in an endless whispered loop while I glared at the empty waiting room that loomed before me. The left wall was covered in pictures of past clients showing off their tattoos, some done in places that defied both reason and sanity. The right wall held similar pictures, only these were of people and their piercings. One girl proudly showed off her double-D breasts and the huge rings she'd had attached to them. The thought of someone shoving a big-ass needle through my tits made me break out in a cold sweat.

On the far side of the wall, where the receptionist normally sat, was a huge display of black photo albums. These were Melissa's personal portfolios. There was also a poster advertising freehand drawings and specialized work for an extra fee. That was all it took. It wasn't working. I couldn't lie to myself. I *was* a chicken, and I was about to prove it. I spun around, ready to make my escape, when I came face-to-face with Melissa, my life partner and the owner of the establishment I was about to flee.

I raised my right hand and gave a little finger wave, like a guilty child with one hand caught in the cookie jar. I wasn't sure I could outrun Melissa. Did I even want to try? "Um, hi."

Melissa raised one pierced eyebrow suspiciously and stared me down. "Kendra, you weren't about to leave were you? You just got here. I closed up early just for your appointment."

I shook my head; my heart hammered harder and harder in my chest until I feared it would burst through my ribs. "No, I, uh, I thought I left my headlights on. I was just going back to check."

She sighed and the blatant disbelief was audible in the weary sound. "You don't have to do this, you know. Just say so and we'll call the whole thing off. No need to lie to me."

I frowned as she saw right through my lame excuse. "Ugh. I know that, but I feel like such a disappointment. I want to show you how much I love you. You mean more to me than some silly childhood phobia."

She smiled and locked the door to the shop, flipping the OPEN sign to CLOSED before stepping toward me. "I know you love me. You've proven it time and time again. This isn't necessary." She leaned down and placed a delicate kiss on my left cheek, a move completely at odds with her look. "And phobias are not silly. Some of the shit that happens to us while we're young can scar us for life."

She held out her right arm and turned it over, the jagged six-inch welt from the shark bite still easily visible after over a decade. She was lucky that was all the damage she'd received. Because of the attack, Melissa still refused to get in the ocean. She wouldn't even get her feet wet. What was a tiny needle prick compared to what she'd endured? How stupid was I being? She put her arm back by her side and the bottom of a heart peeked out from under her sleeve. I knew my name rested in the middle of the design.

I let loose a bit of frustration with a strangled scream. "Yes, it is. You had my name put on your arm ages ago. Now it's my turn to show you how I feel. I want the whole world to know who I belong to." I was surprised to realize I meant every word of my impromptu speech. Maybe I wasn't as big a coward as I thought I was.

I shook with more than fear as she paused before me, less than an inch separating us. Because of her height, I had to tilt my head back slightly to meet her eyes. What I saw there both thrilled and intrigued me. Her face reflected the same desire I felt churning inside my own body. Even after ten years of total monogamy, I wanted her with a passion that defied reason. If her dilated pupils and rapid breathing were any indication, she felt the same way.

Neither of us could be this close to the other and not touch. I wasn't sure who moved first, but suddenly we were pressed against each other, her muscular physique dwarfing my smaller stature. Her lips crashed down on mine, and I groaned from the intensity.

There was nothing subtle or gentle about the kiss. She took what she wanted, plundering my mouth with a fierceness that made me dizzy. My lungs cried out for air, and I ignored the call for something even more important. At the moment, kissing Melissa seemed as necessary to my survival as breathing. Her mouth and tongue dominated mine. I had no choice but to submit and I did so willingly. Hopefully, I'd be able to do the same later on in the back of the shop.

While her lips continued their assault, her hands wandered down my back until she cupped my ass in her sizable palms. After what seemed like hours, we pulled apart, both of us gasping and grinning and turned on beyond belief. She squeezed my rear tight enough to leave fingerprints, and I threw my head back on a moan. If it hadn't been for the glass front of the entryway, I would have gladly lain down on my back and done anything she asked me to.

"Oh god. We have to stop."

In reply, she lifted me effortlessly into the air until we were eye to eye. Our lower bodies were pressed so tightly together, I felt like she was trying to crawl inside me. "Do you really want me to stop?"

I leaned my forehead against hers. The *last* thing I wanted was for her to stop, but I knew if we didn't quit now, we never would. One of us needed to maintain some semblance of self-control; I just wasn't sure which one of us it was going to be.

"No. What I really want you to do is fuck me until I can't walk." I glanced toward the glass front of the shop and the easily visible street. "But someone might see us."

"Let 'em look." She lowered her hands to my upper thighs, forcing me to either wrap my legs tight around her waist or risk falling. She nipped my lower lip with her teeth, her lip ring accentuating the bite even as the cool metal soothed it. When she flicked her tongue stud out and ran the pointed tip back and forth between the seam of her lips, my resolve to remain sensible vanished completely. I knew intimately how that barb felt against my clit and the thought of her face mashed between my thighs while she licked me with her stud had my panties drenched in seconds.

"Oh Jesus." I squeezed my thighs tight around Melissa's hips in a wasted effort to halt the flood between my legs. "Please. Please, let's go home. I'm so wet. I need to feel you inside me. Skin to skin. Hurry."

She shook her head and started carrying me toward the back of the shop. "I can't wait that long. You know what that kind of talk does to me. My clit's so swollen it almost hurts." She took three steps and then had to stop and squeeze her eyes shut as a full body shiver took over. Apparently her hood piercing had just done part of my job for me. When she finally opened those baby blues and hit me head-on with their glare I almost came myself.

Earlier, I'd been terrified about ending up on Melissa's work-bench, but now the actuality couldn't come fast enough. I was so eager I almost asked her to run. The fact that I was about to get fucked senseless probably had a lot to do with my lack of fear.

Melissa pulled the dividing curtain shut behind us and all but tossed me down on the table. She was on me instantly, ripping off my clothes in a fight to get me naked as fast as possible. My flimsy shirt and skirt were no match for her strength or eager-ness. In seconds, I was left in only my bra and thong panties, and even those didn't remain on for long. I sat up in an effort to reciprocate, but Melissa wasn't having it. She was in full control and all I could do was lie back and enjoy the ride.

The minute my panties hit the floor, she grabbed hold of my ankles and forced my legs apart, diving between my thighs like a shark caught in a feeding frenzy. The first touch of her tongue stabbing deep inside my pussy had me creaming all over her face.

I wound my fingers through her spiky purple locks and guided her hardware right where I wanted it. "Oh fuck! Oh shit. More, more. Don't stop. Don't you dare fucking stop."

Melissa took the hint and moved up to my clit, starting off with a few slow licks and sucks until I was begging and writhing on the leather padding like a woman possessed. "Do it. Goddamn it. Just do it. Please. Stop fucking teasing me."

She smiled up at me from her position between my thighs. "I'm not teasing you, baby. I'm just trying to make sure you're completely prepped and ready. I take my job very seriously."

I had no clue what she was talking about, and I really didn't care. As long as she put her mouth back to work on my needy cunt, she could prep me all she wanted to. It was amazing how clueless I could be when I let my pussy do all the thinking. "Okay."

"God, you taste good. I could eat you all night long." She

licked my glistening juices off her lips and patted my leg. "Now turn over, hot stuff, and show me that ass."

My eyes widened in surprise and I flipped over so fast I almost slipped completely off the table. I'm a huge slut for anal play, but Melissa isn't a big fan of it, so it's a rare treat to get those needs met. Melissa caught me easily, before I even came close to hitting the floor, and boosted me back up. The fact that she seemed suddenly eager to play with my rear had me panting.

She gave my right cheek a playful swat. "Up on your knees." The command had barely left her lips by the time I assumed the position. "Keep your head down and your ass up."

I folded my arms and rested my cheek in the crook of my elbow, running through a vast range of possible scenarios in my head. None of them even came close to what Melissa really had in mind. If I hadn't been so blind with lust, I might have figured that out for myself.

She rubbed something cold on my left cheek, followed by a slow swirling movement that felt like a feather dipped in paint. Once that stopped, her hand trailed lower, one finger rubbing along the tight ring of muscle that surrounded my anus before dipping lower in exploration. It wasn't until I heard the buzz of the gun, and smelled the faint remnants of alcohol and marker, that I comprehended my predicament. By then, it was too late.

Before I could utter a protest, Melissa did two things at once. She thrust a well-lubed finger deep inside my ass and lowered the tattoo gun against my skin. As she traced the first line, I hollered out loud and long, caught in a vortex of sensation that rapidly alternated between pleasure and pain. The feelings collided until I couldn't distinguish one from the other. Every time the needle became almost too much to bear, she'd do something wickedly tricky with her finger to distract me. As

I verbally praised her manual dexterity, she wiggled in a second digit and continued to work me over.

The slow glide of her fingers in and out of my ass, combined with the burn of the needle and ink, coalesced into a thrumming, piercing, all-encompassing torture designed to push my senses to the brink and beyond.

"Faster, faster. Oh god. Harder, fuck me harder. Oh shit. Yes!"

I was quickly reduced to a pleading, pulsing, quivering mass of need. My orgasm was rushing toward me with astonishing speed, and there was nothing I could do to push it back. Melissa must have realized how close I was to coming. Her needle sped up in time with her thrusts, her ring finger stretching downward until it slid inside my other entrance like a warm knife through butter. She dug down hard one final time with the tattoo gun as she extended her pinky and gave my clitoris a firm tap. It was a move only Melissa could perform and we'd dubbed the maneuver *the showstopper*. True to its name, I let loose a scream of completion that nearly stripped my throat raw. I'd never come so hard or so long in my life. The spasms just kept coming until I finally collapsed against the table in a boneless heap of sexual satisfaction.

"Oh my god." It wasn't until I started breathing somewhat normally again that I realized Melissa's fingers and needles were gone. I looked over my shoulder and found her at the small sink nearby, washing up her hands and her equipment. She turned and graced me with one of her cocky boi-ish smiles.

"I told you getting inked was a rush."

I couldn't help but laugh and once I got started, I couldn't seem to stop. I finally managed to calm long enough to ask the burning question on my mind. "Do all your customers get such amazing treatment?"

She shook her head and grinned along with me. "Nope. Just one."

The fit of giggles came back, stronger this time, until I was wheezing with each breath. It was like the giddy high of alcohol, only I hadn't had a drink all day. "What the…?"

Melissa rushed to my side, stroking her hand over my back in a soothing motion. "Everything's okay. It's just the endorphin rush. Every person reacts differently. Just try to relax and go with it. Ride the feeling."

"Does this happen often?"

She nodded. "Every time I get a new tattoo or piercing."

I stared at her body and all the tattoos and shiny silver studs that were visible, plus the ones I knew were under her clothes. "Wow."

She nodded. "Though I don't laugh." The look she gave me scorched me to my toes and halted my merriment. "I just get horny." She ran her hand lower, stopping where my back ended and curvier areas began. "Very, very horny."

I followed her gaze to my reflection in a mirror behind me and got the first glimpse at my tattoo. It was a simple design and, under the circumstances, it kind of had to be.

The largest part depicted an ink bottle tipped sideways with Melissa's name flowing out of it in a flowery script. To some, it might have seemed odd, but to me, it made perfect sense. It symbolized our love and commitment as well as Melissa's job and my newest fetish. Now, she was officially in my skin. Where she belonged. Maybe next time I'd let Melissa pierce something. The thought of her prepping my hood made me hot all over. I wondered if I could go ahead and schedule an appointment. I decided to talk it over with her after I showed her my sincere appreciation, one ink lover to another.

STILL FLYING

Andrea Dale

Moments before I got on the plane, Mindy texted me: *I have a present for you.*

I assumed she meant something when I got home, and was only telling me now to distract me from the fact that I had to fly *to* Dallas and then *back again* before I could receive the gift.

You know what they say about *assume*, right? When will I ever learn not to underestimate Mindy? She's the love of my life, my domme, and my wife in everything but a government certificate, and when she tells me the trip will be fine, I'd better damn well believe her.

But the fact is, flying scares the shit out of me. I've even talked to a therapist about this, and the best we came up with is that I hate giving up control. I'm a terrible passenger in any kind of vehicle, but one hurtling through the sky is particularly bad.

Which is a joke, right? Because as a sub, I'm all about giving up control. In fact, I'm all about sub-space and flying.

Just not this kind of flying, apparently.

* * *

My seatmate reminds me a little of Mindy: blonde hair in loose waves past her shoulders, blue eyes. She's a little more solid than Mindy, more farm girl to Mindy's waifishness. Her smile distracts me, and after I fumble my carry-on into the overhead bin, I pull out my sweat-crinkled boarding pass and frown.

Before I can say anything, though, she says, "I'm actually in your seat. But I'm a bit claustrophobic—you don't mind sitting by the window, do you?"

There's a tone in her voice that makes me straighten. She sounds perfectly friendly, making a perfectly logical and polite request, and yet...and yet I can't say no. I'm not allowed to.

"That's fine," I say, even though it isn't, because I don't want to be by the window where I can see the world getting smaller and smaller. At least we're in first class, though, and the seats are bigger, the legroom ample, so I won't feel quite as pinned in.

The décor is muted, in calming shades of blue and gray. The flight attendant, her red hair in a neat bob, asks if I'd like a drink, and on impulse, I ask for champagne. (Another perk of first class: beverage service before we take off.)

To distract myself, I watch her as she walks away. She has a cute ass, though it's difficult for me to truly get a sense of it under her generic outfit. Is it bad for me to think that? Will Mindy think less of me, when I tell her (because of course I must)?

"Before you get too settled," my pretty seatmate says, startling me out of my reverie, "I have something for you, from Mindy."

That pulls an unexpected laugh from me. I'm too stressed, my mind is too befuddled to suss out how Mindy orchestrated this. I manage to stammer my thanks as the woman—"I'm Cerys, by the way"—hands me the box and card.

The card is one of Mindy's, monogrammed with a stylized M. Inside, it says, simply, *Go to the bathroom and put this on.*

And because Mindy has ordered me to, I go.

That's not true. I go because I want to; because I know Mindy's devious, wicked sense of play; because it thrills me. My clit jumped when I read the words. Anticipating.

In the tiny bathroom, I stuff the ribbon into the trash and open the box. It's a hot-pink vibrating bullet, the kind you tuck into the crotch of your panties so it nestles against your lips, your clit. There are no controls, however: only a loop of wire out one end.

It still gives me pleasure, though; it slips and snuggles against my folds, growing slick, as I walk back to my seat, where my flute of champagne awaits me.

And Cerys. I slip past her to my seat.

I don't realize until I lift the glass to my lips that I can smell my own spicy juices on my fingers. Can she smell them, too? I didn't bring myself off—that wasn't explicitly allowed—so why do I feel guilty? She's watching me, and I take a nervous sip.

In my pocket, my phone chimes. Crap, I've forgotten to turn it off. I pull it out, see a new text from Mindy: *Good girl. Now, relax. Cerys will take care of you.*

Before the weight of the words can sink in, the vibrator at my clit shivers. My eyes snap wide and Cerys's hand is on my glass before I drop it. She smiles again.

"Relax," she says, echoing Mindy's words, and I understand, belatedly, that she's taking the place of sweet Mindy for the flight. (Or maybe longer. I can't go there right now.)

I set down the champagne, text back with shaking fingers: *Yes, Ma'am. Thank you, Ma'am.*

Then I turn off my phone and stow it, and, terrified and thrilled on so many levels, drink my champagne.

* * *

The cute redheaded flight attendant takes my empty glass as the door closes. She smiles, oblivious to my turmoil, turns away.

I've tried Valium, other drugs, and I hate them almost as much as I hate flying. It's that loss of control thing. The only thing that calms me down, that grounds me (hah) is Mindy. I feel safe with her—and I recognize the dichotomy, because Mindy will push me to the extremes of my limits, test whether those limits are my true boundaries. I don't know how she'll play with the edges of pain and pleasure, humiliation and delight, fear and rapture.

And yet, I feel safe with her because I trust her. I trust her to recognize which breaking points drive me to new heights and which would be too far. I trust her to take care of me.

Now, Mindy has entrusted Cerys with my care.

But it isn't the same. Cerys isn't Mindy, doesn't have that calming, safe quality that Mindy—the plane vibrates, engines engaging as it poises for taxiing down the runway, and my breath catches—and Cerys's hand comes down on my forearm, her fingers encircling my wrist with a grip more final than metal cuffs. My breath catches for a different reason. I sit up straight in my seat before I realize I've moved.

"Now, here's the thing," Cerys says, her lips near my ear, her voice lower than necessary given the rumbles of the plane. "I know you understand what's going on. You're a pretty thing, and you're mine for this flight, to do with what I please."

She must have thumbed the remote to the vibrating bullet, because suddenly my panties are humming. Not just a taste like before; this time, she leaves it on. I know it's the lowest setting—although immediately arousing, it isn't enough to get me off. (Still, the sound—could anyone else hear?)

How high could this thing go? What would it...she...do to me?

I shudder. Public orgasms are my albatross, my most hated delight.

Mindy knows that—had exploited it on multiple occasions. Which means Cerys knows it, too.

"We have several hours," Cerys murmurs into my ear, her voice light and airy and innocent to everyone but me, who heard the power, the control, "so you might as well sit back and enjoy it. I haven't yet decided if I'm going to make you come, or keep you on the edge the whole time…or even make you come again and again until you beg me to stop. I saw you look at the pretty flight attendant—what would you do if I told you to get her phone number? What if I told you to tell her, in great detail, about the vibrator spreading your sweet, pink pussy lips, snugged up against your quivering clit?"

I squirm in my embarrassment and arousal, staring at the seat back in front of me. The plastic screen, showing the end of the safety message, slides to an ad for the in-flight movie.

I barely see any of it, my mind's eye on the thoughts of the flight attendant's full lips parting, her eyes widening in astonishment at my predicament. Would she be disgusted? Excited?

And then there's Cerys, so cool and calm, whispering the filthy images while looking the epitome of the proper businesswoman. To anyone else, her hand on my wrist probably looks like she's comforting me. To me, it's as good as an iron shackle.

Suddenly the vibration between my thighs stops. I almost cry out from the lack of it, pressing my lips together at the last moment to catch the sound. Cerys chuckles.

And I realize I've completely missed our takeoff. We're already in the air.

The flight attendant—her badge says JANE—returns for another drink order, and I feel myself blush. She *is* cute, but I hadn't consciously processed it until now.

Oh dear lord, is she part of this, too? Has Mindy told her, or has Cerys? *Does she know?*

It doesn't matter if she knows. This is part of the mindfuck, and it doesn't matter whether I'm aware it's part of the mind-fuck or not. What matters is that she might know, and the very idea of her knowing is the turn-on.

I ask for water, and she hands me a foil packet of salted peanuts (nobody with allergies on this flight, apparently), and her smile makes me quiver, deep inside.

"You *do* like her," Cerys murmurs against my ear. "How adorable."

When Jane returns with my water, I reach out for the plastic cup, then nearly drop it when the vibration on my clit unexpectedly whirrs to life.

Once again, Cerys catches my drink. She smiles at Jane. "She hates flying," Cerys confides. "Don't worry, I'll take care of her."

The double meaning makes the heat rise in my cheeks. My flush deepens when Jane says, "Well, let me know if there's anything I can do to help," and Cerys purrs, "Oh, don't worry, we will," in a tone of voice that makes the double meaning that much more obvious.

To me, anyway. Oh, that maddening, delicious, terrifying mindfuck. The knowledge that I'm not in control.

But protected. I have no doubt that Cerys knows my safe-word and will respect it if I use it, if I call the whole thing off.

I have no doubt that Mindy knows I wouldn't do that, and Cerys probably knows, too.

When we're allowed to use approved electronic devices, Cerys produces an iPad and two sets of earbuds, which she plugs into a splitter that plugs into the tablet, so we can both hear what's being played.

"Mindy sent me some fun videos," she says, her voice as natural as if we were going to be watching cute-kitten videos. But I know better. "She promised me you'd enjoy them."

By now, I'm in such a mental state that my brain can't fully comprehend what we're going to watch. But as she takes her time loading the video—deliberately going slow, I suspect, to give me time to think about it—I know it will be something sexy, hot…and potentially embarrassing.

I flush again, a whole-body thing, a wave of hot and cold crashing over me as the first video begins.

Why is humiliation so damn arousing?

I remember the scene well. (How could I ever forget something like that?) We'd gone to the monthly play party, and I'd been cuffed to a spanking bench. There were cutouts in the bench so my breasts hung down, and Mindy had dangled the wicked clover clamps in front of my face, delighting in my reaction.

The camera was before me, getting a close-up of my face and those glittering silver clips. I squealed and I pled with my eyes, *no, no*, and Mindy had laughed. The camera zoomed back a little, to show more of my body, and I was forced to watch myself as Mindy snapped those evil clamps onto my already reddened nipples. My body stiffened—in the video, and now, too, in sympathy—as the exquisite pain coursed through me. I'd screwed my eyes shut, and Mindy had jiggled the infernal chain that linked the clips and warned me to open my eyes and keep them open.

I stare into my own eyes now, watching them glaze over as Mindy went to work on my ass with a paddle. Through the earphones I hear each *thwack,* see my body lurch and the chain swing, and I remember the sting of the paddle, the pain of the clamps that was so close to pleasure.

Hear the humiliating moans coming from my slack-jawed mouth.

I clamp my lips together now, to keep myself from moaning aloud.

Cerys slips the earbud from my right ear and leans in. "You look so amazingly sexy there, darling. And so helpless. What a naughty, naughty girl for enjoying that. Can you imagine if Jane walks by and sees it? She'll know exactly what type of slut you are. Or if someone in the seats behind us stands up and looks over?"

I gasp. I've been so focused on the video that I've forgotten where I am, forgotten that there are other people around to potentially witness this.

"I'm tempted to pull out the earphone plug so everyone can hear you pleading to be allowed to come." Cerys's tongue snakes out to slide along my ear, and I tremble.

Tremble because in the video, even thought it isn't visible, Mindy is teasing me with a dildo, and I am indeed begging for release.

Tremble because the vibrator against my clit surely has been bumped up to a higher setting, and my own need is growing. I would've thought I needed even more stimulation to come, but the public humiliation—even if some of it was only currently threatened—might prove to be enough of an incentive.

I shake my head, just a tiny bit, denying that Cerys should let the passengers hear the video, but I still don't say my safeword, and her chuckle, breathed against the tender flesh of my neck, is painfully erotic.

She turns the vibrator back down, and then off, just in time for me to watch myself come, screaming my thank-yous, my eyes still open because Mindy had commanded it.

If Cerys hadn't turned off the egg, I suspect I would've come in empathy.

Instead, I'm left hanging, desperate, my thighs clenching and releasing, my hands gripping the armrests. My forearms couldn't be tighter against those armrests if I were cuffed to them.

I don't want to come in public.

But I really, really want to come. Need to come.

Thus far, Cerys has kept the remote in her suit-jacket pocket.

Now she takes it out. It's a small thing, black, a rectangle that fits in the palm of her hand.

Oh god, anyone can see it.

She turns it over in her hand as if inspecting it, tapping the plus-sign-shaped toggle that adjusts not only the intensity of vibration, but also the pattern of the vibrations.

Oh. That's new. Instead of a steady hum against my swollen, needy clit, now there are pulsations. Random pulsations. Cerys can't decide on a rhythm, and that's driving me mad with need and lust.

I want to hiss, "Pick one!" but I can't, I'm not allowed.

*Buzz*pause*buzz*pause*buzz*. *Buzz*pausepause. *Buzzzzz*pause.

I want to scream in frustration, but I can't do that, either.

And then, to my horror, Jane is making her way down the aisle again, checking to see if passengers need anything, a trash bag open to accept discards. Her efficiency is my personal hell.

Of course, she stops at our row. "Is that a remote-controlled device?" she asks. "I'm afraid they're not allowed on flights."

"Oh, no, this is Bluetooth," Cerys says. I have no idea if she's lying or not. "I checked ahead of time; it's allowed."

Still, I'm frozen, terrified and aroused. Cerys had threatened to tell the flight attendant of my predicament.

What if Cerys gives her the remote?

The thought of Jane being complicit, of Jane finding out about my torment, would've sent me over the edge if the vibrator had been on. Just the thought of Jane's brown eyes widening as she processed what was going on... Would she be disgusted? Intrigued? Would her lips slowly curve in an evil smile as she held out her hand...?

My entire body tenses; I'm sure my expression is one of pleading and humility and submission.

But Jane's smile is simply efficient and friendly as she says, "Okay, great. Just make sure you've got everything stowed for landing."

Landing. Oh god, most accidents happen during takeoff or landing, and we survived takeoff, and...

That infernal egg buzzes to life again, and I bite my lips together to stifle a moan. I swear I can smell my spicy-sweet arousal; I'm so wet that I fear I'm going to leave a spot on the back of my skirt, which everyone will see when we disembark. My pussy lips slip and slide when I clench against the maddening sensations.

I feel like I'm losing my mind.

It's a familiar feeling, and yet, without Mindy, a petrifying one.

Deep breath. No, Mindy put Cerys in control. Mindy wouldn't have done that if she didn't trust Cerys. If you trust Mindy, you must trust Cerys.

But Cerys, sexy domme Cerys, has put the remote back in her suit-jacket pocket but is clearly still thumbing it to higher and higher settings, and her luscious lips are at my ear again.

Her fingers are at my throat as she tells me how she wants to unbutton my blouse, expose my lace-covered breasts. She knows (she says, and she's right) that my nipples are rock hard and will be clearly visible, distending the ecru fabric, and she wants to take them between her fingernails and scrape and pinch and twist them (and what a pity it is she doesn't have nipple clamps handy). My hips jerk at the concept, at the memory and the desire/hatred for the painful clover clamps on my sensitive nubs.

And then her tongue drags along my ear again and she says, so close, "I'm sorry—well, no, I'm not, not really—but Mindy told me what I had to do. She wants me to report back about how good you were, how you reacted."

Oh, no. Yes.

Please.

No.

Yes?

"It's not my choice to do this," Cerys confesses, "but I'm so glad I get to. Mindy says you're exquisite when you come."

And to my horror, I knew—as I'd probably known from the time Cerys admitted she was working with Mindy—that I would be coming, publicly, on display, on this plane.

And there was not a damn thing I could do about it.

Safeword notwithstanding, I needed to come. That need had superseded any other imperative except my humiliation, and it was rapidly overtaking that.

No, the humiliation was *adding* to my need, and I'm sure the look I shot Cerys was pure desperation, but all she did was lick her plump bottom lip in anticipation and smile, and thumb the wicked bullet vibrator that nestled against my throbbing, needy clit to its highest setting.

My need ratcheted higher, higher, higher, until I cracked apart, shattered, aflight. I clenched and shuddered, my hips rising a fraction of an inch above the seat and then pressing down again, over and over, even as I bit my lips together to keep from screaming or moaning or pleading, although pleading for what? I didn't know.

The humiliation of coming in front of all the passengers and crew was enough to keep my orgasm fucking me as solidly as a dildo.

Didn't care.

Couldn't think.

And when the tremors subsided—and Cerys turned off the vibrations, a relief and yet not, and murmured "Welcome to Dallas, sweetheart"—I knew even though the plane was on the ground, I was still flying.

STRONG

Xan West

For A., who said it deserved its own tale

For both of us, gender is both complex identity and elaborate sex toy. But not just that. It is not easy to grow up breaking the gender rules, to live lives visibly nonconforming. Gender is a dangerous and delicious edge at which we play, knowing that we may inadvertently step on the minefields of our gendered histories and present struggles. Part of the thrill is that danger. We push gender to its own edges, play its sharpness against our throats, fear in our mouths, ache in our guts, building armor against becoming what we fear.

Gender is the core. It drives our relationship. As a transgender butch, for me playing with gender is an edgy and necessary thing. For my genderqueer submissive, whose gender ebbs and flows in life and in play, the conscious choice to play with gender confirms self, breaks boundaries, allows catharsis. My submissive is both my girl and my boy. Tonight she was going to be one and then the other.

When she is my girl, I always start by fucking her throat. It is the most personal hole, and I claim her there first, make sure she knows she is helpless to stop me. Her job is to open to me, give to me, feed me with her eyes. I begin by placing the cuffs on her wrists, then lock them together and force her to her knees. My hands grip her hair, and I force her mouth onto my cock. This is how we start, every time.

Beginning this way every time gives us both a way to go deeper into ourselves, to sink into what we are doing, find ground for the genders we are playing in. My cock in her throat honors how she wants to do girlness, how much we both want her to be open and vulnerable and raw. Her eyes looking up at me and her mouth wrapped round my dick reflect back the masculinity I want to do with her, how much we want me to be cruel and invasive and dominant. I need to see that she wants this, all the way through, and she knows how much I run on adrenaline when we play this way, how it reaches into my core and twists.

I need to start fast and hard, almost dare myself into it, because this scares the shit out of me, and that's the only way to get over the mountain of fear that builds in me as I know we are going there. The more fear there is the rougher and faster I need it. I was especially rough that night, ignoring the gagging and groaning as I forced tears from her eyes.

"That's right, choke on my cock," I said gruffly.

There was rushing in my ears as I watched her choke, tears streaming down her cheeks, her eyes locked on mine, soft, reassuring. I rammed myself into her, cracking her open, thrusting my way inside. I got taller as I fucked her face, wrenching her hair, relentless. I could tell when she started to float, weightless, rapt. I pulled out of her mouth, looking coldly down at her as she took ragged sobbing breaths and offered herself to me.

I lifted her up from her knees, unlocked her cuffs and seated her in the bondage chair, clipping the cuffs to it and attaching her ankles. I put her in this chair when she's a girl. It reminds her to keep her legs spread for me.

It's a rule of mine. When she's my girl she is required to keep her thighs apart. They never touch in my presence. It makes her constantly aware of her body, the position she's in. She is always conscious of her cunt. I want it to feel exposed, even behind layers of clothing. Exposed just by her own awareness. With this one simple rule, I claim ownership of her body, her cunt, her focus. From across the room I am inside her, spreading her thighs, exposing her cunt, deep inside her head.

The chair is an intensification of the rule. More than that, it takes a private thing and makes it public. I always choose to put her in the chair that faces the crowd, the chair that is the most public. I display her body, spread her thighs for all to see.

It was crowded that night. By the time I had her bound to the chair there was a circle of voyeurs behind us, devouring her exposure. Dozens of eyes were on her skin. She was trembling. I wanted to intensify the exposure, use their gaze to push her farther, ride the wave of that. I pulled out my knife and slid it along her cheek, her throat. I began to cut off her clothes. The knife bared her flesh to the room, ripping through fabric, revealing her as she struggled to remain utterly still, biting her lip, eyes closed. I teased the knife along her thighs, taking advantage of her closed eyes to pull something out of my bag and get it ready. The knife edged its way closer to her cunt. I spread her to it, teasing it against her, and then rammed my baton into her cunt in one stroke, pulling the knife away. She trembled, stuffed full, her now open eyes begging.

"Come for me," I said, pulling her hair.

She did, her body contracting, trying to push the baton out, even as I held it there, forcing her to take it. Her eyes were wide and dark. I released her hair and removed the baton, wanting her to be aware she was empty and aching. More than anything, when she is my girl, she needs to be exposed and penetrated, made aware of her cunt and the eyes of others.

"The whole room just saw you come, girl. They know your cunt is dripping, aching to be stuffed full. Their eyes are on you, watching. You can't hide now, girl. We can see you. You are naked to us."

She is so strong. I can't imagine seeking this level of exposure, this level of vulnerability. She awes me.

I pulled out my clover clamps and attached them to her nipples. She hissed when I put them on. I let the chain fall, and tugged on it, watching her squirm for me. I wanted her aware of her skin, feeling me penetrate it with pinches and bites. I leaned in to bite her shoulder, tugging the chain, and felt her writhe, her pulse beating under my tongue, my teeth grinding into her.

I lifted my head and placed the chain between her teeth. She would feel a steady relentless pull on her nipples, and have something to bite down on. She was going to need it.

I pulled out my favorite cane. It is rattan, thin and whippy. Her thighs were exposed perfectly for it. This was no slow, even buildup. It was about opening her up, ripping her open, and that was clear from the start. I drove the cane into her, relishing the sounds it forced from her, slicing into her thighs. The more I drove it into her flesh, the larger I grew. This was more than just dominance. When I take my masculinity and rub it against her girlness, I feel gigantic, and she is so fragile in comparison. This is one of the lines we ride with this kind of play, and one of the many risks inherent in it is that it might actually reduce her in her own eyes, or in mine. That I, or she, might actually be unable to see how strong she is. Part of the intensity comes with the risk. At that moment I stepped outside myself just a bit, to check in with myself, read her a bit closer, before sinking back into it.

I began to breathe with her, building, ramping the pain up, barely pausing between strokes. I rained fire onto her, purple welts forming. Her eyes were closed tight, her teeth gripping the chain, her face contorted in pain, and she finally began to try to get away. Of course she couldn't. That was the point. She was trapped, her legs spread wide, attached to the chair by ankles and wrists, her cunt exposed to all and those naked, vulnerable, sensitive thighs sliced into, relentlessly, no matter what she did. She began to shake her head no, not caring about the pain it caused in her nipples. But she did not say her safeword, did not do the one thing in her power that might free her. Then it happened. The invasive pain spilled through her and out her eyes, tears streaming down her face.

"That's right, cry for me. It will only make me want to beat you and fuck you harder, girl."

I struck harder, repeatedly, watching it sink in. Seeing that she was helpless, exposed, vulnerable. That I would take it all from her. That she was free to move all the way through it and out the other side. It took me a long time to get her to a place where she was willing to cry. Before me, she had not met a top that didn't stop the second the tears started flowing. She still didn't quite trust it, needed me to show her, again and again, that I would keep going, that she could be that strong, give that much, let me see her tears.

The pain moved through her in waves, pouring out her eyes, and I could see the joy spread over her face. She was beautiful in that moment, and I savored it, pouring pain into her and watching it flow through her, riding that. It was time. I set down the cane and took my cock out of my jeans, pulling on a condom. I slid in slowly, luxuriating in every inch of penetration, watching her eyes. I leaned in and licked the tears from her cheeks as I felt her let go. I began to fuck her, my hips ramming into her sore thighs, making her scream, as the chain fell from her mouth.

I growled, "Mine," in her ear as I slammed into her, feeling her body begin to shake as the sensations overwhelmed her. I removed a clamp, ordering her to come for me. She began to sob as she came, my cock driving into her, pain racking her body, her senses on overload. It felt like perfection to claim her.

"Mine," I snarled, as I removed the other clamp, watching her body move, struggling against her bonds, tears streaming down her face. I leaned in and bit her as I fucked her, pounding into her with my cock, driving into her with my teeth, opening her up for my pleasure. I growled into her skin as I bit, my hips slamming into her rapidly, my hands fisted in her hair.

She was sobbing loudly, and it felt so damn good to hear it, the sound reaching right down and stroking my cock in a long velvet caress. I lifted my head and grabbed her eyes with mine.

"You are mine. My girl. Come for me, loud."

She began to shudder and moan, her cunt contracting so hard on my cock, tears pouring out of her eyes.

"My girl," I growled as I came, my hands gripping her hair as I spurted inside her cunt. I closed my eyes and held her, just held her for a long time, savoring the feel of being inside her to the hilt. I carefully pulled out and discarded the condom, cleaned her off gently and gave her some water. I got her down from the chair and brought her over to the couch, seating her at my feet, and stroking her hair.

She laid her head on my thigh, holding tightly on to my boot, and trembled for a good long time. Then she was quiet and still, her hands on my boot slowly easing. She lifted her head to look up at me.

"Sir?" she said.

"Yes?"

"May I please clean up the space and go change?"

"You may," I said, smiling, stroking her cheek, and then watching her as she cleaned the chair and then walked away. She once told me, "Being a girl is like being without armor. Sometimes like being without skin, even. Your power is in your vulnerability and openness. Most of the time, girl is not a safe thing to be. That's why I treasure being your girl, it's a safe place to touch that danger and roll around with it. But sometimes, when I'm putting myself together after you rip me open and poke my soft spots, what I really need is armor. That's one of the best times to be your boy." That's what we had planned tonight. He asked specifically for that, said he wanted to walk out tough and strong and wearing his armor.

He moved differently when he was my boy. His center of gravity was lower, and he swaggered. He strutted over to me, grinning, stopping to stand crisply before me, hands locked on wrists behind him. I eyed him slowly. He was looking sharp in BDUs, tight enough to show the dick he was packing, black ribbed undershirts three layers deep and shiny black Corcs, his hair slicked back. I love a boy in an A-line shirt.

"Grab my bag, boy," I said, and stalked off to claim a semi-private space. I found a perfect corner, where the light was dim and there was no equipment. When he's my boy, I want him standing. He's tough. He can hold himself up. I pulled on my leather gloves and backed him into the wall.

"That's it boy. Just you and me and a wall. Show me how strong you are, boy."

I started steady, pounding him with my fists, going after his muscles. We breathed together, slow and easy. My blows were ramming into his pecs, his biceps. Going after his quads.

Rhythmic, even pounding setting the stage. This was about strength, endurance. Mine, and his.

"Show me what you can take, boy. What you're made of."

I slammed him into the wall with my bulk, reminded him that I have one hundred pounds on him. He stuck out his chin, just a bit. I slammed against him again, propelling my weight into him. Again, taking his breath with my girth. Again. His eyes started to get glossy. I stepped back and began to kick. I drove my boots into his thigh muscles, delighting in the sound of him grunting with each blow. I used my knee to strike his thigh, watching his eyes get darker.

Sinking into *thud* roots me, pulls me deep into myself. Using my whole body helps me reestablish, find my footing. He's not the only one that needs to put himself back together, and he knows it. Knows that this is for both of us, that I need this as much as he does, and his job is to feed the energy back to me, to help keep it cycling between us.

I moved up closer to him, pulled on my SAP gloves and began to pound his pecs. Steady. Repeated. Relentless. Lead shot hammering his chest. Holding his gaze.

"Take it for me, boy."

It was intense for him. I knew it. His breath became more ragged, his jaw clenched. I could see the determination in his eyes. I just kept ramming my fist into him, watching him closely.

He is so strong. I know what it is to endure this, to stay standing through it, to face my own limits and keep pushing them. He awes me.

"That's my boy," I said as I hit him. "Show me how tough you are. Take it for me."

He did. Not a sound. He stood still and took it for me, his jaw clenched down on it, his hands fisted, frustration clear in his eyes as tears slid down his cheeks. We both ignored them. They were meaningless, as unimportant as the people quietly watching us. What was important was that he stood still and took it, for me. He made me proud, and I let it show in my face.

I pulled out my knife and stroked his throat with it, teased it against his lips and grinned at the sight of his tongue snaking out to lick the blade, his lips opening to it, his hand slipping up to hold my hand steady, begging in his eyes. I nodded, and allowed his hand to clasp over mine, holding the knife, watching his mouth engulf it, his eyes wicked and triumphant. Sucking off a knife takes talent, practice, love and deep respect for a sharp blade. My boy was very good. It was a delicious sight, and I savored it, groaning, my dick throbbing.

"That's my good boy," I whispered roughly.

I put my hand on his chin and held him, easing the blade out of his mouth, wiping it on his shirt and putting it away. I pulled out my baton, and flipped him over, slamming him into the wall with my weight. I kicked his feet apart and slid the baton between his thighs, teasing it against his asshole until he moaned. I pressed him up against the wall and growled in his ear.

"Mine."

I stepped back and began to pound his ass with the baton. There is something about that deep thud, right there, that feels like you are getting fucked. He groaned, leaning against the wall, offering his ass to me, luscious sounds leaving his lips with each strike of the baton. I stepped toward him and ground my cock into his ass, pulling him away from the wall.

"Stand up for me, boy. Take it."

I began to pound his biceps with the baton, watching the bruises blossom. He growled and stomped his feet as the blows continued, struggling to take it. As it went on, first one bicep, then the other, he began to shake his head and clench his hands, eventually pounding his fists into his own sore thighs. I did not stop until his arms began to tremble.

When he's my boy, he doesn't want me to fuck around. He wants to be pushed to his physical limits, again and again. To constantly prove to himself (and to me) that he is tough enough, strong enough. That he can stand up and take anything I can dish out.

I set the baton down and pulled my belt from my jeans, snapping it.

"How many months have you been mine, boy?"

"Forty-two, Sir."

"That's right. Forty-two strokes it is. Count 'em for me."

"Yes, Sir."

My belt is serious business. It is always the last toy I pick up because it inspires my most intense sadism. The counting is as much for me as for him. This tool, more than any other, finds me wanting never to stop.

I grinned as the leather bit into his back, and went after his traps first. He was counting steadily as I hurled the belt at him with a red haze around me, and a metallic scent on his skin. I growled, driving the belt into his back, my cock throbbing, his voice grounding me. I stepped forward to rest my cheek against his back, heat rushing off his skin in waves, his adrenaline-soaked sweat setting off a sharp tang in the back of my throat. I snarled and rained fire onto his back with my belt, in roaring relentless flames, no time between strokes, just one long maelstrom of energy building between us.

Some small part of my brain registered we were at thirty-seven. I stopped, wanting to savor the last five strokes. His breath was ragged, and he was shaking. I breathed in slowly, tasting the pain steaming off of him, and sliced into him with all of my strength. Thirty-eight. Drove my hunger into him, raw and ravenous. Thirty-nine. Forty made him scream, sound pouring from him, rendering him unable to count.

"Take it for me, boy. Show me your strength. I know you can do it."

"Forty, Sir," he said shakily.

I growled, "Mine," as I ripped into him with my belt. Forty-one. I carved into his back, the full force of my weight behind the last blow. Forty-two. I wrapped the belt around the back of his neck, lifting it to his lips to kiss, as I pressed him into the wall, breathing him in.

"That's my boy. I am so proud you are mine," I whispered.

I unbuckled his belt and slid down his pants, letting him step out of them and lean against the wall in his jock.

"Stay right there, boy."

I pulled a chair over and sat in it, turning him to face me. I pulled out my cock, suited it up and stroked on the lube. I placed his hands on the back of the chair and pulled his hips toward me, easing into his ass, his boots firmly planted on the floor. Damn did he feel so fucking good.

"Stand up and ride my dick," I growled. He did, growling right back, jamming his ass onto me, riding my cock. He is a delicious fuck, and I told him so, a stream of obscenity pouring from my mouth and egging him on. He rammed his ass onto my cock so hard I began to close my eyes, my cheek resting on his shoulder, my nails gripping him, delighting in the feel of him riding me.

"That's it boy. Fuck yourself on my cock. Show me how strong you are. Give me the ride of my life."

He was magic, my boy. Pulsing with intensity, his eyes locked on to mine, his jaw clenched, as he worked his ass onto my cock, taking it into him, growls and groans getting louder and louder.

"Mine," I snarled. "Mine. My boy. Hold your breath, clench

down on my cock and come for me, boy."

I grabbed his hips and jammed him onto me as I came, feeling him shudder, pouring into him, feeling it build and build as he clamped down on my cock, clamped down on his breath. I held my own breath as long as I could, until I released us both, holding his eyes and watching him explode when I ordered him to let it all go. He began to tremble from head to toe. His eyes held fireworks, feeding me that energy, his hips riding me like there was no way to stop. It went on forever.

We slowly floated back into ourselves. I began to stroke his skin. It felt so amazing. I grinned into his eyes, hugging him close to me.

"You sure are strong, boy," I said, laughing delightedly. He grinned back at me. We breathed together, settling back into our own skin. I whispered praise in his ear as I stroked him, easing him off my cock gently and standing up to gather him close into a deep hug that lasted a good long time.

THE LAST LAST TIME

BD Swain

It was the sound of her boots on the sidewalk that buckled me. Goddamn her. Coffee. Seemed innocent. "Let's talk," she said, as if we could manage that without the sudden swerve and crash. Big fucking joke. Every time I saw her face, I thought, *Too much damage,* and then fell right into the middle of it all again. Over and over. The swerve. The crash. All that damage.

We sat there. She stared at her coffee. Poured too much milk and too much sugar in. "Candy coffee," I said, like I always said, and kicked my own goddamn shin under the table for saying something I always said. I drank my tea. Fuck her and her coffee. She mumbled. I had to ask her to repeat herself. She stared up at me, sad eyed, and mumbled something about how things were good with her and her new girlfriend. And I thought, *Fuck you and your fucking girlfriend,* and said, "That's cool. I'm good too." And then she stared back down at her coffee and stirred it and sipped it a little and wiped her mouth. She wiped her mouth after every sip. Every bite. I used to think it was adorable. Now I wondered what the fuck was wrong with her.

We held our dialogue close to the script.

"How's your job?"

"It's stupid. It's not my real job."

"Are you quitting?"

"Yeah, I need to quit."

"But are you looking?"

Silence. She looked out the window pretending that she recognized someone, which I knew was just a bullshit way of avoiding the question.

"Fuck it. Find something else."

Silence. A sip of coffee and her napkin across her mouth.

"I'm serious. You hate that job. You should find something else." I kicked myself again. What the fuck do I care? I'm not her goddamn mother. I'm not her girlfriend.

"I'll work it out."

It went like this. On and on. Pointless. Irritating. Me saying shit I didn't really want to say, her avoiding my stupid questions. Rubbing our raw wounds up against one another. Stupid. I got another cup of tea. We sat mostly silent. I tried to remind myself why I was sitting there. "Let's stay close," we'd decided, "Let's not be stupid and ignore each other and pretend this never happened or feel like we have to hate each other." I was so sick of that bullshit. The scene was too small for that crap. So many people you had to call up before a party and tell them, "So and so, your ex, will be there," and blah blah blah and then phone call after phone call about what a shit this or that person was and how they can't stand her anymore and won't be in the same room and fuck that fucking crap. Fuck it.

Right. Okay. That's why I agreed to go sit down over coffee and watch her stare silently and mumble about her new girlfriend and pretend that we're all casual with each other and it's cool. I blew out my breath and ran my fingers through my hair. I leaned way back in my chair and spread my knees wide. Butch to butch, here we were. We could be buddies, right?

I cleared our glasses and we headed out for a cigarette. I hate smoking, but I always smoked with her. It seemed sexy. Still does. I liked the way we walked down the sidewalk together. Side by side, boots hitting the pavement hard. Jeans slouched down resting on the curves of our asses. Her vintage shirts. Her perfect cuffed sleeves. I usually had my jacket on. Zipped up tight. Shoulders hunched. We walked in silence. Smoking. I crushed my cigarette out under my heel while she lit up another. I jammed my hands deep in my jeans pockets and nudged her with my hip. She laughed. I looked at her. "C'mon," she said and jerked her head toward one of the dozens of bars open in the morning in the city. Our city. The city that felt like ours, together, because we met the first week we both lived here.

It felt so good, so right, to drink those beers together. It wasn't ten in the morning yet, and I felt the buzz hit me halfway into the bottle. We didn't say anything. We drank and read all the words on the coasters, the labels on the bottles, the signs behind the bar. She turned around and leaned her back against the bar and looked at the empty tables and the one old man sitting there with his drink. She stared at him when she talked to me. "Listen. I'm glad we're going to do this. Stay friends, I mean. I don't know what I'd do without you," she said. That felt like bullshit. She started fucking some other girl and dropped me without warning weeks ago. I was pretty sure what she'd do without me was exactly what she was doing already. But I didn't want to lose her either. "Yeah," I said. "Me too."

"You're my best friend, you know," she said, and I shoved her hard enough that she fell off the bar stool and had to grab the spinning seat to keep from landing on her ass. "Fucking jerk," she said, and we laughed. I ordered us two more beers and two whiskeys. Fuck it. We were going to get drunk enough, I guessed. We deserved it. I didn't think we'd fall out like we did. But we did. Fall out of line, I mean. Fall out of our senses. Maybe I should have known. I just didn't think she was still into me in that way. So I didn't look for it. Or maybe I did. Maybe it's what I had planned the whole time. Sitting there with my knees wide and my hand resting between my legs. Sucking on the bottle good and hard. Looking stoned. Looking dead to everything. Hard and stiff, just like she always liked me. Just like I wasn't.

"I need to piss," I said and slid off the bar stool, walking slowly toward the bathroom, knowing my ass looked great in those jeans. I had a drunk smile on my face when I pushed the door open. I stood there to take it in. I love dirty bathrooms in bars. I love them. The sticky floor with wadded-up toilet paper jammed into corners. The tiny porcelain sink that would pull right off of that wall any day now. The floor was tiled with square-inch black and white tiles. Filthy. The toilet bowl permanently stained with a rust-colored ring. I wanted to stand to pee but I've never been good at that and especially not when I'm drunk. I squatted over the toilet with my jeans held at my knees. "Maybe we'll fuck in here before we go," I thought. Stupid idea. I shook my head to rattle the thought out of there. The water in the tap was hot, really hot. I cupped my hands and splashed my face over and over again. I ran wet hands through my hair until it was all slicked down. I combed through it with my fingers and wiped my face on my shirttails. I looked at my teeth. "I'm stalling," I said out loud and turned to go back.

"Rudolph Valentino," she said, and whistled at me. I slicked my hair with a smile. "Errol Flynn," I answered. I never liked Valentino. She never remembered anything. Why was I sitting here strutting for her. Preening. Fuck her. Nothing was right between us when we were going out. Nothing. The fucking was great. It was everything else that was a total disaster. But when the fucking is great. When you hook up the way we did. Lost little puppies in a big new world. Well, the fucking can get you pretty far. The fucking was unlike anything I'd ever known before. Jerk my pants down, bend me over, shove spit-covered fingers into my holes. That kind of fucking. Nothing about sweet kisses and polite little pets. No more fawning about how soft each other's cheeks were. This was fucking. Like boys. Our tiny little cocks. Ramrod stiff. Stiff jeans. Shiny boots. Thick belts. Slicked hair. Fall in line, little boy, because this is how you show it here. I fell in line for her. Or she fell in line for me. Or we both fell in line because that's what you fucking do.

The fucking. The way we fucked. Tossing back and forth. You fuck me. No, you fuck me. We both wanted to be fucked. We both wanted someone stronger than either of us. Or weaker. We both wanted something that was more opposite. Maybe. I don't know. I don't think she knew. How could we know anything? How can you figure anything out when the fucking is so good and you're both new? I remember the time she grabbed my stiff, black comb out of my back pocket and held it against my neck. It hurt like a knife. It felt dangerous. I didn't feel like a kid playing dress up. I felt tough. Dangerous. How I wanted to feel. She cut my back with that comb. Raking it across my shoulders, she let it bite into me. Jagged red lines.

I felt the booze swirl around in my brain. The warm rush in my belly. I stared at her with my wet lower lip hanging open. A dog. She was telling me some story. Something dumb. She was shaking her head and laughing and telling me about some asshole on the bus. Something about makeup. Or maybe it was a pregnant lady. I wasn't listening to her. "I want you to fuck

THE LAST LAST TIME

me," I said, too loud, in the middle of her story. She looked at her knees for a second and then grabbed my arm and we headed out the door.

She walked ahead of me, still gripping my arm, and led me to her place. She stumbled off the curb once and nearly took us both down, but she never looked at me. Not until we got inside her apartment. When the door closed she turned around and shoved me up against it. She grabbed my crotch and spat her words at me. "You want me to fuck you? You don't hate me yet?" she hissed. The words stung. Prophetic. I was going to hate her after this, I knew. It didn't matter. Or maybe it did. Maybe that's why I wanted it.

I moved slowly as I turned around and put my palms flat on the door. My boots slid apart as I stuck my ass out for her. I closed my eyes and opened my throat when her arm snaked around me. Her hand grabbed my belt. All the anger left me. All the frustration and hurt melted. I had her. Now. Right now. She wanted me, and I was right here. Any thought of how she didn't love me disappeared. All my tortured images of her fucking someone else vanished. Whatever pain I had would be made physical.

She punched at my clit through my jeans. Her head pushed into my back between my shoulder blades. I could hear her crying. "Shut up and fuck me," I said. I needed her angry or desperate, not sad. She shoved my head against the door. Pain shot through me. We were both suddenly struck as if by light-ning. She unbuckled my belt but left my jeans buttoned as she scraped them down and off over my thighs. My underwear was pulled down too. She left it just below my ass. The elastic bit into my thighs. One hand held my head against the door and the other jerked my ass back against her. She slammed her hips against me. Slamming her jeans, her cunt up against my bared bottom. Without warning, her fingers jammed into me. Her other arm gripped me tight around my middle. Her head sunk against my back. I heard her boots scraping the wood. I heard her grunt. "Fuck me," I spat out anytime I wanted to say something else.

I rolled my ass higher for her. I wanted her to see how I craved her fingers deep inside me. "Don't you want to fuck this ass?" I snapped. She pulled her fingers out of my pussy and grabbed my neck, starting to drag me down the hall. I straightened up and stumbled toward her bedroom. Shuffling with my pants still around my knees. I crawled onto her bed without being led and pulled my jeans down to my ankles for her. "This," I said, and wagged my ass at her on all fours, rolling my back. I heard her open the closet. I felt the hairs on my neck stiffen as I listened. Her box. The glove snapping onto her hand. The wheezing sound of her nearly empty bottle of lube. "This?" she said hoarsely, and I felt her in my ass. "Yes," I said, and now my own big fat tears rolled down my face. I buried my hot, shameful face in her blanket and brought my fists to my chin. I pounded my ass against her as much as she slammed into me. "Harder," I spat through my teeth, "Harder. Harder. Harder."

I wanted her to hurt me until I couldn't feel anymore. None of the pleasure was there. Nothing left of the way it feels when you're in love or think you're in love or at least aren't in that category of ex, lost, already used. That's how I felt. Already used. The empty wrapper of something that tasted good a long time ago. I was crying. She was yelling. No words, but something animal. Something hurt.

This is what I needed. This last fuck where everything felt desperate and wrong. The one that would remind me not to do it again. This is what I wanted. I don't know about her. I didn't care.

She fucked me hard in the ass for a long time. I finally reached down between my legs and jerked my aching clit off for an orgasm that hurt like a pulled muscle, a deep cramp. I doubled over on my side and held my knees to my chest. I felt the snot dripping on my upper lip. I didn't care. She was on her back in front of me. Her chest heaving up and down. I saw her smile. Her wide grin. Her eyes open and darting around. That clean look she gets after she fucks me.

I fucked her too. Her knees thrown up by her shoulders. All of my fingers and nearly my whole hand inside her. I leaned my weight onto her shins. She held her knees. I fucked her hard and fast. Nothing mattered but her feeling the ghost of me in her cunt after I left. The raw places on her skin.

She held her breath just before she came. The veins bulged in her neck. I watched her. I waited. It was time. She jerked her whole body and nearly knocked me off the bed. I slid off the mattress onto my feet, pulling up my pants. I didn't say anything as I turned to go. "Wait," she started to say but the word got cut off halfway. "Yeah, never mind," she ended.

Walking home, I lit a cigarette and took a deep drag and very suddenly felt more drunk than I'd thought I was. My stomach pulled back into a tight ball and I knew what was coming. "Just get home," I said to myself. A mantra I chanted block by block until I turned the key in my door and ran to the toilet to throw up. "Fuck," I said to myself, my head in my hands, and let the tears cleanse my sweet face. I was okay. I really was. I knew it.

ABOUT THE AUTHORS

NAN ANDREWS is a trained pastry chef who finds food and women equally erotic. Her stories have appeared in numerous anthologies, including *Spankalicious*, *Voyeur Eyes Only* and *Where the Girls Are: Urban Lesbian Erotica*. She is a member of Sapphic Planet, the Erotic Authors Association and ERWA; she lives in Northern California.

AVERY CASSELL (averycassell.wordpress.com) is a writer, painter and cartoonist. Their work has appeared in *Anything that Moves*, *Whipped: 20 Erotic Stories of Female Dominance*, *Sonic Erotica* and *More Five Minute Erotica*. They live in San Francisco and are currently working on a memoir, a graphic novel and an erotic novel.

Called a "legendary erotica heavy-hitter" (by the über-legendary Violet Blue), ANDREA DALE (AndreaDaleAuthor.com) writes sizzling erotica with a generous dash of romance. Her work has appeared in twenty years' worth of Best volumes as well as about a hundred other anthologies from Soul's Road Press, Harlequin Spice and Cleis Press.

ALEXANDRA DELANCEY has had a passion for words ever since she could first speak, and in later years developed no less a passion for sexuality. After graduating in English Lit, she's worked as a commercial writer by day, while combining her twin passions by night. She has just finished writing her first novel.

SACCHI GREEN (sacchi-green.blogspot.com) has published stories in a hip-high stack of erotic books, and edited nine anthologies, including *Girl Fever, Women with Handcuffs, Lesbian Cowboys* (winner of a Lambda Literary Award) and *Wild Girls, Wild Nights*, all from Cleis Press.

TINA HORN is a writer, educator, and media-maker who produces and hosts the sexuality podcast *Why Are People Into That?!* She holds an MFA in creative nonfiction writing from Sarah Lawrence. Her publication credits include *Vice, Nerve* and *Best Sex Writing 2015*. Born in Northern California, Tina now lives in Manhattan with a very sweet bear.

THEDA HUDSON's (thedahudson.com) work has appeared in *Best Lesbian Erotica 2011*, *Best Lesbian Romance 2011* and *2012* and *Dyke Valiant,* an erotic urban fantasy novel. For those wishing to learn more about cancer or folks just wanting to poke a stiffy at the Big C with "Fuck Cancer" merchandise, visit letsfcancer.com.

CAMMY MAY HUNNICUTT is Mississippi choirgirl and athlete corrupted by beauty pageants, lingerie modeling and much worse. She writes erotica, mostly scantily disguised memoirs. Her first book, *Considerations Prior to Shooting Your Boyfriend Right in The Nuts* was a flash-in-the-pan best seller on Amazon.

DEBORAH JANNERSON's work has been published in *Bitch, Curve, Vertigo, Redlands Review, Bust, Nola Live, BookByYou, Deconstructing Glee, A Room of Her Own, Crazy with a Side of Awesome Sauce and Women's Review of Books*. Jannerson resides in New Orleans.

LEE ANN KEPLE is an educator and comedian. Strategist by day, she inhabits any number of characters by night, as part of Vancouver's vibrant improv scene. She is an aficionado and defender of all manner of human communications—including porn.

KATIE KING, a longtime member of the common name club, is probably not the Katie King you are looking for. Her most recent writing project is inspired by the misdirected erotic emails to her doppelgangers worldwide that end up in her inbox—beware! Her favorite writing location is in bed.

CATHERINE LUNDOFF (catherinelundoff.com) is the author of *Silver Moon: A Women of Wolf's Point Novel* (Lethe Press, 2012) as well as the short-story collections *Night's Kiss* (Lethe Press, 2009), *Crave* (Lethe Press, 2007) and *A Day at the Inn, A Night at the Palace and Other Stories* (Lethe Press, 2011).

JEAN ROBERTA (JeanRoberta.com) has taught English in a Canadian university for a quarter century. Over one hundred of her erotic stories have appeared in print anthologies, including five previous editions of Best Lesbian Erotica, plus *The Flight of the Black Swan: A Bawdy Novella* (Lethe) and three single-author collections.

MIEL ROSE (mielrose.com) is a rural queer femme raised in the wilds of Vermont. She is a witchy healer, textile artist and hair-stylist. Find her writing in various erotica anthologies including *The Harder She Comes* and *Leather Ever After*, or look for her book *Overflow: Tales of Butch-Femme Love, Sex, and Desire.*

LISABET SARAI (lisabetsarai.com) writes in many genres, but F/F fiction is one of her favorites. Her lesbian erotica credits include contributions to Lambda Award–winner *Where the Girls Are*, Ippie-winning *Carnal Machines*, *Best Lesbian Romance 2012* and *Coming Together: Girl on Girl*. Lisabet currently lives in Southeast Asia.

BD SWAIN (bdswain.com) is a butch dyke who started writing queer smut because of a deep need to do so. Pushing her sexual expression is what makes her feel the most alive.

ANNA WATSON sends big big love to her queer brothers and sisters in Western Mass. For more sexy butch/femme lovin', see *Best Lesbian Erotica 2012, Take Me There, Best Lesbian Romance 2012*, and *The Harder She Comes* among others. Also, take a look at Laz-E-Femme Press on Facebook. Kick off your pumps and read!

XAN WEST (xanwest.wordpress.com) is the pseudonym of a Bay Area kink/sex educator. Xan's "First Time Since" won honorable mention for the 2008 NLA John Preston Short Fiction Award. Xan's erotica appears all over, including the *Best SM Erotica*, Best Gay Erotica and Best Lesbian Erotica series, *Daddies and Say Please.*

NICOLE WOLFE's work has been previously published by Cleis Press in *Best Lesbian Erotica 2010, Girl Fever* and *Twice the Pleasure*. She loves vintage pinup art (which inspired this story), women of all shapes, Thai food, Radiohead and her amazing wife.

Erotic author/editor **BETH WYLDE** (bethwylde.com) writes what she likes to read, which includes a little bit of everything under the rainbow. Her muse is an equal opportunity smut bunny that believes everyone, no matter their kink, color, gender or orientation deserves love, acceptance and scalding HOT sex!

Jamaican-born **FIONA ZEDDE** currently lives and writes in Atlanta, Georgia. She is the author of several novellas and novels of lesbian love and desire, including the Lambda Literary Award finalists *Bliss* and *Every Dark Desire*. Her novel *Dangerous Pleasures* was winner of the About.com Readers' Choice Award for Best Lesbian Novel or Memoir of 2012.

ABOUT THE EDITOR

LAURA ANTONIOU's publishing career began when she started writing gay men's smut to promote safer sex practices during the early '90s. Emboldened by getting paid to do this, she then edited the groundbreaking three-volume Leatherwomen series, highlighting tales of kinky women. This was rapidly followed by half a dozen other anthologies and the Marketplace series of erotic BDSM novels, which never reached the sales level of the 50 Shades books, but she's not bitter. Instead, she just wrote the sixth in that series, titled *The Inheritor.* In 2013, she turned her mind to mysteries and came out with the Rainbow Book Award–winner for Best LGBT Mystery, *The Killer Wore Leather.* Now that she has achieved nearly mainstream success with it, she plans a sequel to be released via Cleis Press. Follow her on Facebook and Twitter or check her out at lantoniou.com.

More of the Best Lesbian Erotica

Buy 4 books, Get 1 FREE*

Sometimes She Lets Me
Best Butch/Femme Erotica
Edited by Tristan Taormino

Does the swagger of a confident butch make you swoon? Do your knees go weak when you see a femme straighten her stockings? In *Sometimes She Lets Me*, Tristan Taormino chooses her favorite butch/femme stories from the Best Lesbian Erotica series.
ISBN 978-1-57344-382-1 $14.95

Lesbian Lust
Erotic Stories
Edited by Sacchi Green

Lust: It's the engine that drives us wild on the way to getting us off, and lesbian lust is the heart, soul and red-hot core of this anthology.
ISBN 978-1-57344-403-3 $14.95

Girl Crush
Women's Erotic Fantasies
Edited by R. Gay

In the steamy stories of *Girl Crush,* women satisfy their curiosity about the erotic possibilities of their infatuations.
ISBN 978-1-57344-394-4 $14.95

Girl Crazy
Coming Out Erotica
Edited by Sacchi Green

These irresistible stories of first times of all kinds invite the reader to savor that delicious, dizzy feeling known as "girl crazy."
ISBN 978-1-57344-352-4 $14.95

Lesbian Cowboys
Erotic Adventures
Edited by Sacchi Green and Rakelle Valencia

With stories that are edgy as shiny spurs and tender as broken-in leather, fifteen first-rate writers share their take on an iconic fantasy.
ISBN 978-1-57344-361-6 $14.95

Essential Lesbian Erotica

The Harder She Comes
Butch / Femme Erotica
Edited by D. L. King

Some butches worship at the altar of their femmes, and many adorable girls long for the embrace of their suave, sexy daddies. In *The Harder She Comes*, we meet femmes who salivate at the sight of packed jeans and bois who dream of touching the corseted waist of a beautiful, confident woman.
ISBN 978-1-57344-778-2 $14.95

Girls Who Bite
Lesbian Vampire Erotica
Edited by Delilah Devlin

Whether depicting a traditional blood-drinker seducing a meal, a psychic vampire stealing the life force of an unknowing host, or a real-life sanguinarian seeking a partner to share a ritual bloodletting, the stories in *Girls Who Bite* are a sensual surprise.
ISBN 978-1-57344-715-7 $14.95

Girls Who Score
Hot Lesbian Erotica
Edited by Ily Goyanes

Girl jocks always manage to see a lot of action off the field. *Girls Who Score* is a winner, filled with story after story of competitive, intriguing women engaging in all kinds of contact sports.
ISBN 978-1-57344-825-3 $15.95

Wild Girls, Wild Nights
True Lesbian Sex Stories
Edited by Sacchi Green

Forget those fabled urban myths of lesbians who fill up U-Hauls on the second date and lead sweetly romantic lives of cocoa and comfy slippers. These are tales of wild women with dirty minds, untamed tongues and the occasional cuff or clamp. And they're all true!
ISBN 978-1-57344-933-5 $15.95

Stripped Down
Lesbian Sex Stories
Edited by Tristan Taormino

Where else but in a Tristan Taormino erotica collection can you find a femme vigilante, a virgin baby butch and a snake handler jostling for attention? The salacious stories in *Stripped Down* will draw you in and sweep you off your feet.
ISBN 978-1-57344-794-2 $15.95

Best Erotica Series

"Gets racier every year."—*San Francisco Bay Guardian*

Buy 4 books, Get 1 FREE*

Best Women's Erotica 2014
Edited by Violet Blue
ISBN 978-1-62778-003-2 $15.95

Best Women's Erotica 2013
Edited by Violet Blue
ISBN 978-1-57344-898-7 $15.95

Best Women's Erotica 2012
Edited by Violet Blue
ISBN 978-1-57344-755-3 $15.95

Best Bondage Erotica 2014
Edited by Rachel Kramer Bussell
ISBN 978-1-62778-012-4 $15.95

Best Bondage Erotica 2013
Edited by Rachel Kramer Bussel
ISBN 978-1-57344-897-0 $15.95

Best Bondage Erotica 2012
Edited by Rachel Kramer Bussel
ISBN 978-1-57344-754-6 $15.95

Best Lesbian Erotica 2014
Edited by Kathleen Warnock
ISBN 978-1-62778-002-5 $15.95

Best Lesbian Erotica 2013
Edited by Kathleen Warnock
Selected and introduced by
Jewelle Gomez
ISBN 978-1-57344-896-3 $15.95

Best Lesbian Erotica 2012
Edited by Kathleen Warnock
Selected and introduced by
Sinclair Sexsmith
ISBN 978-1-57344-752-2 $15.95

Best Gay Erotica 2014
Edited by Larry Duplechan
Selected and introduced by Joe Manetti
ISBN 978-1-62778-001-8 $15.95

Best Gay Erotica 2013
Edited by Richard Labonté
Selected and introduced by Paul Russell
ISBN 978-1-57344-895-6 $15.95

Best Gay Erotica 2012
Edited by Richard Labonté
Selected and introduced by
Larry Duplechan
ISBN 978-1-57344-753-9 $15.95

Best Fetish Erotica
Edited by Cara Bruce
ISBN 978-1-57344-355-5 $15.95

Best Bisexual Women's Erotica
Edited by Cara Bruce
ISBN 978-1-57344-320-3 $15.95

Best Lesbian Bondage Erotica
Edited by Tristan Taormino
ISBN 978-1-57344-287-9 $16.95

More of the Best Lesbian Romance

Fuel Your Fantasies

Carnal Machines
Steampunk Erotica
Edited by D. L. King

In this decadent fusing of technology and romance, outstanding contemporary erotica writers use the enthralling possibilities of the 19th-century steam age to tease and titillate.
ISBN 978-1-57344-654-9 $14.95

The Sweetest Kiss
Ravishing Vampire Erotica
Edited by D. L. King

These sanguine tales give new meaning to the term "dead sexy" and feature beautiful bloodsuckers whose desires go far beyond blood.
ISBN 978-1-57344-371-5 $15.95

The Handsome Prince
Gay Erotic Romance
Edited by Neil Plakcy

A bawdy collection of bedtime stories brimming with classic fairy tale characters, reimagined and recast for any man who has dreamt of the day his prince will come. These sexy stories fuel fantasies and remind us all of the power of true romance.
ISBN 978-1-57344-659-4 $14.95

Daughters of Darkness
Lesbian Vampire Tales
Edited by Pam Keesey

"A tribute to the sexually aggressive woman and her archetypal roles, from nurturing goddess to dangerous predator."
—*The Advocate*
ISBN 978-1-57344-233-6 $14.95

Dark Angels
Lesbian Vampire Erotica
Edited by Pam Keesey

Dark Angels collects tales of lesbian vampires, the quintessential bad girls, archetypes of passion and terror. These tales of desire are so sharply erotic you'll swear you've been bitten!
ISBN 978-1-57344-252-7 $13.95

* Free book of equal or lesser value. Shipping and applicable sales tax extra.
Cleis Press • (800) 780-2279 • orders@cleispress.com
www.cleispress.com

Ordering is easy! Call us toll free or fax us to place your MC/VISA order.
You can also mail the order form below with payment to:
Cleis Press, 2246 Sixth St., Berkeley, CA 94710.

ORDER FORM

QTY	TITLE	PRICE
_____	_____	_____
_____	_____	_____
_____	_____	_____
_____	_____	_____
_____	_____	_____
_____	_____	_____
_____	_____	_____
_____	_____	_____

SUBTOTAL _____

SHIPPING _____

SALES TAX _____

TOTAL _____

Add $3.95 postage/handling for the first book ordered and $1.00 for each additional
book. Outside North America, please contact us for shipping rates. California residents
add 9% sales tax. Payment in U.S. dollars only.

* Free book of equal or lesser value. Shipping and applicable sales tax extra.

Cleis Press • Phone: (800) 780-2279 • Fax: (510) 845-8001
orders@cleispress.com • www.cleispress.com
You'll find more great books on our website

Follow us on Twitter @cleispress • Friend/fan us on Facebook